# HALLOWED GAMES

C.N. CRAWFORD

*For the readers who crave a shadow king to match their own darkness...*

I don't need to sell my soul; he's already in me.

STONE ROSES

Join the C.N. Crawford Mailing List

# GLOSSARY

**Archon:** the only god permissible to worship, represented by a sun.

**Eboria**: A semi-autonomous city-state in the north of the kingdom, not fully controlled by the Order.

**Lirion:** An island to the west of the Kingdom of Merthyn.

**Luminari:** Religious soldiers, akin to the Knight's Templar, who form the military wing of the Order.

**Magister Solaris:** Head of the Order's army and all the Luminari.

**Merthyn:** A kingdom that spreads across the majority of the island.

**Mistwood Shire**: The seaside county where the book opens, south of Penore.

**The Order:** A monotheistic religious sect that took over Merthyn centuries ago, until gradually usurping more power until they controlled the entire kingdom.

**The Pater:** Merthyn's ruler and religious leader; the head of the Order. He seized control during a civil war known has the Harrowing, when he executed the former king.

**Penore:** The capital city of Merthyn.

**Raven:** A cleric of the Order who hears confessions.

**Raven Lord:** Head of the witch-hunters.

**Ruefield:** An ancient castle and former university that has become the center for witch trials.

**Sumaire:** A kingdom to the north of Merthyn, walled off.

**Tyrenian:** An empire that invaded Merthyn centuries ago, conquering the polytheistic tribes and bringing with them the monotheistic religion of the Archon.

**Tylwith:** A kingdom to the west of Merthyn, also walled off from Merthyn.

**Serpent-touched:** Anyone with magic; a witch.

\*\*\*

CORVUS

# CHAPTER 1

*A*s my life was about to spill out of me on the floor of a musty little cottage, a realization hit me like a fist: I'd forgotten how all this was temporary —the sunlight, the smell of grass, the feel of cold rain on my skin. In a few seconds, it would be gone for good.

The witch-hunter was holding a dagger to my throat, and I wanted to scream at him that my life wasn't supposed to end this way. That someone was waiting for me at home, a boy who'd be waiting for me every night until he was at least old enough to shave. So, I *had* to get out of this because I wasn't done yet.

Clenching my teeth, I gripped my attacker's wrist tightly in place. Straddling me, he had the upper hand —the extra body weight, the weapon. Slowly, inevitably, I'd be bleeding out on the hearth soon if I didn't gain control.

Blood spattered the man's black tunic, and it glistened in the firelight.

The edge of the man's blade touched my skin, and panic screamed in my mind. His hands shook as he tried to force himself to push the steel in further. But he wasn't like me. Death didn't run in his veins, and his eyes looked wild with the horror of what he was about to do. This close, it was hard to kill someone—when you could feel the warm breath, see the beads of sweat. Despite their name, the hunters usually had someone else finish the job for them.

Sweat ran down his temple, his jaw moving soundlessly. The edge of the blade pierced my skin just a little. My blood roared.

My thoughts spun wildly with everything that had gone wrong tonight, each misstep that led to exactly this moment. When the Baron sent me on this mission, he'd told me there would only be one hunter in the cottage. Now, two of them lay dead on the floor, bruises covered my body, and I'd been stabbed in the shoulder.

The third was trying to work up the nerve to end my life. His hesitance was a weakness I could exploit.

I stared into his green eyes. He looked about my age. In another world, one without dangerous magic like mine, we might be friends. We might meet at the tavern to drink and sing bawdy songs with the bards.

But not in this world.

My chest cracked beneath his weight. I needed to

use my magic. The problem was, every time I used it, it felt as if a hole was ripped open in my soul, leaving a ravening hunger. Magic was a dark and dangerous addiction that would tear my life apart if I gave in.

On the other hand, I *really* had to get home. Sometime tonight, the little boy I looked after would be waking and searching around for me, wanting to tell me about his nightmares. I needed to sing him a lullaby, to reassure him that monsters weren't real.

I needed him to forget that I was one.

A sharp pain shot through my neck as the dagger pressed harder. I was out of options. By the tensing of this man's muscles, he was working up the nerve to slit my throat. A lock of his hair brushed my cheek as he leaned over me. The way his hands were angled, all I had to do was move my head up a little...

I hadn't touched another person in years. The pathetic thing was, I yearned for the contact. Magic was evil—especially mine—but I craved it like a starving man craves food. And I didn't really have another choice here, did I?

I lifted my head, feeling the blade nick my skin. But it was close enough. I brushed my lips against his hand. It was barely a kiss, a gentle skim across his knuckles. A little taste of warmth that made me feel as if, for just a moment, I wasn't alone.

A kiss of death.

His muscles constricted, and he jerked the blade away from my throat. Lurching back, he dropped the dagger. A purple bruise formed where I'd kissed him, and then dark veins shot out along the contours of his hand like paint racing under his skin. As his body started to convulse, he slumped off me. I stood as shadows spread along his body. He stared up at the ceiling, twitching, lips growing blue.

I closed my eyes, forcing myself to look away. A forbidden pleasure roiled through my body. Once I used my magic, I always wanted more. I wanted to run through the village knocking on doors and caressing the warm, sweet faces of anyone who answered, brushing my fingers over their lips to watch their last breaths...

I tightened my jaw, and my eyes snapped open again.

Sadness carved through my chest, and I forced myself to walk to the door of the cottage. I tugged my cloak tight against the cold and pulled up my cowl.

By the hearth, the witch-hunter was still gasping for breath. But at that point, it didn't matter if I was there. Everyone died alone.

# CHAPTER 2

*M*y nerves jangled from the chaos of the night, and I craved another taste of my magic. But I had to rid my thoughts of that exhilarating hum. Before I went in to see the Baron, I needed complete mastery over myself.

I breathed in deeply, thinking of a sun-kissed afternoon by the lake, throwing stones with Leo. My muscles relaxed.

I pushed through the door into the courtyard, my feet crunching over the snowy cobbles. Pain shot through my shoulder where I'd been stabbed, but it wasn't a serious wound.

With a deep breath, I surveyed the wintry rose garden, trying to rein in any last crackles of magical cravings. White and thorny, the garden spread out beneath a star-flecked sky. Our village of Briarvale stood close to the sea, and when I licked my lips, I could always taste the salt.

When I was a kid, my father had planted the pear trees in this very garden, saying they did well in the coastal air. They still reminded me of him, even if he was long gone. Even if it was just the Baron now, with all his threats and shitty information.

Earlier tonight, the Baron had told me I'd find only one person in that cottage. And yet, when I stepped into his office, I'd have to do my best not to scream at him about his mistake. Whether I liked it or not, he was the one with the real power.

Ahead, the Baron's manor house loomed over the courtyard. Made of thick stone, its sharply peaked towers gave it the look of a grand castle. From its diamond-paned windows, warm light crowned the gargoyles' heads with gold.

A night patrolman was standing by the entrance already, and I tried not to think of how thrilling it would feel to put my hand against his face. With a smile, I nodded at him, then pushed through the heavy door.

In the vast stone hall, I could just about make out the tapestries in the candlelight. In some of them, people danced around maypoles—life before the Harrowing. Back then, you could dance in public without the Order accusing you of fornicating with the Serpent. I'd been born in the wrong decade because Merthyn's dancing days were long over. Even this art was forbidden, and the Baron was risking everything by keeping it on the walls.

I turned into a winding stairwell as shadows crept over the halls. On the upper floor, the moonlight gave the portraits a spectral appearance.

As I reached the Baron's ornately carved office door, I paused for a deep breath. Then I knocked twice.

"Open it!" he barked impatiently from the other side of the wood.

I pushed through the door into his office, where smoldering firelight wavered over white walls and dark wood beams. The Baron sat at his desk, cradling his closely shorn head in his hands. When he looked up at me, I felt the familiar flutter of nerves at his piercing green stare. "We have a problem." He leaned back in his chair and folded his arms across his green velvet tunic.

"Besides the three Ravens I just killed, my lord?" Ravens—that was what everyone called the Order's witch-hunters—the clever, shadow-clad harbingers of death. Their leader, the Raven Lord, would murder anyone caught with magic.

His eyebrows shot up. "Three?" He scrubbed a hand over his jaw. "Only one of them came to the manor today."

"One of them nearly slit my throat. Another stabbed me in the shoulder. The first went down without a fight."

"Well, you seem fine. And they are dead, yes?"

"All dead, my lord." Of course, I'd never expect

sympathy from the Baron. I tightened my fist, forcing myself to shut down all my fantasies about stroking his forehead with my death-touch.

"Good. I hadn't expected a Raven to visit today. If I'd known he was coming, I would have taken the tapestries down. But once he saw the art...you know what? I'll take the weavings down first thing in the morning." He arched an eyebrow. "Can't have that obscenity, can we? The Raven Lord will burn anyone with too much beauty in their life."

He still hadn't told me what the *new* problem was, and my chest tightened. Had someone learned I was Serpent-touched? That I was a *witch*, as the common folk said?

"Elowen." He sighed. "Sometimes, I sense you are uneasy around me." He gave me a twisted smile. "My father would have absolutely terrified you."

Probably. Once, I'd seen the Baron's back as he'd bathed in a river. Scarred from top to bottom with ridged lines from lashes.

"Anyway, let me get to the point." The Baron's gold brooch shone brightly in the firelight. "I know you care about my Lydia."

I nodded, even though it wasn't entirely true—at least, not anymore. But I always knew what to say to keep him happy.

His forehead creased. "So of course, you'll be as concerned for my daughter's welfare as I am. And now, the Raven sniffing around here today has me on high alert."

A sharp thread of regret wound through me. "I'm delighted for her upcoming nuptials, my lord." I played my part like I was supposed to, feeding him the right lines.

He sighed. "Of course, I understand there is some awkwardness."

At one point, Lydia's betrothed and I were supposed to marry. The Baron never approved of that. Anselm was the son of an earl, and I was common, with hardly a penny to my name.

The corner of his mouth curled in a faint smile. "It wasn't to be, was it? Everyone has their place in Merthyn. Yours is in the barracks. My daughter belongs by Anselm's side."

I schooled my expression to calm. According to the Baron, I'd become a witch ten years ago because I'd crossed the class lines. I had a different theory.

"She'll make a beautiful bride, won't she?" he added.

I cocked my head, not answering. But I knew what he meant. Lydia was tall, with golden hair and fair skin like Anselm's. A classic Merthyn beauty.

"Even if you hadn't been cursed," he went on, "you'd have made an odd pairing, I think. Dark hair, olive skin, eyes the color of dirt. Appropriate for the peasant classes, I suppose. The Archon made you all unremarkable."

Often, like right now, the Baron was more interested in mind games than he was in conveying useful information. And sadly, he always knew just which buttons to push to get my heart racing. My chest felt tight as he tested me.

But what did it matter, really, if the Baron thought I was unremarkable? Anselm never thought I had a boring peasant face. Years ago, my lover used to tell me I was the most beautiful person he'd ever seen.

The Baron wanted to see how angry I was. He wanted to see if a shadow of bitterness trailed after me wherever I went. Would I snap, or would I tell him what he wanted to hear, like always?

I raised a gloved hand. "As you say, my lord. Lydia and Anselm are perfectly suited. And if the Archon above had wanted me to marry, he wouldn't have cursed me." I cleared my throat, because technically, Lydia was as much of a witch as I was. "At least, not with lethal magic. Now, I'm destined to remain a spinster. It is the Archon's will."

Another dramatic sigh. "You're not really young anymore, either."

I was only twenty-nine. But in Merthyn, you were supposed to be married at sixteen.

From across the desk, he studied my face, trying to read subtle signs of anger.

I showed him nothing. After all, I'd learned from the master of deception. I'd learned from him.

"Of course, my lord," I added calmly. "It would be easier for me to protect Lydia if I knew what the threat was. I assume there is one, or you wouldn't be talking for this long in the middle of the night."

His jaw tightened. He didn't like my directness. "Today, Lydia and Anselm went for a walk in the weald." He arched an eyebrow. "A nighttime forest walk. Archon knows what they were up to. Of course, they should be chaperoned before marriage, but they are deeply in love, so who am I to stand in the way? You must remember what it's like to be in love. Hard to keep your hands off someone." The corner of his mouth curled. "You probably ruined yourself a long time ago."

This time, I could feel my body growing hotter, and I could only hope it didn't show as heat in my cheeks. Ten years ago, Anselm and I had lain beneath the shade of a yew tree, and he'd covered my neck in soft kisses and told me our love was written in the stars.

"What is the new problem, exactly?" I asked, the tightness in my voice betraying some of my irritation.

I slowed my breathing, trying to force the memory out of my thoughts. When the Baron knew my true feelings, he always found a way to use them against me.

"Lydia brought her hound on the walk with Anselm." His eyes were narrowed as he stared at me. "You know, she brings that mongrel everywhere. And it seems while they were walking, Hector ran ahead. A wolf attacked, ripping into the hound's neck."

My breath caught. "Did Lydia heal him, my lord?"

The Baron nodded. "Of course. The dog is fine. But

Lydia believes someone saw her using her magic. While she was tending to the hound, Rufus Wrenbrook passed by. You know him?"

"I know of him."

"If he sells this information to the Order, not only will Lydia be thrown into the trials, but they'll likely come for me, too. The Order would love to get their hands on this estate, turn it into another institute for their witch-hunters." He drummed his fingers on the table. "Of course, if they find Lydia, they'd likely discover your dark magic. And that orphan boy? He's been marked by them, hasn't he? A little suspect, that one."

My blood pounded hot. Here it was—my worst fear spilling out before me.

I'd been looking after Leo since the Order had burned his parents, and I now loved him like a little brother. Back then, the witch-hunters had marked him with a little tattoo on his wrist. Everyone in the family of a witch was considered suspect—even a sobbing two-year-old who just wanted his parents. I wanted nothing more than to keep him safe from the Order, and the Baron knew it.

It was the strongest weapon he used against me. It was how he kept me here, working for him, protecting him at all costs.

"You want me to kill Rufus, I take it." I flexed my fingers.

"You've been one of my most trusted soldiers for

the past nine years. And your powers are incredible—when you're willing to use them. As they say, one man's curse is another man's gift."

No one said that. I'd literally never heard anyone say that.

I flashed him a small smile. "Thanks to your training, Baron, I am skilled in many other ways of killing that do not risk losing my soul to the Serpent."

"Fine. I don't care how you take care of it. But it must be you. You're the only one in the barracks who knows about Lydia's...situation. But Elowen? I don't want you to kill him tonight. Rufus isn't the real risk. The Order is, and what I need is information. I want you to follow Rufus and listen in to hear what he says to the Order. Find out what they have planned for me."

My heart skipped a beat. "You want me to go into the heart of the Order? Into the Dome of the Archon itself?"

He nodded. "After the visit today, I think I could be a major target. Their Luminari soldiers go after the poor, yes, because the poor are a nuisance. But now they're going after the wealthy, too. They want to confiscate all our property. The Order grows rich off our land. If they are coming for me soon, I plan to flee across the sea to Aquitania. But I need the appropriate warning. That's where you come in, Elowen, my most loyal soldier. You can get me the information I need."

My stomach tightened at the thought of this mission. The Baron wanted me, a Serpent-touched witch, to walk right into the Ravens' headquarters. Right into the Order's army.

I inhaled deeply. "And if Rufus informs one of the Order's Ravens, what should I do? Kill them both right there, in the Dome of the Archon? If I'm caught, the entire Luminari army will descend on me. The Raven Lord himself will be there."

He stared at me. "So don't get caught. Elowen, why do you think I've spent the past nine years training you? Why have I kept you fed and safe in my barracks all this time? Why have I allowed you the indulgence of keeping your orphan boy? This is exactly why you're here. You can kill better than anyone, and I can trust you."

By "trust," he meant "control."

"I'll go to the Dome tomorrow." There was no other option.

The Baron frowned. "I've raised the drawbridge tonight. I'll increase night patrols." He drummed his fingertips on his desk. "We're all at risk, of course, if the rumors get out." He flashed me a faint smile. "We don't need any of us to burn on the pyre, do we?" His smile faded fast. "Me, Lydia, you, or Leo. Dreadful thing when a child is killed. Of course, most of the world wouldn't mourn a wretched little witch like him."

My blood turned to ice. "I'll take care of it, my lord. Lydia's secret will remain safe." Even as fear hummed through my bones, I'd mastered a soothing, velvety tone. "There's no need to imagine the worst."

He raised his eyebrows. "Just observations. Just facts, my dear." Another wistful smile. "I know what it's like to love a child so much you would do anything to keep them safe. Goodnight, Elowen."

"Goodnight, my lord." Dread coiled through me as I turned, stalking out of his office.

I almost felt as if the scars under my gloves were igniting with flames again.

I should have taken Leo out of here years ago—as far as possible from the Baron's influence. But the Baron was a master manipulator, and my secrets were his puppet strings. One little tug, and he had me dancing to his tune. The moment he'd learned of my lethal power, he'd issued a decree among the other barracks soldiers: if the Baron was killed, they were supposed to take Leo's life. According to the Baron's will, the soldier who murdered Leo would earn fifty gold coins.

And that was how the Baron ensured that I protected his life with my own.

Leo was all I had in Merthyn.

I tightened my cloak around me as I crossed back to the barracks where Leo would be sleeping right now. A few snowflakes twirled in the air, stinging my cheeks. Fear settled in my stomach. Could I really assassinate people in the Dome of the Archon and make it out of there alive?

I pushed through the barracks door, sneaking past the sleeping soldiers. Their snores echoed off the ceiling.

I climbed the stairs and found Leo sleeping sideways across his bed, his head hanging off one side, feet off the other. My chest grew warm, and I found myself smiling at him. Here, at least, everything was in the right place—the colorful rug I'd scavenged to cover the wood floor, the soft lantern light casting a warm glow over Leo, the shelves of books with bright spines in emerald and blue.

With gloved hands, I shifted him into position and pulled up the covers. He yawned loudly and stretched his hands above his head. "Elowen, what's your favorite instrument?"

His desire to talk to me always came alive long before his body did. To satisfy his curiosity, I'd needed to identify a favorite of everything: color, tree, cake, mythological monster. He'd even wanted to know my preferred way to die, which was something I hoped to avoid for a while.

Sadly, tomorrow's mission didn't bode well on that front.

"Shhhh, love. Go back to sleep. It's still the middle of the night."

He'd already gone completely still, snoring quietly. I stared at him. He always looked so beautiful when he slept, his dark hair sticking up in tufts, his face half-mashed in the pillow. He was small for an eight-year-old. Bony, despite all the extra tarts he got by working in the kitchens. I needed to see him grow up strong enough to hit back if anyone messed with him.

I swallowed hard. I always wished I could kiss his forehead when he slept, but that would never happen. Ever.

I knelt at the side of my bed, feeling around in the dark for the bandages I kept there.

I wouldn't be sleeping again tonight. Before dawn, I'd be lurking outside Rufus's house, waiting to undertake another deadly mission.

But as much as I loathed the Baron, he was right. One little whisper into the wrong ears could bring us all down.

# CHAPTER 3

The late morning sun stained the old Tyrenian road with coral and rose. Wattle and daub houses crowded either side of the snowy lane, bathed in gold light. I'd been following Rufus Wrenbrook on foot for several hours at this point. I had to stay just far enough away that he wouldn't see me, but not so far that I'd lose sight of him.

As I glanced at the smoke rising from the chimneys, I wished I were still curled up warm in my bed. Instead, I was out here undertaking a stupidly dangerous mission—a Serpent-touched witch marching right into the heart of the Order.

In the March air, my breath clouded around my face. At this point, I didn't have high hopes for Rufus's chances of surviving the day. He'd woken up this morning, and then he'd started taking the long, ancient road from Mistwood Shire all the way to Penore. It took four hours to walk the route from the southern coast to the capital city.

And what would a country farmer like Rufus need from Penore? Likely, it was the silver he could earn in one of the Order's whispering chambers. Two pounds for every name he gave, for every witch he turned in...

The longer I followed him past tidy squares of farmland and sleepy villages, the worse it looked for him. And sadly, the worse it looked for me.

Dread slid over my skin as I walked.

The Order was half witch-hunters, half soldiers. The Dome of the Archon would be heavily protected. The Ravens heard confessions, read from the codices, and hunted witches. They decided who did and did not get into the heavens after death. If they suspected anyone, they reported directly to the Raven Lord. While they weren't technically soldiers, they were still trained to kill as part of the inquisition.

Then there were the Luminari—the Order's armored soldiers. Legions of well-organized killers who marched in perfect formation and defeated every enemy they encountered. The Magister Solaris commanded them, a terrifying warrior who probably spent most of his free time torturing people.

And at the very top of the Order's hierarchy was a man known as the Pater. Our new great leader, the only one who could shepherd us through these dark and sinful times. So they said. He was the man who'd burned a king, silenced the music, and stolen a crown.

In the *best-case* scenario, I'd be killing only two people today: Rufus and a Raven. In the worst-case scenario, I'd be frantically trying to cover up one assassination after another until the Luminari chopped me into pieces right in their temple. Or I'd be brought before a Magister and made to endure horrific torture until I accused every person I'd ever met.

*Stop it, Elowen. Stay calm.*

I pulled my gray shawl tight around me as I walked. Instead of my usual soldier uniform, I was dressed like a housewife: a gray dress belted at my waist, a thick wool cloak, and a shawl draped over my head. Completely boring to look at. And according to the Baron, that included my brown-eyed peasant face.

As we walked closer to Penore's gates, the houses grew more crowded together along the road. Thatched houses and timber-framed inns nestled alongside the thoroughfare, and the scent of bread coiled through the air. A horse-drawn carriage rolled ahead of me, but I was careful to keep my gaze on Rufus.

I kept my focus on him, even as buried memories of the times before I'd become Serpent-touched sparked to life. Those sun-kissed days seemed unreal now, like a fever dream.

In my mind's eye, I could almost see the three of us —Lydia, Anselm, and me—when we were Leo's age. We were a triumvirate of childhood wildness. Once, we slipped out of the manor's gates to walk along this road without our parents' permission. Lydia thought we should go all the way to Penore for the white gossamer gowns the ladies were wearing back then, dressed like spirits from another world.

When we'd walked this road, it had been a scorching summer day, and the sweat had rolled down my reddening skin. I'd nearly fainted from thirst, and Anselm had insisted on trying to carry me back. I think he'd half-dragged me. Lydia had demanded a turn in his arms, but he'd held me tightly. She'd hissed at him that she didn't want anything to do with him, anyway, that he was grotesque and stupid. Maybe that had been the first time she hadn't gotten what she'd wanted. Maybe that was when her hatred for me had started to bloom from a little seed into something bigger, thornier.

A scream interrupted my thoughts, and my attention snapped back to the present.

"The witches killed him!" A woman's voice pierced the air, and my gaze landed on a crowd gathering by an alley, just next to a tavern.

I so desperately wanted to stop to investigate, but I had to keep my eyes on my target. As I passed by, I caught a glimpse of a woman cradling a body. The victim's skin was white as snow. Bizarrely, his head had been nearly torn from his body, and yet he had not a drop of blood on him. My stomach turned with disgust. You'd think I'd be used to death by now, but this murder seemed grotesque. Unnatural.

And what's more, it made no sense. Unless someone

had cleaned the body and moved it, it must be the work of someone Serpent-touched.

Someone like me.

I swallowed hard. This wasn't good. The Order would be on a rampage soon, slitting throats and building pyres.

When I looked up again for Rufus, he was gone.

# CHAPTER 4

*W*e were nearly at the gates, and I hurried onward, frantically searching for the blue cloak. Crowds pressed in front of me, bustling into Penore. A larger man in a butcher's apron shoved me out of the way.

My pulse raced as I scanned for signs of Rufus, and I picked up my pace, pushing my way through the crowd. I wasn't tall enough to see over most people's shoulders.

Just before the city entrance, I finally spotted the royal blue of Rufus's cloak and exhaled a sigh of relief.

The Tyrenian road led up to an entrance charmingly known as Gropecunt Gate. When we were little, Lydia and I were fascinated by the beautiful, brightly dressed women who lingered at the gate to ask men if they were lonely. We'd crush up rose madder to dye our lips and cheeks like theirs. Anselm would blush when we'd ask if he needed a friend for the night, though none of us really knew what we were saying.

Those ruby-lipped women disappeared eleven years ago with the Harrowing. A city ruled by the Order would not tolerate prostitutes.

My blood pumped harder as I drew closer to the city walls. Hundreds of feet high, Penore's sheer stone walls cast a long shadow over the Tyrenian road. Darkness slid over me, and the stench of the place slammed into me. Ringing the city walls was a ditch filled with rubbish and old animal carcasses.

Just before the gate, my gaze flicked up to the severed heads that hung above it, faces covered in pitch to preserve them. Enemies of the Order—a brutal reminder of the witch-hunters' power.

Fear skittered over my body, making my skin grow cold. I swallowed hard and pulled my gaze away from the heads, trying not give in to the dread of imagining my own up there. But after what I was about to undertake today, it was a distinct possibility. The Order's Ravens and Luminari lurked in every shadow in the capital city, radiating out from the Dome of the Archon. The witch-hunters and soldiers alike sent ripples of terror around them wherever they moved.

As I crossed the threshold of the city gates, my pulse fluttered with the assault on my senses. The acrid scent of the ditches outside mingled with roasting meat and woodsmoke. In Penore, everyone seemed to shout instead of speaking, the sounds echoing off the cobbles and timber-framed houses. Steeply peaked buildings and shops looked as if they might topple into the narrow road. Gables and archways jutted overhead, some hanging with drying laundry. In the throng, I worked to keep my eyes on Rufus from twenty feet behind.

After a few twists and turns, the narrow road opened up into the cobbled square of Sootfield. Here, the scent of penned animals and blood hung in the air —a thriving livestock market. Ashes floated on the wind, and I tried not to breathe them in or look at the pyres that stood on the far side of the square. I didn't want to imagine myself there, condemned to burn.

I could only thank the Archon that no one was being executed today.

By Sootfield's eastern corner, I passed the golden statue of Lust, represented by a naked woman, her gilded hands covering a bit of her modesty. The Order had commissioned that a century ago, long before they killed the king. A terrifying plague had run rampant through Merthyn. Because the sickness had caused a swelling of the groin, the Order had blamed the lethal disease on the sin of lust, so they'd put up the statue to remind us of our sins. Now, the Ravens could stare at the alluring curves of a woman's naked backside and still feel pious about the whole thing.

I let out a long, shaking breath as I passed stalls of brightly colored textiles and spices.

All these strangers around me sent dread swirling

through my gut. These days, anyone could be your enemy, and the Order had built walls of suspicion. You couldn't trust your neighbor or uncle or daughter. Swallow your secrets, or they'll be used against you.

Loneliness was the greatest weapon wielded by the order, a hole they'd ripped in each of us. Because who was easier to control than those who were half-mad with isolation? Who was easier to manipulate than the empty?

I tuned out the din of the city, the butchers hawking their meat, the screaming of the animals.

Rufus was heading straight for the great Archon's temple at the north side of the square. I could see it from here, a massive dome that stretched up to the heavens, casting the rest of the city in shadow.

I quickened my pace as he crossed through the gatehouse, an archway carved with stars and a crescent moon, and towers of stone rising high on either side. Inside the gate, the temple's stark grandeur made my breath catch. It was taller than the city walls, and its central dome looked like the skull of a giant. On the exterior walls, master masons had carved grimacing stone gargoyles. To either side of me, the soil was six feet higher than the path, and crooked tombstones faced the east. If the Archon ever returned to raise the dead from the soil, he'd descend from the skies over the ancient eastern city of Ebeline. The rising dead would see the Archon beaming in glory the moment he returned—a second sun over the sky. Here, centuries of bones lay beneath the soil, each generation of the dead on top of the one before. A sprawling necropolis spread out beneath my feet. In the old days, they said you could learn from the spirits of the dead, that you could become a brilliant painter or poet. All that was forbidden now.

The temple's towering doors gaped open, and I watched as Rufus disappeared into the shadows inside. I followed, slipping in after him into the cool rotunda. Inside the dome, awe electrified me. I hadn't been here since I was eighteen, and I'd forgotten its vast size.

I swept my gaze over the vast interior space, one of sleek cream marble and bright light. In the center of the temple stood a circle of blindfolded torchbearers. Their flames cast wavering light over the hundreds of tombstone effigies that spread out across the floor from the center, stone memorials of the Order's most prominent Luminari. An army of marble lay with their arms crossed over swords, feet stepping on serpents.

But most breathtaking of all, sunlight beamed in through an oculus hundreds of feet above. I couldn't see what it illuminated because the torchbearers blocked it. But I knew it beamed into a chasm no one was allowed to see. Once a month, blindfolded torch-bearers sacrificed a bull over that hole, letting the blood drip down into it.

The Ravens said that if you looked into the hollow, you could see the divine face of the Archon himself—and that was why no one must ever do it. Mortals weren't meant to see him, and the vision would rob you of your sanity. Only the dead could lay their eyes upon the glory of the Archon.

Lydia also once told me the torchbearers wore blindfolds because they'd been forced to carve out their own eyes, but I'd never known if that was true or one of her gruesome exaggerations. She'd *also* said that if one of them ever let their torch go out, he'd be tossed into the chasm to starve to death among the dried bull blood. I wouldn't put it past the Order, really.

I followed Rufus past soaring columns, and my gaze drifted over rows of gargoyles—monstrous dragons with fangs, each being slain by a Luminarus of the Order. In the dancing torchlight, the carvings seemed alive, shifting and snaking over the walls.

I shuddered. But luck was on my side today because the temple seemed fairly empty.

Rufus's footfalls echoed off the stone as he crossed into the atrium that jutted off the rotunda. I followed after him, slowing my gait a little so I looked relaxed, aimless.

When I reached the atrium, my heart skipped a beat at the sight of not one but two Ravens. Cloaked in black, they stood by a wall of flickering candles. Shadows writhed over an image of the sun, the symbol of the Archon himself.

Rufus cleared his throat, and the sound echoed off the rib-vaulted ceiling.

I kept my face hidden as I wandered over to the

candles and picked up a taper. From the corner of my eye, I watched as one of the Ravens acknowledged Rufus with a nod. Together, the two of them walked with Rufus to the wooden stalls on the other wall. The whispering chambers were Merthyn's central hub of betrayal.

I lit a candle in service of the Archon.

What I needed to do now—my mission—was to cross to the whispering chambers and listen in. But the second Raven was a problem. Morally, I had no qualms about killing Ravens, but three dead bodies in the atrium was risky...and messy.

I glanced at him, catching his eye for just a moment. Tingles danced up the nape of my neck. Had I seen his face somewhere before? Candlelight sculpted his high cheekbones and flickered in his piercing blue eyes. His sweep of dark hair contrasted sharply with his pale skin. There was something otherworldly about his penetrating gaze, almost heavenly.

And when I glanced down at his chest, my heart nearly stopped. He wore a silver Raven pendant around a chain. He was no ordinary cleric. Standing before me was the bloody Raven Lord himself. No wonder I could practically taste his dark power on my tongue.

I slowed my breathing, mastering control over myself.

I lit another candle, racing through the options in my mind. A dagger out here would be too messy.

I could kill him with a simple stroke of my fingers, just like the Baron wanted. Watching the Raven Lord spasming to death on the marble floor was a temptation I almost couldn't resist. That lovely pale skin…

How would he react to it at first? Like me, the Ravens were forbidden from touching anyone—a sacrifice to the Archon. Did the Raven Lord crave human contact, too? Of course, the pleasure wouldn't last long for him.

This was the Serpent speaking in my thoughts. Once, the Serpent's voice terrified me, but now, he was like an old friend. And it scared me how much I wanted to listen to him.

But it was a bad idea because I didn't want to send the Order on high alert. After the magical death of their Raven Lord, they'd start to purge the city, killing relentlessly. Slaughtering children in their beds. Better to make all this look like an ordinary murder.

When I chanced another glance at the lord, I found him still looking at me, pale eyes burning, like he was peering into my very soul and examining each one of my dark secrets. My breath left my lungs.

At last, he turned smoothly and stalked out of the hall. His graceful movements reminded me so much of a predatory animal. He pushed through a wooden door. Sunlight streamed into the atrium as he crossed outside, and then the door closed again with an echoing boom. I let out a long, slow breath as my heart rate slowed. *Thank the Archon.*

I scanned my surroundings, relieved to find that no one else had crossed into the atrium. This was my chance.

Under my cloak, I pulled a dagger from the scabbard.

Silently, I crossed the stone floor toward the whispering chambers. I leaned in close and tuned in to hear what they were saying.

The Raven was speaking, I thought. He had the clipped accent of nobility.

"As a faithful servant of the Archon, a pious tiller of the land, can you please consider again if there could be more in that manor? Are you quite positive it's only the daughter?" He sighed. "Dark magic runs in families. It's hard to believe her father would not also summon these evil arts. Surely he has also made a bargain with the Serpent? I could pay you very handsomely. We are at war, Rufus, with the Serpent. We've been finding bodies all over Merthyn. Unnaturally killed, drained of their blood. We must fight back."

I swallowed hard. How many of these bodies were there?

Rufus cleared his throat. "It's just that I haven't seen him use magic…"

At least he was honest, I supposed.

"But there's a small boy," he added. "He lives in the soldiers' barracks on Baron Throckmore's estate. The boy has been marked by the Order. I saw it on the back of his wrist. It's a symbol like the sun, yes? In a circle?"

Fear iced my veins, then slowly heated to molten anger.

My jaw clenched. I'd heard enough.

Gripping the hilt of my dagger, I pulled open the carved wooden door to the whispering chamber.

Two sets of eyes turned to me, and the Raven began to stand.

I slashed his throat before he got a chance to call out. Rufus made a choked, terrified sound, and I whirled, bringing the dagger up beneath his ribs into his heart. Swift and brutal, just as the Baron had taught me. Both taken out within seconds.

I stared into Rufus's eyes, fury still humming through my bones.

Blood trickled from his mouth, and his gray eyes snapped wide open.

"You're willing to kill a child," I whispered into his ear, "for silver?"

His body went limp, and he slumped forward onto me. I pushed him back in the chair, and his head lolled. I pulled a second dagger from my scabbard and planted one in Rufus's hand, laying it limply on his lap.

I added a few more stab wounds in his chest, some across his palms to give the appearance that the Raven had attacked him first. Then I cleaned my bloodied hands on the Raven's black cloak and used the fabric to wipe off the soles of my boots.

Blood had spattered all around me. I pulled off my thick wool cloak and turned it inside out, hiding the stains. I peered out through the chamber's wood latticework.

The atrium looked empty. Quietly, I pushed through the chamber door. Silence hung heavy in the air, and my heart still slammed against my ribs.

My breath was shallow as I crossed to the door leading to the garden. Right now, I was desperate to be out of here.

I reached the door, pulling it open into the overgrown garden. My breath caught. There, under a yew tree, stood the Raven Lord. "Are you all right, mistress? You seem as though you've had a shock."

Was there a hint of mockery in his tone?

I raised my eyebrows and pressed my hand to my chest. I'd been trained to keep my expression neutral, but inside, my pulse raced wildly.

Why did I have the sickening feeling that he knew what I'd done, that he could sense my fear?

When I glanced at the far end of the garden, I saw a family strolling through. If I killed him, they'd see. Inwardly, I cursed. Killing in the Dome had been a reckless idea.

"I heard shouting in the whispering chamber," I said. "It sounded like an argument. It disturbed me. I visited here for quiet contemplation, and they sounded..." I breathed in deeply. "Agitated. Someone was angry about heresy. It sounded like...well, I don't want to suggest it was a fight..."

He stepped closer, peering down at me. This close,

the lord towered over me, and his blue eyes glowed with a fervent, holy gleam. The air seemed to vibrate between us, charged like lightning. Was this the power of the Archon himself, radiating from the Raven Lord?

But it didn't feel like the Archon. It felt forbidden.

The lord breathed in deeply, closing his eyes, and a faint smile curled his lips. He looked as if he was inhaling the spring air.

His eyes snapped open again, and his jaw tightened. His smile disappeared completely.

"You should get as far away from me as possible," he said in a deep, husky tone.

As if I didn't want to.

He held my gaze for another second too long, then walked past me back into the atrium.

I did as the lord suggested, moving as fast from the temple as I could.

Rufus was dead, Leo was safe, and I never wanted to set foot in Penore again.

# CHAPTER 5

*T*wo *and a half months later.*

Spring was arriving in full, and a few shoots of green grass were beginning to spring up in the courtyard. Outside, Father's pear trees were starting to burst with white blossoms. A gorgeous spring day, and a wedding I would rather not attend. Today, it would be official—I'd lose Anselm forever.

But it had been my choice, hadn't it? There was no other way.

I stood and tried to get a glimpse of my reflection in the glass, but the light wasn't quite at the right angle. When I looked down at the dress, my mood immediately started to brighten. Its delicate beauty delighted me—blue and silver, with billowing sleeves and a tight velvet bodice. As a soldier, I almost *never* got to wear beautiful things like this. And silk gloves—how lovely and smooth they felt against my scarred skin.

The creak of stairs behind me turned my head.

Leo stood at the top of the stairwell, his eyes widening. "Elowen. Look at that dress! You look like a queen."

Leo wore a royal blue tunic with a silver surcoat to match my dress. I'd saved a full year for these outfits. "And you look like a prince."

Leo tried to suppress his grin.

"How's my hair?" I asked.

He cocked his head. "I think I have a comb. Can I try to fix it?"

Not good, then. "Put some gloves on first."

He crouched down, peering under his bed until he pulled out a pair of leather gloves and a small comb made from cow bones.

I sat on my bed so he could reach my hair, and I felt a tug from behind. "Wait. Are the gloves on?"

"Yes, Elowen. You always ask that."

*So you don't die, love.*

I exhaled and I let Leo tug at my hair with his comb. I was pretty sure he was making it worse, turning the dark curls into frizz. But since Father died, it wasn't often that I had anyone looking after me. I wasn't in a hurry to interrupt this rare luxury.

"Elowen, who's the smartest person in the world?"

"Pretty sure it's me."

"But I mean, seriously." His comb snagged in my hair.

"You don't think it could be me? I'm definitely the

smartest person in these barracks, and that is our world. I don't think any of the men have read any books." I waved at my sparse wooden shelves tucked behind the bed. "Look at the wealth of information at my fingertips. Three books of philosophical musings about the Archon and the Serpent. A military treatise on war tactics from four centuries ago, and a romantic poem that the Order banned years ago. Which, by the way, you're not allowed to read until you're twenty-one."

"I meant at learning about the stars. How to make gold. Things like that."

I shook my head. "Ah, love. That sort of knowledge is forbidden now, too. Only the old people remember."

"Elowen, I learned how to make butter yesterday. I can make you some. I think it was the best butter I've ever had."

"I love butter."

He paused, trying to smooth my hair with his gloved hands, then he let out a loud sigh. "I'm not sure this looks good. Maybe we could pick some wild-flowers outside? I think you need a flower crown to cover it up."

My lips curled. "You seem very invested in how I'm going to look for this wedding. I'm afraid to tell you, no one will really be looking at us. All eyes will be on the golden couple."

I rose from the bed, running my fingers through the frizz.

"But you were supposed to marry Anselm," he said. "And when he sees you, he should remember that. Is it too late for you, do you think?"

My smile disappeared. "How did you know that, Leo? That was all a long time ago. You weren't even born then."

He shrugged. "Everyone talks about it in the kitchen. Everyone knows. And we all think you're prettier than she is, even if she has pale hair."

"Don't say that. She's beautiful. And she's very clever, too. And you know why I can't marry anyone." I sighed. "But I don't really care, darling. Having a husband would probably be tedious, and I've got you instead. You're much more fun."

"So you're not sad?" he asked.

A hollow ache opened up in my chest.

"No," I lied. "And you're right. We should make a flower crown. The Archon's temples are always somber and depressing, and we'll need to liven it up."

HOLDING LEO'S HAND, I walked past the crooked-stone cemetery to Briarvale's village temple. Gravestones radiated out from all sides of the dome, the earth piled high with bodies over the years. Budding trees arched over them, and honeyed light streamed through the branches onto our path. White petals littered the ground.

We crossed inside, blending into the crowd. Our village temple was like a mini version of Penore's—just as ornately carved, with gargoyles jutting from the interior walls and effigies spread out over the floor. Light streamed in from the oculus in the roof.

With Leo's hand in mine, we found a spot in the circle of guests that crowded the temple.

My chest went tight as I waited for Anselm to arrive. In the past nine years, I'd done my best to avoid him. Why had they even *invited* me today? I'd hardly spoken to either him or Lydia.

Leo tugged at my arm, and I leaned down so he could whisper. "You said there would be sweet buns and cakes."

Is that why he'd been so desperate to come?

"After," I whispered back, and I put a finger to my lips.

The wooden door on the eastern side swung open, and Anselm crossed inside. Immediately, I felt my heart crack. He'd grown his hair long, and he looked like gorgeous royalty in his purple brocade doublet and fur-lined mantle. His gaze slid to mine, lingering. I felt like my heart was going to leap from my chest. I couldn't breathe.

Before the curse, Anselm and I could almost speak without words—just a look or a smile or a brush of fingertips on my arm was enough to say everything we'd needed to say. And that one little look he'd given me just now told me he'd searched the crowd for me.

Leo tugged my sleeve, and I knew he wanted to tell me that Anselm had looked for me—as if I hadn't noticed. But I was already the source of enough gossip as it was.

Anselm waited before the torchbearers as a Raven joined him, clutching the sacred codex. On the other side of the chasm, a harpist began to play, the beautiful sounds echoing off the dome. The crowd parted among the effigies, and I watched as Lydia strode in, carrying a bouquet of lavender.

Heavens above, she was made for this. Jealousy pierced me as I watched her, dressed in an ivory gown with an emerald bodice. A jeweled crown sparkled on her head, and a gossamer veil draped over her face and hair. She looked like a princess, perfectly suited for the son of an earl. She'd make a perfect noble wife.

For a moment as she walked past, I was sure her gaze flicked to me under the veil.

My heart pattered hard. Did she wish I hadn't come? Or when she saw me here, did it feel like a triumph?

I dropped my eyes, wishing I'd stayed at the barracks. I tried not to think about the time years ago that Anselm and I had staged our own wedding under a rowan tree, with rings made of twisted dandelion stems. I absolutely would not remember how it felt the last time we'd kissed.

Because Anselm was the last person I'd ever kiss. Unless, of course, I wanted the person to die.

My chest felt tight as the Raven intoned the prayers. He spoke in the ancient tongue of the Tyrenians, so I had no idea what he was saying. Probably for the best. I didn't want to hear about twin souls and eternal love. The Raven droned on, and my mind wandered back to the time the three of us wandered to the beach near Briarvale and we'd swum in the salty waves. Lydia had dared us to jump off the cliffs, but anyone who'd done that would have died on the rocks.

When I looked up again, Anselm was lifting Lydia's veil, and he kissed her on the mouth. My breath stilled in my lungs. Lydia's cheeks shone like burnished pearls as she kissed him.

At least it meant the ceremony was ending.

Despite the towering height of the dome, I felt as if there were no air in here at all.

As soon as it was polite to do so, I slipped my gloved hand into Leo's and dragged him outside.

Sunlight streamed through apple trees, and tables had been laid among the graves with cherry tarts, sweet buns, and spiced cakes. The scent made my mouth water, and I guided Leo over to one of the tables.

"How much are we allowed to have?" he whispered.

"As much as you like. Eat it all." It was on the Baron's tab.

I picked up a cherry tart and bit into it, the sourness and sweetness delighting my tongue. And just as I'd taken an enormous bite, the bride and groom crossed outside. Lydia looked positively glowing. I quickly swallowed my bite.

I smiled at her and mouthed, "Congratulations."

She narrowed her eyes at me, pure ice.

So, she hadn't wanted me here. Of course she didn't really want Anselm's former lover at her wedding. Turning away from her, I left Leo by the table of cakes, wandering further into the cemetery. With a lump in my throat, I crossed around the temple. Sunlight dappled the raised, grassy earth. More comfortable among the dead here than it was lingering around Lydia and Anselm.

My gaze trailed over the old carvings of skulls on the graves, some with ancient Tyrenian text. The temple itself probably dated back over a thousand years, back to when the Tyrenian emperors ruled the island. And before it was a temple for the Archon, it might have served the Old Gods.

Yew trees arched over me.

"Elowen." The familiar, gravelly voice made my heart race.

I swallowed hard, and I turned to see Anselm. My stomach swooped at the sight of him. Sunlight streamed through the trees, dappling his hair with flecks of gold.

My mouth went completely dry. "Congratulations."

"I didn't think you'd come. I'd hoped you would."

I shrugged. "We were all best friends once." At those

words, a jolt of sadness pierced me. "I couldn't miss it. Anyway, you look beautiful together."

His eyes shone. "Elowen, I waited for you as long as I could."

Oh, heavens above. What was he doing? "I know, Anselm. I'm glad you moved on. We couldn't be together. Now you're with someone who won't hurt you, and I'm happy for you." Was I happy for him? I didn't know. I was so used to playing a part with the Baron, of feeding him the right lines, that I could hardly remember what I actually felt anymore.

Sorrow shone in Anselm's eyes. "You know I never gave a fig that you were common, or that the Serpent cursed you. I would have kept waiting if I thought there was a chance."

Regret pierced me as I turned over what he was saying. Had I made the wrong choice? What if I'd simply taken the risk, run off with Anselm, and lived a chaste married life of separate beds? What if we'd looked after Leo together? "You're married, Anselm. It's too late now." I was reminding myself as much as I was reminding him.

"It was always you."

To my horror, I caught a glimpse of Lydia stalking up behind him. I held out my hand to caution him. "Anselm, now is not the—"

"It was never the right time to speak, according to you," he said.

Panic started to rise, and I raised a finger to my lips.

My eyes darted behind him in a warning as Lydia approached. "Your wife is—"

"I never stopped thinking about you." His voice rose and broke.

My heartbeat faltered. Lydia stood behind him, her cheeks reddening. Tears sprung into her eyes.

At last, Anselm noticed his wife. He turned slowly toward her. "Lydia," he said softly.

"On our wedding day?" Her pale skin had turned splotchy. "Can I remind you that she nearly killed you, Anselm? And who was it who saved you when her curse poisoned you? Her magic is the work of the Serpent. You should have seen how you looked. Like a corpse. I thought you were dead." Tears clung to her pale eyelashes. "I was the one who healed you. Anselm, you wouldn't be here without me. Do you still want what kills you?"

"I know, Lydia. Of course."

Coming to this wedding was one of the poorest decisions I had ever made.

She turned to me, blinking tears out of her eyes. "I was always in your shadow when it came to him. You didn't even have a dowry, but it didn't matter. You always shone like the North Star to him. I thought with your curse, things would change. But sometimes, I wondered if when he kissed me with his eyes closed, he was thinking of you. So. Now, on my wedding day, I think I know. It was *always* you. The little gardener's child. The witch."

Oh, Archon. I shook my head, at a loss for words. "No," I started to say, at the same time Anselm said, "Of course not." But I wasn't sure he sounded genuine.

Her mouth closed, and her lips pressed into a thin line. "She's Serpent-touched, Anselm. She shouldn't even be here."

She turned and stalked out of the cemetery. Anselm hurried after her, and I watched him leave—the last man I'd ever kiss.

My chest ached.

I blinked to clear my blurred vision, my thoughts scrambling. She wouldn't tell anyone my secret, would she? We'd once vowed to always look after each other, always, mingling blood from our fingertips…

As I walked to the cemetery exit, my gaze landed on a brand-new threat. The bloody Raven Lord was here. My heart stuttered at the sight of him stalking closer to me, his pale gaze locked on me like a hunting falcon locked on its quarry.

What was he doing *here*?

My blood roared to life as I wondered if he'd come for me—or for Leo. Had someone else informed on us? My breath quickened.

A muscle twitched in his chiseled jaw as he moved closer. His eyes danced with what looked like curiosity, and I had the disturbing sense again that he was peeling back my layers, reading my secrets. Was that one of the dark powers of the Raven Lord?

He stopped just one foot from me, and I arched my neck to look up at him. "Hello again."

"The last time I saw you, mistress," he murmured, "two people ended up dead. And now, after a moment of speaking with you, the new bride is running away in a flood of tears. Should I be concerned about your presence?"

My skin felt alive and sensitive around him with the sense of power he exuded. Maybe an effect of his pent-up sexual energy. After all, he was a young man forbidden from carnal desires, but it wasn't as if lust just went away.

My heart slammed against my ribs, but I kept my expression serene. "We're a few hours from Penore. Seems a strange coincidence to find you here."

The lord's mouth looked too full and soft for his chiseled features, his hair a little too long. It fell down around his sharp cheekbones at the front. "What, exactly, did you overhear in the whispering chamber that day?"

I breathed in a slow, steady breath. "Something about heresy. I'm not sure who was speaking." The less I said, the better. "I can hardly remember now."

Sunlight washed over his pale skin, gilding his sharp jawline. "Why don't you tell me why I make you so nervous?" A knife's edge of a threat slid under his silky voice.

*Because you Ravens are a plague on our kingdom,*

*spreading fear and death in your wake and leaving a trail of innocent dead behind.*

But of course, saying what you really thought could be a death sentence.

So instead, I gave him a small smile. "You don't make me nervous."

A faint smile played over his lips. "Mistress, I can quite easily tell when a person is lying. I can feel your fear like a caress."

I searched around for Leo, my breath shallow. Now, he'd really be able to sense my fear. "Do you encounter many liars? I would guess that many people are nervous around the Raven Lord." *Maybe it's to do with your habit of rounding up people and burning them.* "Apologies, my lord. I must go."

"Maelor."

I stared at him. "Pardon?"

"My name is Maelor."

"If you'll excuse me, my lord." As if I'd call him by his name, like we were friends.

"Take care, mistress," he called out after me. "I do hope to see you again."

Maybe he could have been charming in another life. But in this world, he was a vicious hunter—and for once, I was the prey.

# CHAPTER 6

*J* woke to the sound of shouts echoing off the barracks' arched ceiling. Dawn light hadn't yet pierced the sky, and chaos reigned in the dark.

One of the night guards was shouting at us all to wake. "Get up! Get up!" The frantic, ragged tinge to his voice set my teeth on edge.

My first thought was that something was on fire, but I couldn't smell smoke. I turned to see Leo still fast asleep. Of course, the boy would sleep through a stampede of wolves.

I grabbed his shoulder, shaking him. "Leo, get up." He tried to pull the covers back over his head, burying himself under the blankets again.

As he did, the soldiers below shouted a word that sent fear racing up my spine—"Luminari!"

No.

They were here. The order's military wing was

descending on the estate like a living nightmare. Dread coursed through me, making my muscles shake. Had they come for Leo and me? Was it that bloody Raven Lord turning me in?

I had to get him out of here. "Leo," I shouted. "Get up, now."

He was alert suddenly, his eyes wide. His face went pale.

"Grab your cloak."

Just as I snatched my own, the door to the barracks swung open, slamming against the stone wall. Five Luminari marched in, metallic armor creaking. In the moonlight, their breastplates gleamed with the symbol of a golden sun. The sight of them sent jagged fear coursing through my veins.

"Out!" they shouted, the sound echoing. "One by one. Line up in the courtyard, all of you. Everyone out. Everyone must be accounted for. No one is to be left behind. We'll be searching every building. Anyone found hiding from the Archon will be killed immediately."

My hands were trembling. It was a witch-finding. They'd be gathering us all in the town square today, demanding names from the crowd. And if the people of Briarvale offered nothing up, the Luminari would start pulling people out randomly, killing them one by one. They'd get their names one way or another.

Those accused would be carted away for trial or burned at the stake. My hands were shaking wildly, but

I had to make sure not to scare Leo too much. If he saw my fear, he'd feel completely out of control. His terror would only draw attention to us.

"What do we do?" Leo whispered. His eyes shone with tears.

"Act normal," I whispered back. "It will be okay. Just do what they say, and everything will be fine."

I pulled on my cloak, praying to the Archon that no one would look for Leo's mark.

These days, the most important skill in Merthyn was the ability to go unnoticed, to hide in the shadows. There was no greater gift than looking unremarkable. If the Luminari sensed fear, they'd close in on us. Whatever happened today, I had to keep Leo relaxed.

"Put your head down," I whispered to Leo, then grabbed his hand to lead him down the stairs. "Stand behind me, slightly outside."

I led him outside the barracks to the courtyard, where I tried to calm myself by breathing in the scent of pear blossoms mingled with the briny sea air. I clutched hard to Leo's hand as if this firm gesture alone could keep us from ever being parted.

A knight of the Luminari stalked up and down the courtyard. Crowned with a golden wreath, he bellowed, "The Pater has ordered that we round up every living person from Mistwood Shire today. Today marks the beginning of our Purification. We must purge Merthyn once more of the Serpent's touch."

As his voice echoed off the stones, everyone filed

out of the manor—the cooks, the servants, the stewards and stable hands, the butler and new gardeners. We all stood dazed, shadowed by fear among primroses and brambles.

Who in this crowd would turn on their neighbors today? Because when the Order wanted names, people always cracked. There was no way around it.

Ten years ago, the civil war ended—a war we called the Harrowing. And for a moment, everyone thought peace would reign. It lasted only until the Pater publicly burned the defeated king. That's when we knew no one was safe, and we understood how the Pater would rule. From that point on, the Order maintained complete control over Merthyn, wielding terror as a tool. Public displays of cruelty kept everyone in line.

Four years ago, he'd called the first Purification. The horror of it all had been seared into my memory, and I'd learned then that they spared no one. It didn't matter if you were a baron or an earl's son or a little orphan boy who worked in the kitchens—everyone was suspect now.

Back then, Leo was only four. I don't think he'd understood that the Order had killed his parents a few years before. And when the Luminari had started running their swords through random victims, I'd told him we were playing a staring game, and that he needed to look into my eyes the whole time. He hadn't seen a thing.

This time, how would I keep the truth from him?

I watched as Anselm and Lydia crossed outside in their dressing gowns, followed by the Baron. Unlike his daughter, the Baron looked dressed for battle, leather-clad. He kept his expression neutral, as he'd always taught me to do. But if I looked closely enough, I could see the tension in his fists. This intrusion enraged him. Fifteen years ago, he had been a truly powerful man.

I pulled my gaze away, glancing at the wood anemones that grew in a carpet of white around the pear trees. For a moment, a shiver rippled up my spine. Why did white wood anemones always remind me of death? Maybe it was just the nightmares sifting through the air around us like ghosts.

I smoothed Leo's hair with my gloved hand.

One of the Luminari strode across the cobbled courtyard, shouting, "Everyone will be present for the Purification today! The Pater, in his wisdom, has declared we shall begin here, but we continue on through the Shire. Today, we leave no one behind except the dead."

How lucky for us to be first.

Anselm stood by Lydia's side, their blond hair caught in the wind. She leaned into him, hugging herself in her deep purple robe.

When we'd all lined up among the garden paths, a Luminarus began chanting in Tyrenian, walking up and down the paths. The scent of incense spilled from him as he droned on.

While he chanted, a white-haired Raven walked along the lines, asking each of us our names, writing them down. My pulse raced as he moved closer to us. Would he check Leo's name against his records? Could we lie?

His heels clacked on the stones, and his rheumy gaze slid down to Leo. "Your name?"

Leo answered quietly, "Leo Silverlock."

The Raven nodded.

As I gave my own name, I couldn't stop wondering how good their records were. Would Leo have a mark next to his name—a child of the convicted?

Through the manor's stone walls, we could hear the sounds of crashing and banging. Inside, the Luminari must be searching for anyone hiding. I'm sure they were also helping themselves to whatever they found— gold, jewels, anything that struck their fancy. All in the service of the Archon, of course.

We all should have left for Aquitania years ago, or at least fled to Eboria. The gated city in the north had never fully been conquered by the Order, and Eboria still maintained a semblance of independence.

By the time the Raven had taken everyone's names, the sun had risen, spreading pale amber light over the Shire of Mistwood.

I clung tightly to Leo's hand as the Luminari barked orders at us. With swords drawn and gleaming in the morning light, the soldiers herded us through the gate-house. Behind me, screams echoed through the air.

Who was screaming? *Archon save us.* Someone had tried to hide.

Somberly, we crossed over the drawbridge.

The Luminari herded us into the town square. Leo and I found ourselves walking silently with soldiers from the barracks. For a moment, I locked eyes with Anselm.

If anyone from Mistwood Shire should be high up on the Order's most-wanted list, it would be me. A few months ago, I'd murdered four of them. If only I'd been able to kill them all…

I glanced at Leo, who walked with his shoulders hunched. On a normal morning, he bombarded me with questions and ideas: "What's the fastest animal in the world? Could someone make wings to fly like a bird? What if someone made wine out of strawberries? Don't the gold suns on the Luminari make their armor heavy?"

Today, he didn't say a word. His forehead was creased with worry. And that wasn't ideal, because under the searching gaze of the Order, I needed him to look guiltless. The Luminari seemed to be all around us, watching our every move.

"Leo." He loved riddles. "What can run, but never walk? What has a mouth, but never talks? What has a head, but never weeps? And a bed, but never sleeps?"

He looked startled at the question. Biting his lip, he stared at the ground as we walked.

"I know this!" One of the Baron's soldiers turned around.

"Shh," I put my finger to my lips, and I nodded at Leo. "Let him figure it out."

As we walked, Leo whispered the riddle to himself as we turned into the town square.

At last, Leo smiled and said, "A river!"

I grinned. "Good. Now, you think of one for me."

His gaze trailed over the shuttered houses as we passed, and I could almost see his mind turning as he tried to think.

But when he turned to me, he asked, "Will we be together during the Finding?"

I held his hand more tightly. "Yes, and I will be here the whole time. There might be times I tell you to close your eyes, okay?"

His frown deepened. "Why? Why would I need to close my eyes?"

"So you don't see things that have nothing to do with you, love," I said. "So when I tell you to close your eyes, you need to close your eyes. Even if you're curious. Do you hear me?"

He nodded.

I cleared my throat. "If we do get separated for some reason…" I trailed off for a moment. "I mean, if it happens, just because the crowd is so big and there's so much chaos, it will be better if we met somewhere."

"Back at the manor?" His cheeks had gone completely pale.

"No." I didn't trust a single person around us to hear what I was about to say. I cupped my gloved hand and leaned in close, taking care not to brush my lips against his ear. I whispered, "Not far from here, at the Derunis River. It's five miles east of Penore. Meet me under the moss-covered bridge that spans the river. Do you remember where we went fishing last summer? Stay hidden, and meet me under the bridge." I pulled away from him and smiled brightly. "Just think of today as an adventure. Something you could write about someday."

He stared at me. I could see the worry written on his face, but he kept his questions to himself.

Even at the age of eight, he knew better than to trust strangers.

# CHAPTER 7

*I* gripped Leo's hand as the sun rose higher above the town square. On the cobble-stones, surrounded by crooked buildings, the people of Briarvale pressed together, each of us hoping we could float away like ashes on the wind.

The middle of the crowd seemed the safest space to be. Lydia and Anselm stood a few feet away from us, holding each other's hands. The Baron's shoulders were squared, defiant, as if he still commanded the village.

Towering over the square, a stone platform cast a shadow over the crowd. They'd set up witches' pyres, with wooden stakes jutting up to the skies like bony fingers. When Leo asked me what they were, I told him they were stocks where people would be pelted with rotten vegetables. He'd never seen stocks before, so he might believe it. But he was a clever boy, and he might have wondered why stocks would require driftwood, straw, and kindling at the base, or why all the Luminari on the platform held torches in the daylight.

They probably wouldn't burn anyone today, but they wanted us to remember that they could.

My gaze swept over the Ravens, landing on Maelor. The torchlight danced over his masculine features. My breath caught in my throat. For a moment, I was sure he looked directly at me, and a shiver ran up my spine.

Beside him stood the Magister Solaris. I recognized his authority by the sun pendant around his neck. He wore a black cloak, too, but his was a rich velvet, an almost sensual material. Given the broadness of his shoulders, I could tell that under his cloak was the powerful body of a soldier. And like a soldier, he wore a sword slung around his waist.

I stared at him, and his terrible beauty sent a shiver down my spine. He reminded me of the Serpent himself—a sensual face marred by the cruel gleam of violence in his eyes. Maelor had the pale blue eyes of the heavens, and the Magister was a shadowy warrior from the abyss.

The Magister's eyes scanned the crowd—strange amber eyes so bright, they almost looked like gold. And they were the only thing about him that moved; the rest of him was as still as the marble statues in the Dome, lending him an otherworldly presence. Had I seen him before? In a nightmare, perhaps? In the old Tyrenian style, he wore his long hair pulled back, with just a few wisps escaping to his strong jawline. He looked like a warrior who'd traveled through the centuries to be here, with a cold beauty that made my blood turn to ice.

Maelor and the Magister stood taller than the rest. Two of the most powerful men in the entire kingdom. Really, they looked exactly how I'd always imagined the old gods in the myths would look, the divine conquerors who demanded sacrifices and seduced mortals to ruin. Celestial and infernal alike. Was that why the Order had chosen these two to stand front and center? To remind us of our inferiority?

Fear slid down my skin like cold rain, and my thoughts flashed with a buried memory—blood spattered across bone-white wood anemones. I inhaled a shaky breath. Was I remembering a nightmare?

I blinked, refocusing my attention on the village scene. It wouldn't do any good to let my nerves get the better of me.

Overhead, the skies had clouded over to an iron gray. A fierce wind whipped through Briarvale, whistling through the alleyways and tearing at our hair and cloaks. A few of the Ravens' torches were snuffed out in the gale.

All around us, a wild hum of whispers filled the town square.

I smiled down at Leo, feigning nonchalance. "Everything will be fine." I wished to the Archon I actually meant it.

Anselm stole a quick look at me. His forehead creased in worry, and I knew what he was thinking: both of the women he loved were Serpent-cursed. Lydia glanced at him, and she hugged him more tightly.

Dark panic hung in the air like a miasma, making it hard to breathe.

"You know me as your Magister Solaris, commander of the holy Luminari army." The Magister stepped forward with an unnerving grace. "The Pater Sanctus has ordered a Finding to purify our kingdom by the divine will of the Archon. All around the kingdom, we've been finding dead, bloodless bodies. We know who to blame." His deep, smooth voice seemed to float on the wind, carrying over the crowd. In fact, the timbre of his voice was deceptively soothing for a death knell. When he spoke, he rolled his *R*s faintly—an accent I couldn't quite place. "The Order depends on you to identify evil among your neighbors and root out the dark poison of the Serpent. As the Archon has taught us, we must resist the Serpent's temptations. Power. Greed. Lust." He delivered that last word in an almost velvety tone that made me wonder exactly how much he'd thought about lust in all his chaste days with the Order.

The Raven Lord stalked forward, scanning the crowd with his torch aloft. "And most of all, the Archon forbids magic that humans were never meant to wield. That power comes from the Serpent. But we are fortunate that the Pater Sanctus is here with us today so that he may restore us to grace in the eyes of the Archon."

A frantic murmur rippled through the square, and the crowd started to part. The Baron held out his hand protectively before Lydia, and the two of them pushed back against me. From behind the Baron's shoulder, I watched the Pater Sanctus slowly process toward the platform. My heart slammed hard.

Unlike the others in black, he wore a long, white cloak embroidered with the gleaming gold insignia of the Archon. Beneath his flowing cloak, burnished armor gleamed. The sound of his shifting metal hinges was the only thing to pierce the silence. There he was, killer of kings, the man who'd spread a gray mantle of death over the kingdom to suffocate us all.

Unlike the Magister and the Raven Lord, he looked ordinary—about fifty, with a close-cropped salt-and-pepper beard and rugged features. His dark, silver-streaked hair reached his chin. His thick black eyebrows knitted together, and he kept his gaze locked on the platform completely, as if the crowd didn't exist.

In his white-gloved hands, he gripped an aged copy of the Luminis Codex as he climbed the stone steps toward the stakes. When he turned to face the crowd, he held his gaze above us. He might want to kill us, but he didn't want to have to actually *look* at the rabble before him. The Pater clutched his codex against his chest with one hand. With the other, he signaled to the Magister.

The Magister's gold eyes slid around the crowd. "We'll have the names, now. The Pater wants twenty accused from Mistwood Shire."

It made no sense to have a predetermined number of the guilty, but no one ever accused witch-hunts of excessive rationality.

Silence met the Magister's demand.

The cool wind whipped over the platform, and the gleam in the Magister's eyes looked almost predatory. "We shall have to begin persuading you, then."

"Leo," I whispered. "Close your eyes, love."

"Why?"

I gritted my teeth; I thought we'd already gone over this. "Because I said so."

Leo closed his eyes, and I pulled him in closer. I wrapped my cloak around him.

From the platform, the Pater stared at the crowd while a Raven whispered into his ear. A few moments later, the Pater pointed at someone.

"Agnes de Vray!" The Magister's deep and resonant voice carried out over the square. "The Archon summons you."

"No!" A woman's voice, tinged with panic, rang out. Around me, the crowd jostled as armed Luminari led a woman to the platform. With the metallic ring of their armor floating through the air, two Luminari gripped the arms of a white-haired woman. I could see the terror in her face, but the soldiers' expressions were shielded by their steely helms.

The crowd shifted from them as if they exuded poison.

Agnes wore a meticulously tailored dress of deep burgundy embroidered with gold and a bodice of saffron yellow. She shouted, "Archon save me! I am innocent. I live in the light of the Archon."

Her feet and gray cloak dragged up the stairs to the platform as they pulled her along.

I swallowed hard, cupping my gloved hands around Leo's head. He wrapped his arms around my waist. How long would he have nightmares after this?

The Magister drew his sword. "The Archon has guided the Pater to select this woman. And if anyone wishes to save her, you can offer up to us the names of the wicked among you."

Thorny tension sharpened the air, and Agnes seemed to be frozen on the platform. She stood hunched, a bright figure against the grim surroundings. Visibly shaking, she folded her arms and clutched at the billowing sleeves of her gown.

"Anges de Vray, do you wish to name a Serpent-touched heretic from Mistwood Shire?"

She shook her head, and sweat beaded on her brow. She croaked, "I do not know anyone who is Serpent-touched, and I, myself, have no magic. May the Archon save Merthyn."

Archon bless that woman. She knew what was coming next, and she chose not to give a name. Fear rattled through my bones. Would I be so brave in the face of death?

The black of the Magister's cloak seemed to devour the light. He pulled his sword, the hilt engraved with sinuous carvings. Something stirred in the darkest recesses of my memories...

"Elowen," Leo whispered, "what's happening?"

"Shhhh. It's fine." Yet another lie today. "Everything is fine."

The wind whipped at Agnes's lace headdress as she stared at the Magister's gleaming blade. "Archon save me."

I could have looked away. But somehow, I felt that we owed it to this woman to watch her die. She could have easily saved herself, but she was refusing to condemn another. This was a sacrifice she was making for us.

In a blur of movement so fast it almost seemed divine, the Magister swung his sword. The blade carved through Agnes's neck. A scream erupted from the crowd as her head tumbled forward. Agnes's head-less body fell to its knees, then slumped backward on the platform.

Leo kept his arms around me and his eyes pressed closed. "It's fine," I whispered again.

"Why did they scream?" he asked into my dress.

"Shhhh." I was all out of plausible lies at this point.

I swallowed hard. Did the Archon delight in blood, or was this all the twisted work of mortals? I had no way of knowing. None of us were meant to see the true face of the Archon or understand what he wanted.

The Pater hardly looked at the body at his feet or the blood spilling over the platform. Once more, he lowered his gaze to the crowd. With one hand, he clutched his codex to his armored chest. I prayed to the Archon that the Pater wouldn't notice me. I lowered my eyes, hoping to go unnoticed. Chills rippled over my skin as a heavy silence filled the town square.

The deathly quiet seemed to stretch on until sharp gasps broke it. When I looked up, fear clawed at my chest.

The Pater was pointing in our direction—directly at the Baron. My blood roared, pounding so hot, I could hardly think.

If anything happened to the Baron, I needed to get Leo into hiding immediately. I pulled him in closer to me. Could I stop this?

A silver-haired Raven crossed to the Magister, whispering in his ear. I watched with frozen horror as the Magister drew his sword, then called out, "Baron Morvel Throckmore!"

*Oh, Archon save us.*

The crowd shifted away from the Baron. Only Lydia clung to his arm. "No! Not him. He's innocent."

The Baron pulled his arm from his daughter. "Get a hold of yourself, Lydia." Standing tall, he climbed the platform.

He didn't look scared. Unlike Agnes, he would

never sacrifice himself. He'd kill half the people here before he risked his own throat. And I hoped to the Archon he would make it out of here alive because Leo's life depended on it. But who would he accuse?

My mind whirled as I frantically tried to think of a way to save him, or to at least get Leo out of here.

The Magister towered over the Baron, dwarfing him. I'd never seen him look so small before.

The corner of the Magister's mouth curled like he was enjoying himself. "Baron Morvel Throckmore, do you—"

"Wait!" Lydia screamed. "I have a name. I'll give you a name if you give me my father."

Time seemed to slow down, the wind whipping at her pale hair. Anselm turned to Lydia with an expression of horror. "Lydia, no."

She raised her hand, and wild hysteria tinged her voice as she repeated, "I have a name."

*No.*

My heart slammed against my ribs, and I leaned down, whispering to Leo, "If I say run, you disappear into the crowd. No questions. Get to the mossy bridge where we went fishing."

"You said you'd stay with me," he said, a little too loudly.

"No questions."

The crowd started to shift away from Lydia, and furious whispers rippled out around us.

I reached for one of the many sheathed daggers in

my cloak, and I handed it to him by the hilt. "Don't use this unless you have to. I'll meet you," I said through gritted teeth.

Slowly, Lydia turned around to stare at me.

"Run." I pushed Leo away from me. "Now."

To my immense relief, he did as I'd told him, and he started to push his way through the crowd.

"No," Anselm said again as he reached out to touch her arm. "Lydia, no."

Leo disappeared into the crowd, and my chest unclenched. *Please, Archon, let him escape.*

"Not her," the Baron said from the platform.

But Lydia wasn't listening to her father right now. "Elowen Wrothmere."

All eyes turned to me, and ice poured through my blood.

My fingers flexed as rage simmered.

Time seemed to slow down as the sea-swept wind rushed over me.

Lydia's voice cracked as she pointed at me. "She kills with her touch. She's Serpent-touched. She's the worst of them all."

# CHAPTER 8

$\mathcal{M}$y blood roared in my ears, pounding so hot and loud, I could hardly think straight.

Those around me were shouting about the boy I'd been holding close, that he could be "a familiar."

"Someone, find the boy!"

Panic choked me. I needed complete anarchy to distract everyone from Leo. Chaos would be my best weapon right now.

I pulled off my gloves, my heart pounding like a war drum. It was so rare that I slipped the leather off my hands, so rare that my scarred skin saw the light. I flexed my fingers.

Armored Luminari walked toward me, metal creaking. But they weren't the ones I wanted to touch.

Right about now, Leo might be reaching the edges

of the square, and Luminari would be blocking him in. Only total panic would give him the chance to flee.

"She's right," I bellowed. "I can kill with my touch. I'm a witch, as Serpent-touched as they come. Who wants to see?"

The Baron was screaming at me, but I tuned it out. In this moment, I needed anarchy to reign in Briarvale. The Serpent inside me commanded me to touch someone, and my addiction called to me. My power thrummed and crackled through me, raising goosebumps on my skin. Darkness welled in me, the tempting allure of death.

Lydia stepped back, raising her hands. Anticipation surged in my veins. I wanted to caress her delicate, milky skin, to watch her gasp.

"See?" she screamed. Her face had completely drained of color, and she was visibly shaking. "The witch comes for me. Soldiers! Luminari!"

I lunged, reaching for her face. When I touched her cheek, my dreadful power pooled in my chest. It slid down my shoulders, my arms—a shadowy ecstasy. Death spilled through me, rushing down the length of my arm and coursing from my fingertips right onto her pretty face. Her eyelids fluttered. My breath quickened, and the air grew cold around me. Evil breathed in me like a living thing.

Lydia's back arched, and her eyes opened wide. As her body convulsed, she looked terrified, like a frightened animal. Veins of midnight blue slid through her skin, and shadows lashed the air around me.

When I pulled my hand away from her, I discovered that my plan had worked. Pandemonium ruled Briarvale.

Anselm held Lydia in his arms, and her body glowed with the pearly, shimmering light of her own magic. Just as I'd known would happen, she was healing herself.

Because, of course, I wasn't the only Serpent-touched person here.

I turned to run, hoping to get to Leo in the chaos. But it was too late, and a crowd of Luminari surrounded me, blocking my way. They drew their swords.

"Elowen." A deep voice I recognized rang out from behind me.

I whipped around to see the Raven Lord stalking closer. The wind whipped at his dark cloak, and the corner of his mouth curled slightly. "It seems we keep running into each other."

The Serpent's voice croaked in the hollows of my skull, *More chaos. Use his dead body as a shield. Make your escape.*

Dark magic still crackled through my bones. I darted closer to him. Hunger danced at my fingertips, and I reached up for Maelor's high cheekbones. As I cupped his cheek, magic spilled from my body into his.

A thrumming pulse of shadow slid into him, a charge of lethal power.

He tilted back his head, breathed in deeply. His dark eyelashes stood out starkly against his pale skin. The morning light cast shadows beneath his cheekbones, his sharp jawline. My breath caught.

How strange that only as I was killing him did I realize exactly how beautiful he was.

Shadows writhed around me, and a chill spread through the air. My breath clouded.

To my shock, his eyes opened.

The expression in his blue eyes was almost euphoric. A lazy smile curled his lips—satisfied, like I'd just kissed his throat and he liked it.

Confusion whirled in my thoughts. Why in the Archon's name was he still alive?

"You have true Serpent-power." He sighed, looking rapturous. He slid his hand down to the small of my back. "And the Pater demands you come with us."

Then, abruptly, he twisted my arms behind my back. I felt the rough rope tighten over my wrists.

With a hammering pulse, I faced a line of armed Luminari, each with their swords pointed at me.

Maelor's bare skin still touched mine, fingers warm against my flesh as he finished tying my wrists together. From behind us, he barked an order: "Lydia Throckmore comes, too. Pull that witch off the ground. The Purification continues throughout Mistwood Shire all day."

I glanced back at her to find her looking nauseous but recovered.

Ice flowed through my blood. Here we went—my oldest friend and I, marched off to our deaths. We'd always said we'd stick together until the end.

\* \* \*

# CHAPTER 9

Among the accused, I walked at the rear of a cart, hands tied behind my back, a rough rope around my neck. Maelor, immune to my touch, had carefully slid the gloves back onto me, handling my lethal hands as though they were delicate.

I loathed him.

Luminari walked on either side of us, some mounted, some on foot.

My worst fears were now blooming into a dark reality, a garden of nightmares. Captured by the Luminari, and Leo out there on his own.

A mounted Luminarus rode a horse just ahead of us, dragging the cart through a small city called Thistlehaven. The Order was intentionally taking us through populated areas—four to a cart, a public display. *See what happens when you defy us?*

My little group led the grim parade. We'd be

walking all the way to the trials, past ramshackle houses with curious faces in the windows and streets lined with spectators.

Just ahead, a woman hung out of a window from an upper story that jutted out over the street. A faded sign swung in the breeze, painted with the blazing fire of the Archon. "Witches!" she screamed. "The Serpent walks among us. The monsters who curse us."

I'd love to think I *wasn't* evil. But the truth was, the Serpent's shadowy magic still whispered through me, hungering for death. I bared my teeth at her, delighting a little too much at the look of fear in her eyes.

They marched us slowly over the cobbles. I had no idea where the trials would be held, and I didn't intend to find out. As soon I got the chance, I'd be breaking free.

They hadn't searched me quite as thoroughly as they should have. I'd arrived at the Purification armed to the teeth because I always was. Maybe they thought someone who could kill with her touch wouldn't bother with daggers.

Trying to look casual, I glanced over my shoulder, catching a glimpse of Lydia. She walked behind the cart following mine. She'd been weeping so hysterically that guilt started churning in my gut.

But what else could I have done, really? Behind my back, I tugged off one of my gloves. Then the other.

At the back of my cart, three more accused walked with me. Penitents, the Order called us. Unlike me, the others had the good fortune of being bound by their wrists only.

I had the distinction of being tied by my neck, since my arms were bound behind my back. I supposed the others weren't as dangerous, but one of them looked like an ogre of a man. His head was shaved, tattooed all over with the sun symbols of the Order.

He'd been silently glaring at me the entire time.

I strained my arms behind my back, reaching for my hip. From there, I could tug my cloak inch by inch until my hands reached one of the internal pockets. My fingertips brushed the hilt of one of my daggers, and then I was able to draw it out from my pocket.

Flipping the dagger upright, I began to slowly saw at the ropes.

The woman to my left glowered at me, but she wouldn't be able to see what was going on behind my back, and my face was completely impassive.

The woman looked young, but her hair was so pale, it was almost white. With her pale skin, she looked like a ghost. She wore a stern gray headdress, and when I glanced down at her dress, I noticed how worn and threadbare it was at the knees. A woman who spent her days on her knees could mean one of two things. In her case, I suspected it was piety.

"So." Her mouth pressed together into a thin line. "You are Serpent-touched."

"We're all Serpent-touched," said the man next to me. He looked about my age, with short hair and bronze-brown skin. "According to the Order, we are all guilty. Isn't that why we're all here, tied to the arse of a cart?"

"I'm not Serpent-touched," said the woman. "I'm Gwyneth Ableworth, a pious servant of the Archon."

"I'm not touched, either," snarled the bald man. "And it's witches like her that got us into this mess. Some of us are innocent, but these Serpent-whores have brought enough evil into this world that we all have to suffer."

"*Serpent-whores*," I muttered. That was a new one to me.

The blonde woman lifted her chin. "The Archon will see to it that I survive these trials. And really, my lord Percival, is it proper to refer to yourself as Serpent-touched? I heard your father, the Viscount de Montfort, give a speech about the problems with modern society. He said Merthyn was changing too quickly. Do you know what they were getting up to in the cities before the Harrowing? *Degeneracy*. The Pater is restoring things to the way they were. He's bringing us back to the purity of the holy Tyrenian emperors. I believe in the work of the Order. I am fully confident that the Archon's light will keep me safe during these trials, as it keeps the Ravens safe." She shot me another sharp look. "Even you couldn't kill the Raven Lord. It is because the Archon protects them when they're faithful enough."

Percival looked bored with her already. "What did

you say your name was? *Gwyneth?*" He managed to make her name sound like the worst sort of insult. "I wouldn't count on the Archon saving you." His hazel eyes slid to me. "You both realize that only one among us survives, right? Shall we place bets on who among us will die first?" He frowned. "Though I suppose we'll never get the chance to make good on those bets. The dead won't pay."

"What do you mean, only one survives?" Gwyneth asked sharply.

"This is her fault," growled the bald man.

Gwyneth's eyes looked wild with terror. "Surely *all* the innocent among us survive. That's the purpose of a trial."

"As I said." Percival brushed some dust off the front of his robe, and I noticed his family sigil embroidered into the front of it. A dragon. "According to the Order, none of us are innocent. We are all Penitents. All guilty."

He didn't seem particularly scared. Maybe he expected to be the single one chosen.

As I hacked at the ropes binding me, I realized I recognized his name. *De Montfort.* His father had left blood-soaked fields and ravaged cities in his wake during the Harrowing. It was their family banner that gave rise to the phrase "raising the dragon" when no mercy was shown on the battlefield and prisoners were slaughtered.

Gwyneth smiled at me. "If there is only one, it shall

be me. I serve the Archon. It's my whole purpose for living. I don't suppose it is yours."

"I am the Archon's humble servant," the bald man shouted.

Every now and then, the tip of the blade would nick the skin at my wrists, but I masked any reaction to it. "I fear the Archon, but no, serving him isn't my reason for being."

"Heathen," Gwyneth whispered.

The rough rope chafed my skin as I worked away at it. "Some philosophers say that we are driven by pleasure, others say we're compelled by power. I think we just need a purpose, but it doesn't need to be the same for all of us. For you, it's serving the Archon, but not for me. The Order tells us he loves us, except I've only felt his wrath. For me, the Archon is terror."

My purpose was to keep Leo safe and happy. In the darkness of Merthyn, I lived to help him see the beauty in the world—the warmth of sunshine on his skin, the rushing sound of water over stones, the perfumed triumph of spring over winter. The Archon scared me, but I didn't love him.

So right now, all I could think about was that little boy waiting by that fishing bridge, terrified I'd never show up.

And the moment the final thread of my bindings snapped, I was ready to get to him.

With my wrists freed, I pulled off my gloves. The

dark magic inside me was delighted that I was going to kill again.

I shifted closer to the cart, giving me a good amount of slack on the rope that bound my throat.

I glanced at the armored Luminarus walking next to me. He wore no helm, and the scars on his jaw suggested he'd seen a number of battles.

Still, magic scared the shit out of even the most hardened soldiers.

I stared at him and began chanting in a made-up language. *"Irsira molu locci lira Nior montele beddu..."*

He glared at me, gripping his sword. "You stop that. What's she doing?" Panic broke in his voice.

I flared my eyes open wide. *"Omini spiritu iddi libiri diritta hanno..."*

Gwyneth shrieked by my side. "What is she saying?"

"Stop it!" the Luminarus barked. "She's cursing me. You shall not curse me!"

*"Serpenti!"* I shouted the final word of my spell.

Just as he gripped his sword to swing for me, I dodged sharply backward, making the rope go taut.

His sword came down cleanly through the rope.

Exhilaration ripped through me. *Free.*

Screams erupted around me, and I leapt onto the empty cart itself. In the next heartbeat, I was on the back of the horse, behind the mounted soldier. I pushed my hand into his face. Shadows surged from my fingertips into him. As he fell, I reached down to rip his sword from his scabbard. I inched forward on the horse. Turning, I slashed the sword through the rope behind me.

I pulled the horse's reins, and we took off through the cobbled streets. I was heading south again, back near Penore. Back to Leo.

# CHAPTER 10

*T*he Luminari pounded the narrow dirt roads behind me as we whipped through a small city. My body was electrified with the exhilaration of escape twined with the fear of getting caught.

The wind tore at my hair, and I sucked in the scents of woodsmoke and baking bread. How long did I really have left in this world to take air into my lungs?

But I couldn't let myself think like that. I simply had to survive to get to Leo because there was no other option. This *had* to work. Anything else was unthinkable.

Without a sheath for the sword, I had to fling it to the side so I could take the reins in both hands. I couldn't waste a single moment. Behind me, the Luminari charged over cobblestone, bellowing for me.

The pounding of my heart slammed in time with the hooves beneath me. Gritting my teeth, I stole a quick look behind me. My stomach flipped at the sight of them so close.

None of this would be any good at all unless I could lose the bastards. As I raced, my gaze flicked over narrow passageways and the timeworn, mossy stone of an ancient village. Guiding the horse, I careened into an alley. Wooden eaves swooped overhead, casting me in shadow. Thistlehaven was a maze of narrow passages, which was perfect for me right now.

Leaning forward in the saddle, my body moved along with the horse's frantic gallop. I nudged her with my heels, urging her on faster. The Baron had taught me to ride like this. I gripped the reins, navigating the labyrinth of alleys with rapid little shifts and tugs, until the horse and I were almost of one mind. My cloak whipped at the air behind me.

With my breath ragged in my throat, we hurtled through winding turns. Gasping for breath, I was desperate to lose them without trampling anyone. When we veered around a corner, I found a woman carrying a basket of laundry.

"Get out of the way!" I shouted.

Yelping, she leapt back into her doorway, dropping the laundry. The twisting alleys turned into a blur of brightly colored signs and stones. Shopkeepers scuttled out of my path, and I guided the horse to leap over a loose barrel.

In my wake, I left complete chaos, broken tables

and shouting merchants. If I'd had time, I'd have flung off my wool cloak.

We swung wildly around a corner, and the alleys gave way to a wider road. The horse's hooves pounded the dirt. Around me, the buildings thinned, steeply peaked houses interspersed with a few birch trees blending to checkered farming fields.

As I fled, iron gray storm clouds rolled in overhead, and a chill rippled through the air. The first few drops of rain felt like a blessing on my overheated skin.

I glanced behind me. No one was following now.

Ahead of me, patchworks of green fields spread out, lined by stone walls. They stretched across the landscape all the way to a dark forest of oaks.

*Leo, stay where you are. I'm coming for you.*

When I glanced behind me again, relief spread through me. I'd lost them—for now. But it might not be long until they found trackers and hounds to map my route out of Thistlehaven.

I sped toward the line of oaks until I felt the shadow of branches envelop me like an embrace. I breathed in the moss and soil of the forest. Overhead, rain began to hammer the canopy.

I sucked in a sharp breath, heading west toward the mossy bridge.

EVEN AS I rode through the forest, I kept up the relentless pace. It wasn't just about escaping the Luminari; I also wanted to get to Leo as soon as possible. What if he gave up after waiting too long? My mind was a frantic whir of worry, and I hardly noticed the dampness of my coat as the rain slid down my skin.

I didn't have my gloves. Normally, I never went anywhere without them, but I'd left them behind in Thistlehaven. Honestly, the idea of being around Leo without gloves on made me want to vomit.

And all this because Lydia had decided to shout out my name today. Maybe she thought she had no choice with her father's life at risk. But we both knew Edward Mounthorn beat his servants to death, and Greynard Hough forced himself on young women. Surely they'd have been better sacrifices than the one person looking after an eight-year-old boy?

The shadows grew longer as I drew closer to the Derunis River, the rain letting up. In the woods, there was enough moss growing to tell me which way was north.

At last, at the forest's edge, I slid off the horse and tied her reins to a tree.

I stepped out of the shadows, surveying the landscape. Outside the cover of trees, a few rickety houses dotted the landscape, all shuttered windows and crumbling stones. There were rumors that long ago, monsters from the west ravaged this land, and that's why we'd put up the walls. Walls cutting off Western Tylwith. Cutting off Northern Sumaire.

No idea if that was true, but no one lived out here anymore.

I slipped back into the cover of the forest anyway, my heart slamming hard. I *had* to find Leo here. If he wasn't by the bridge, I couldn't bear it. Really, he must be mad with hunger by now. The poor boy hadn't eaten all day. I bit my lip, wondering where I'd get him something to fill his stomach out here.

When I thought back to our little loft space where I'd been just that morning, it already felt like years ago.

The sun broke free from the clouds overhead, and rays flecked the forest floor with gold. When I glanced down at the dirt path, I wondered how long it would be until the soil wrapped me up in its embrace. It's where we were all destined in the end, wasn't it? If it weren't for Leo, I'd feel like the earth was the only thing that wanted me.

Closer to the bridge, I almost wanted to stall. Until I got there, I could live in a suspended reality where Leo was waiting for me. But once I learned the truth, there would be no going back.

I sighed and forced myself on.

As the bridge came into view, anxiety crackled through my veins, and I couldn't wait a moment longer. I broke into a run and skidded down the steep, rocky slope to the stream beneath the bridge.

He stood there, crouched on the rocks, half-covered in mud.

"Elowen!" He leapt up to run for me.

Tears sprung to my eyes, and I held up a hand. "Wait, wait. I don't have my gloves on. Don't come closer."

He beamed at me. "You escaped. You're amazing."

"I will always try to find you, Leo." I cleared my throat. "I've got a horse. We can take the back roads up to Eboria, but we have to stay discreet. And you have to be very careful about my hands. Are you thirsty?"

"I drank from the stream. But I'm starving."

"We can collect some acorns. We'll have to make a fire and boil them before we eat them, though. And we might be able to find berries."

His forehead creased. "I know. But I'm hungry *now*."

"We have to wait. I'll feed you when I can, love."

"I don't understand why we can't go home, back to the barracks."

I shook my head. "Because Lydia accused me, and we're on the run now. The Order will be looking for us at the manor. No one can know where we are."

He rubbed his stomach. "But what's in Eboria?"

"It's a free city...sort of. They still have Ravens and temples, but they have their own king and their own laws. They have walls and gates if they're under attack. Eboria is almost as large as Penore, and your Uncle Hamelin lives there. He couldn't take you in when you were little, but maybe now we could help him." My words were coming out in a frantic rush, still bubbling from the euphoria of finding him.

"We'll stay together?" he asked hopefully.

"Of course." I beckoned him. "Come with me. We need to hurry, Leo."

But the moment I started climbing the bank, an uneasy feeling started creeping over my skin like icy shadows snaking over my body. The hair on the back of my neck stood up, and goosebumps rose on my arms. A cold, uneasy breeze moaned through the trees. I surveyed the forest, looking for signs of movement, feeling a sharpening in the air.

I nearly reached for Leo's hand before quickly pulling it back. *No gloves.*

"Leo," I whispered, "if anything happens, if we get separated again, this time, I want you to go directly to Eboria. Can you do that? There's an old Tyrenian road that leads all the way from Penore to the northern kingdom. You won't get lost. It's a straight shot."

"You just said we would stay together," he said.

Unease swirled in my thoughts. "Right. I'm just saying *if* anything happens. And you must be very, very careful not to touch my hands, okay? You'll ride behind me and hang on to my cloak."

He nodded. "I'll be careful."

"But *if* we're separated, Leo…your Uncle Hamelin lives on Boar Street. If anyone stops you at any point, you have to act like you know exactly what you're doing. You can't let anyone see the tattoo on your wrist, and you can't let anyone think that you're on the run. You just need to tell people that your Uncle Hamelin hired you as an apprentice and you're on your way there, and act like everything is fine. And you need a password to get into Eboria. *The Archon watches over us.*"

"It won't matter," he said quietly, "because we'll be together. So *you* can say all of that."

"Say it, Leo," I ordered sharply.

"The Archon watches over us."

As we drew closer to the horse, I felt as if a cold shadow were snaking up my spine, an unnatural power that spilled through the forest like a billowing fog. Rising dread stole my breath.

Where was that chill coming from?

I turned. Maelor, mounted on a horse, prowled from the shadows.

When the Order comes for you, there is no escape.

# CHAPTER 11

*I* held out my arms, shielding Leo behind me. "Leo. Get on my horse," I shouted. "It's just to the left of here. Go where I told you. I will find you when I can. *Now.*"

Never before had Leo done exactly what I'd asked without a discussion. But I'd never spoken to him in quite that tone before, and the sharp edge in my voice had him frantically scrambling onto the horse.

I heard the snapping of twigs as he rode away, and I loosed a breath. I hoped to the Archon that he'd find the Tyrenian road.

Shadows darkened the forest, bleeding into the air around Maelor.

My gaze swept over him, looking for points where I could make contact with his skin. With his long cloak on, only his hands and face were exposed. A cold breeze whistled through the trees as he dismounted.

I reached into my cloak and slowly pulled out a dagger.

"I do admire your commitment," he said. "But there is no escape from the Order, Elowen. If I didn't capture you, the Magister would. And honestly, he's really not as nice as I am."

My gaze flicked to his throat, and I found my target. I hurled the dagger. To my shock, his hand whipped up, and he caught it in midair by the hilt. How did he do that?

"Elowen," he said softly, "I told you there is no escape."

The air left my lungs. That rapid movement had seemed so fast, so precise, so...*inhuman.*

Somewhere in the depths of my skull, a voice whispered that I'd found the Serpent incarnate. What if he'd been hiding among the Order all along, delighting in the blood and the death and the agony...and I recognized him so easily because his darkness lived in the worst parts of my soul. The Serpent was part of me.

Maelor prowled closer to me, and a lethal surety imbued his every movement, sending alarm bells clanging in my mind.

At least he didn't seem to have any interest in chasing after Leo.

I reached into my cloak for another dagger.

He arched an eyebrow. "The Archon protects me, Elowen. You're wasting your efforts."

I lunged for him, but he flitted out of the way,

dodging back with alarming speed. It was almost as if he disappeared into the shadows. I pivoted.

As the blood roared in my ears, I hurled my last dagger at him. He snatched it from the air, then twirled it between his fingers. "I feel as if you're not listening to me."

"What are you?"

His eyebrows rose. "Untouchable."

He shifted through the air too quickly for me to react.

He pinned me against the tree trunk, and my back slammed into the bark. One of his arms pressed against me. With otherworldly power, his strength and speed sent a shock through my system.

*What the hell am I dealing with here?*

"Elowen, if I don't capture you, you will be killed by someone far worse. With me, at least you'll get a chance to live. Trust me."

Absolutely not. I could never trust him.

His blue eyes shone with a mournful innocence. Cloaked in shadows, he towered over me.

My fingers twitched, hungry to kill again. I wondered if he was still immune to my power, or would he fold if I hit him with all the magic I had?

I reached up and pressed my palm over the beautiful planes of his face. Shadows churned in me, desperate to devour him, to suck the life from him. A shiver rushed over my skin, making the air cold around me. I could grow addicted to this dark pleasure. It rippled through me, cool and electric, and shadows darkened the air around him.

I looked up, searching for the spread of dark veins over his skin, the poison rushing through.

The Serpent's voice rasped in my mind. *Bring this beautiful man to his knees. Make him beg your forgiveness.*

I watched as his eyelids fluttered closed and he exhaled. Time seemed to slow, an icy breeze rushing over us. Thunder rolled over the horizon, but still, I kept my palm pressed against his skin—cool to the touch, marble-smooth. Darkness breathed around him like bellows exhaling smoke, and forbidden pleasure rolled through my body. As a charge passed between us, visions flitted through my mind until they crystallized on one image—the Magister, bare-chested, with a spiked crown tattoo on his chest. Blood spattered a pendant that hung from a chain around his neck, the little silver surface etched with a butterfly—

What the hell was that? Whatever the case, Maelor wasn't dying.

His eyes snapped open once more, and he covered my hand with his. "It's been a long time since I felt my heart race. It seems like a dangerous thing." His murmured words felt like a dark caress up my spine.

A violent, holy sort of ecstasy burned in his eyes. His cloak had opened a little, exposing his clavicle. As much as I loathed him, the man was hauntingly beautiful. And the Serpent must be whispering in my mind because I had the most bizarre desire to lean in closer and kiss him.

"Why don't you die?" I croaked. "I've never met anyone who can live through my touch."

He pulled my hand from his face. "Don't you believe the Archon protects those of us who serve him? That he empowers us?"

I nodded, feeling the blood drain from my face. What I wanted to say was that sometimes, I couldn't tell the difference between the Archon and the Serpent. Both were powerful, destructive, and demanded fealty.

"I appreciate your reasons for wanting to escape, Elowen," he said quietly. "The Pater wanted me to kill you. I had to persuade him that I should bring you back alive. But it won't be easy in the trials. Now, the others will have you marked as the biggest threat after your public displays of magic. No one has ever escaped after a Finding."

I had no regrets, but my heart pounded in my chest anyway. "Maybe the Archon will protect me as he does you."

"Maybe so." He glanced over my shoulder. "The boy is gone."

"He's only a child." I forced a calmness into my voice that I didn't feel. "And he has no magic."

He cocked his head. "I need to get you to Ruefield Castle. Trust me when I say there is no escaping the Magister. Sion is ruthless." He arched an eyebrow. "So will you come with me the easy way or the hard way?"

Out of weapons and outmatched, I didn't have many choices. "Whatever."

Maelor gripped my shoulders and spun me around. Pressing me against the tree trunk, he bound my hands —this time with iron. I wouldn't be carving my way out of these manacles.

As the sound of a horse's hooves drew closer in the darkness, Maelor called out, "Sion!"

I turned to see the Magister weaving between the shadowy trees, mounted on his horse. A cloak hid his face. Sion. Even that sounded lost to time, dredged from the past.

"Call off the Luminari," said Maelor. "Elowen has realized the error of her ways, and she's giving herself over willingly to the trials. She's begged forgiveness."

I did no such thing.

"She's still an escape risk. Or at least a risk of trying." Sion dismounted with an easy grace. Cloaked in shadows, he crossed closer to me. His amber-flecked eyes danced with amusement, and his lips curled in a faint smile. "Though I don't know how she thought she could escape us. This little one with the deadly touch is completely devoid of sense, I'm afraid."

My jaw tightened. I hated the way he was speaking about me like I wasn't there.

He stalked closer to me, towering above me as he lifted my chin with his fingertips. Under his cowl, I glimpsed a strong jawline and a dimple in the center of his chin. Gold flecks blazed in his honey-kissed eyes.

He'd be beautiful if it weren't for the sense of brutality that radiated from every one of his muscles.

"What a pair you two will make." He chuckled softly, a disturbingly sensual sound. "A Raven Lord who thinks of nothing but forbidden touch and a witch who can kill if she does."

Inwardly, I was rattling off prayers for Leo's safety. *Please, Archon. Please get him to Eboria. Keep him safe with a full belly and someone to look after him.*

"You should know that you can't run from us." Sion dropped my chin. "The Order will always find you. *We* will always find you."

Ice ran through my blood.

It was another ten minutes before I realized that Sion had touched my skin, unflinching.

Was I supposed to believe the Archon protected him, too?

# CHAPTER 12

Maelor rode behind me on the horse with his arms wrapped around me to hold the reins. The muscles in his chest and his steely arms moved against me as he guided the horse through the storm. Rain droplets shone on the skin of his hands.

A powerful gale whipped the rain at us from behind, but Maelor's body shielded my back from it. Here, on the west coast, the sea air smelled different. Sharper.

What I hated more than anything right now was how much I loved the feel of this evil Raven Lord's body against mine—and I knew it was only because I'd been starved of touch for so many years. I'd grown ravenous for it.

Lightning flashed in the dark, illuminating the Magister a few feet ahead of us. A ripple of dread snaked up my nape at his dark form. When he turned back to look at us, the eerie brightness of his eyes reminded me of a nocturnal animal hunting in the shadows.

The stormy wind whipping over us felt unnatural, like the Archon was punishing us. But if I could thank him for one thing, it was that Leo had made it away from these people. They didn't seem particularly interested in hunting him down, either. Maybe they hadn't seen his tattoo. For all they knew, he was just an ordinary boy, unmarked.

My gaze flicked to the pale skin of Maelor's hands. I wanted to reach for them, to stroke my fingertips over his knuckles. I wanted to try my curse on him again, but he had unfortunately made that impossible with the iron manacles.

I shifted my hands behind me. Maelor smelled of sandalwood, smooth and rich. Calming, almost. I should hate it, but I hadn't been this close to anyone since I was a teenager.

Being a Raven, his body was nearly as covered as mine was, head to toe in a black cloak. But the cloak was open behind me. And if I slid my fingertips under his shirt—

As I brushed my fingertips against his finely cut abs, Maelor tensed, then inhaled sharply.

He looked like an ordinary Raven, but beneath his tunic was the muscled body of a soldier.

"What are you doing?" Under that smooth murmur

was the knife edge of alarm. It was the reaction of someone who thought he might be tortured.

And given how much I loathed him, torturing him felt like a fantastic idea.

"Testing again," I said, pulling my fingers from his bare skin. "For the past ten years, I've killed anyone I touched, but now it seems the two of you are protected."

His voice was husky as he responded, "Sion and I are strongly protected by the Archon due to our station. But if you keep using that cursed magic, you won't survive long. Your magic will kill most of the Ravens and Luminari, and all the Penitents."

I frowned. Either they *were* protected by the Archon or they were witches just like me. Just two more cursed humans, twisted by the darkness inside.

"You don't move like any person I've ever seen before," I said.

And my real question was why had he allowed me to live at all? What did this Raven Lord have in mind for me?

Maelor's body felt unyielding behind me. "I've been with the Order so long, I've almost forgotten what it's like to be a person."

That sounded eerily like the feeling I got when I used my cursed magic. Empty inside. Soulless. "You don't look that old."

"I try to keep some of who I was, to remember who I was before. To remember it every day and every night." He breathed in deeply. "Elowen, how did you end up cursed? You weren't born like this, were you?"

Unease rippled through me at the way he said my name, like we were friends. What was his game, exactly? I didn't know him yet, and he was much harder to read than the Baron. I didn't know what he wanted to hear from me. And for some reason, that left me with a strange, destructive desire to just tell him the actual truth. To tell him *everything*.

But I swallowed it instead, tasting the bitterness. It would be stupid to tell the Raven Lord more than I had to. "Who could say?" I asked. "Lord, can you tell me anything about the trials?"

"They will be brutal. The Order views all of you as guilty, and all the other Penitents will try to eliminate you first. Everyone will be attempting to kill you."

I swallowed hard, thinking only of getting back to Leo. "So I've been told."

"But you do have a chance. The Archon, in his mercy, allows one Penitent to live. Whoever survives will be stripped of magic and allowed to return home."

My heart raced. There was a chance—an infinitesimally small one, but a chance nonetheless—that I could get rid of my curse. That I could actually hug Leo. "One out of how many?"

"A hundred or so."

I closed my eyes, not loving the odds. "How does the Archon choose?"

"Most of you will die in the trials. Usually five or

ten survive all three. From those, the Pater chooses one to live. Because only one lives, the other Penitents will want to reduce the number of people left at the end. The trials are a bloodbath."

I nodded, and rain slid down my face. "I've heard as much." I could only thank the heavens that Leo wasn't here. The boy didn't have a fighting bone in his body, and I prayed that he *never* ended up here. "The Archon chooses those who are the best at killing," I said, raising my voice over the wind. "That's who he wants to live?"

"The Order believes that those who make it out of the trials have been guided by the Archon. He protects those with faith. And as for the final one, the forgiven one…only the Pater knows how that works."

"Theoretically," I ventured, "I could touch all the other accused and remain the only one standing."

"No." His deep voice resonated in the air around me. "You won't be able to use your magic. The Luminari will kill you."

I wanted to ask him why, if the Archon truly controlled everything, I'd ended up with a curse that he loathed, but I kept my mouth shut.

Nearby, lightning cracked the black sky, illuminating dark, rolling meadows that spread out in either direction. Thunder pealed over the shadow-cloaked kingdom.

"What happened to your wrists?" Maelor asked in a quiet murmur.

"Burned." I didn't need to tell him that the Baron

had held each of my arms over an open flame while I screamed. That he'd wanted me to feel a real terror of fire so then he could use my fears against me.

"It must have hurt a lot."

I clenched my jaw. What was this ridiculous pretense of sympathy? "Not nearly as much as it will to burn at the end of the trials."

Rain weighed down my wool cloak against my skin, making me shiver. When the lightning flashed, I caught a glimpse of a towering castle on a hill on the horizon.

In the relentless storm, my thoughts kept flicking back to Leo, wondering if he'd found the right road or if he'd found shelter in the rain. I didn't know how well he'd managed to find the acorns, of if he'd remember to boil them, or—

"I can feel your fear," said Maelor quietly.

"I'm not afraid," I lied. I made my voice calm, almost singsong.

Leo must be out of his mind with hunger. I had no idea if his uncle would take him in, even if he made it there. There wasn't a lot of protection for an orphan boy in Merthyn.

But I had no reason to say all of that to the lord. Here, it was always a mistake to let strangers know what you truly cared about.

Up ahead, gold lights glittered from some of the castle's narrow windows.

"What is Ruefield Castle?" I asked. I'd never even heard of it.

"Long ago, in the dark ages, it was a center for philosophy and worship of the old gods. Once the Tyrenian Empire arrived to teach us about the one true god, the Order took over. Apart from the trials, it's a place where Ravens can quietly study the Luminis Codex."

Pious studying to the pleasing sound of human screams. Sounded *just like* the Order.

"Elowen." Maelor's deep voice had a soothing quality that made me want to lean further into him, even if he was a monster. "If you want to get back to that boy, you need to do everything you can to survive. Think about nothing except survival. If others die... that is as the Archon chooses."

I let out a long, slow breath. "Any other words of advice for me, Raven Lord?" I might not know what his agenda was, but if he was willing to tell me things, I'd use him for every ounce of information I could get.

"Be brutal," he replied bluntly. "You have no friends here. You have no family. You are not Elowen anymore. You are just another witch."

My mouth went dry as I thought of Lydia. Maybe, within the next few weeks, my oldest friend would die at my hands.

Maelor guided the horse onto a cobbled road that led to the castle gates, which glistened in the rain.

Lightning reflected off the soaked walls and towers of Ruefield Castle. Standing on top of the hill, the castle towered over the dark landscape. The lights I'd spotted from farther away were still just pinpricks of gold, even from closer up. Its highest spires disappeared into the storm clouds. As it loomed ahead, I felt tiny and powerless in its presence. Ruefield Castle was the size of a city, fortified like a kingdom.

Another burst of lightning had me gazing up at the stone walls surrounding the castle, dizzyingly high and made of golden stone. The gate barring entry looked a hundred feet high, with thick wood and iron reinforcements. I shivered as we approached, hoping Leo would soon be drying off in a home much cozier than this.

Guards flanked the enormous doors. Wearing hooded cloaks, they shielded their torches beneath the large gargoyles that jutted from the walls. The flames whipped and danced in the darkness.

I flexed my wrists, imagining that I had the strength to break free from these manacles. But all I could do was scratch at my skin.

Moving closer, I let my gaze flick up at the colossal door, its surface marred with dents from battles in centuries past. Rivulets of rain streamed down the front of the iron bolts across the door. On either side, the towering battlements and walls stretched out across the dark landscape.

Just a few feet from the door, the Magister called out, "The Magister Solaris returns."

A creaking, groaning sound rolled through the quiet night, metal cranking against metal as the iron bolts shifted upward like the fingers of a great monster.

The deep rumble of heavy wood against stone sent a shiver through my belly. Slowly, the giant doors opened. Despair settled in my stomach as we crossed over the threshold.

The horses' hooves clacked over cobblestones. Behind us, the great boom of doors closing had my shoulders sagging. As the horses carried us between towering stone walls, the iron bars slid into place at our backs.

I scanned my surroundings, searching for spots I might use to hide. Walls rose up on either side of us, their battlements lined with archers. We followed the curve of a path between them. In alcoves along the way, torches flickered, casting writhing light over rain-soaked cobbles. I breathed in the scent of moss and stone. After the hours I'd spent in the saddle, the pain in my arms was a sharp jolt that ran from my shoulders down to my wrists.

At last, a break in the inner wall opened into a stone courtyard. On a sloping hill ahead, the dark castle rose to the stormy skies like a god of stone.

Sion turned to me. "Welcome to your new home. Ruefield Castle. You will be imprisoned in the Mauber-geonne Tower."

I inhaled a shaky breath. There was no going back, now, and there would be no escaping this place.

Fear wrapped its bony fingers around my heart. In all likelihood, this would be the place I'd die.

# CHAPTER 13

My legs burned from what seemed like an endless march up a winding stairwell, following just behind Maelor. When he finally pushed through a door into a small corridor, I exhaled with relief. My thighs ached.

He turned back to me. "I'll take the manacles off you once you're inside." In the flickering torchlight, Maelor's pale blue eyes and beautiful features looked haunted. "I think you are capable of a great many things, some of them terrifying. But I think you're too smart to try to escape again. I won't put them back on you."

Given the way the Raven Lord had spared my life, and now the way he spoke to me—with something almost like respect—I could only imagine he'd already devised some sort of use for me. Perhaps, like the

Baron, he planned to use my curse as his own weapon. What a great gift for those who wanted to kill...

He pulled out a large set of iron keys to open the door to my tower room, then pushed the door open.

As I followed Maelor inside, the musky, damp air made it hard to breathe. There wasn't much in here— just a rough wooden table, a bed of hay, and etchings on the walls. Candles in iron sconces cast dim light over the room, but the darkness seemed to swallow it. A narrow window the size of an arrow slit let in a crack of white light when lightning flashed.

Maelor stepped behind me, and I heard the clink of the keys against my manacles. When he loosened them, I groaned and turned to face him. I rubbed the raw skin at my wrists. My shoulders burned.

"What happens tomorrow?" I asked.

"You'll have attendants to clean you and dress you. Then you'll meet the other Penitents. You'll be well fed. Between the dangers of the trials, you'll be looked after here. But during the trials…"

*Treated with gentle care right up until we light you on fire.* And why, exactly, would that be? Kindness in a place like this didn't make any sense, but I was sure I'd learn the real reason for those comforts soon enough.

Candlelight gilded the angles of his gorgeous face. "Goodnight, Elowen."

He stepped back into the hall, closing the door behind him. I heard the sound of an iron bar sliding over the door, leaving me alone with only the flickering light and shadows. I crossed to the window and cupped my hands against the diamond-paned glass to try to peer outside.

From what I could see in the dark, this place was a meandering labyrinth of stone, a city of towers and buildings surrounding a vast courtyard. Lightning kept flashing outside, and I caught a glimpse of the rambling hedge maze that stretched out over the courtyard. Rain lashed the narrow window as I peered outside.

When I turned back to my little tower room, my gaze roamed over the carvings. I traced my fingertips over some of them, and ice slid over my skin. Names had been carved into every inch of the walls in here— of the imprisoned, of the dead.

The old, blocky Tyrenian alphabet from centuries ago marked some of the stones. Others had engraved prayers to the old gods or to the Archon. A beautiful family sigil of a sinuous dragon was chiseled in the stone, along with stars and planets.

I traced the names with my fingertips, and my skin prickled with the feeling that thousands of ghosts lingered here. Centuries of the condemned had picked up blades, demanding to be remembered. A monument to the fallen. If I had a dagger, I'd do the same. It felt like my tomb, too.

I sat on the bed. Without knowing where Leo was, I'd never sleep. I stared out the window, trying to picture him safe in the shelter of a cave, filling his stomach with boiled acorns. I'd never forgive the people who separated me from him.

As I pictured him, a burst of white light illuminated the room, and a deafening boom shook the walls. Shifting on the bed, I peered out the window. The lightning had struck a tree a few hundred yards away. In the courtyard, it blazed like a torch in the dark. That didn't seem like a great omen, did it?

A second strike ignited the air just outside the window, the following boom of thunder loud as a drum. I clamped my hands over my ears at the sound. It must have struck the tower itself because the vibrations rumbled through the rocks around me. When I breathed in, the air smelled scorched, the stones hot beneath me.

Cracks spiderwebbed across the wall, shooting up toward the vaulted ceiling. The lightning, I thought, had to have struck this very tower. Definitely a bad sign. Dust rained down on me, and I covered my head with my hands.

I heard the sound of iron shifting, and the door swung open. Maelor stood in the doorway, frowning at me. "Are you all right?"

I glanced at the cracked stones. "Lighting struck the tower, but I think it's fine."

"Right. Well, you're coming with me, anyway." He turned and stalked into the hallway, expecting me to follow him.

My eyebrows flicked up as I walked tentatively after

him. The Raven Lord *definitely* had an agenda in mind for me. And as I followed him through the vaulted hall, I began to piece together what it might be.

People with nothing to lose were harder to control. You couldn't take anything from them. And that was where the comforts came in. A nice bed, good food, a bath—the respect of a powerful man like the Raven Lord. These were all things that could be taken back.

Maelor, I thought, intended to use me. Whether it was for information or destruction, I had no idea. But it would take more than good food and some kind words to get me dancing to his tune.

The cold castle air chilled my skin through the damp cloak, and he led me from the Maubergeonne Tower into a soaring corridor with mullioned windows. Bronze sun sigils hung on the walls, the symbol of the Archon. Through the windows, I could see some of the stone buildings jutting from the darkness. Lightning flashed, and I caught the faint golden hue of the towering boundary walls in the distance. They practically pierced the clouds, impossible to scale. My gaze swept over to the Maubergonne Tower to the right, where we'd just escaped. Chunks of rock were tumbling off the roof where the lightning had struck it.

Maelor glanced back at me. "I don't know if the Archon wants you dead or protected, but lightning striking your exact location is surely a sign."

He stalked through the hall, his cloak billowing behind him, and I followed. He stopped before an arched oak door, then pulled out an iron key to unlock it. When he pushed open the door, he revealed a vast domed room with a ceiling supported by lofty columns. I stepped inside after him, smelling sandalwood.

My first thought was that he'd taken us into a temple, but this dome had no oculus. Instead, its faded blue and gold paint looked like the night sky. An enormous brass telescope stretched all the way up to a glass aperture in the ceiling. Around the room, candles flickered, casting warm light over the space. Sheer spheres hung from the dome on delicate strings, representing our seven planets. In the center of the room stood something I thought was called a meridian circle, its rings etched with symbols to track the stars.

Stunned, I let my gaze trail over the gilded instruments that littered the place. Leo would *adore* this... well, if it weren't for the grim presence of the Raven Lord. Leo loved books about the stars and planets. I'd been over the old texts I could find with him. They'd all been written before the Harrowing, when scholars were allowed to study the heavenly spheres.

Columns flanked starry stained glass windows. An enormous brass celestial globe rotated near one of them, a complex series of rings that shifted around a sphere. Papers scrawled with writing and numbers littered every surface—the desks, the floor, even a bed.

"Is this your room?" I asked.

He ran his hand through his hair and looked around

as if noticing the mess for the first time. He turned to organize a pile of books and papers strewn over the desk. "When I joined the Order, it was empty, so I moved in."

"It was empty because the Order forbids this knowledge."

He flashed me a rueful smile. "Well, it seemed a waste to let the room go unused."

"And I'm here, in your room, because you believe the lightning strike is a sign from the Archon?"

He splayed his fingers out, his mournful blue eyes locked on me. "Precisely."

I didn't believe him for a second.

I crossed to the celestial globe and ran my fingers over the etched surface. "Raven Lord, what drew you to this line of work, exactly?"

I turned to look at him again, and my heart jumped a little at the way he was watching me. Like he was *hungry*.

His pale gaze burned with an unnerving intensity. "The Order teaches us that we must resist the things our bodies crave because if we give in, we lose our souls. You know what that's like, don't you?"

I tightened my jaw, not answering him.

"We become like animals," he went on. "Driven only by primal cravings. Hunger. Lust. Violence. We become beasts that feed on sex and death." His voice had a tension in it, and he pulled his gaze away. In the candlelight, shadows sculpted his high cheekbones. "If I take what I want, I will lose my divine light—or what's left of it. The Order gives us control over ourselves."

I felt my cheeks flame. Anger, perhaps. If the Archon didn't want us to feel lust, then why would he create us with it? What was wrong with the way we were?

I turned away from Maelor and surveyed the crooked stacks of books strewn over desks and shelves. The chaos in his room seemed completely at odds with his determination to have control over his life.

"So, I'm staying here?" I asked.

"I think it's best that I keep an eye on you." Now, his soft voice had a quiet edge. He pointed to the rumpled bed with deep blue blankets tucked under the window. Open books lay strewn around it, along with parchments scrawled with writing. "You can sleep there. I'll sleep in a chair."

I crossed to the telescope, feeling a pang again that Leo would never get to see this. "Maelor, how many days do I have until the first trial?"

"Tomorrow is a day of rest. There'll be a ritual bath to purify you of sin, to spiritually cleanse you. The first trial begins the next day. And you will need all the rest you can get to survive it."

I closed my eyes, and my insides twisted.

# CHAPTER 14

By the time the sun rose above the observatory, I felt half-mad. Without knowing what had happened to Leo, there was no way I could sleep. Instead, I'd been poring through books to find out whatever I could about Ruefield Castle and the trials. All I'd learned was that ancient tunnels had been carved under the lands around here. The tunnels were tombs, monuments to the dead from the days before the first Tyrenian emperor arrived. Once, monoliths rose above the tunnels, hymns to the old gods.

I found little that was useful in the books. And as the hours wore on, the texts had started to shift and blend in my mind until nothing made sense anymore. Maelor hadn't slept, either. He was still at his desk, frantically writing something.

With heavy eyelids, I leaned against the diamond-paned window, staring out at the endless castle grounds of golden stone. I'd arrived in the dark. The sun was now rising, kissing the castle with honey and rose. Still resting against the window, I let my eyes shut. The room smelled so alluring, of sandalwood and old books.

In the hollows of my mind, a vision bloomed to life. White wood anemones carpeted a forest floor, awash in golden light. But as I looked at them, a lash of blood spattered across them, a violent streak of red.

When I lifted my eyes from the forest floor, I was staring at the Magister Solaris. He moved inhumanly fast, shifting closer to me. He was going to kill me. Terror clawed at my heart.

My eyes snapped open, and I gasped, nearly falling from my chair. When I glanced at Maelor again, I found that he stood facing away from me. Shirtless, he wore only leather trousers. I took in his powerful back and arms, my gaze lingering over a deep scar in his flesh. I wondered how he'd ended up with that thick red ridge on his left side.

I shouldn't be staring. The Raven Lord stood for everything I loathed, and it wasn't fair that he looked this good.

But could I really be angry with myself when I hadn't seen a shirtless man in over a decade? When I hadn't touched one? Maelor's muscles shifted as he pulled on a white shirt. It slid down to his waist—

When he turned back to me, I realized I was still

staring. "What?" I said, a little too sharply, as though it were his fault.

The corner of his mouth twitched. "I thought you'd finally fallen asleep."

I shook my head. "Just for a minute."

A light knock sounded at the door.

"You won't survive if you refuse to sleep," he muttered as he crossed the room.

He pulled the door open, then he took a tray from someone's hands. The smell of freshly baked bread wafted into the room, and my mouth began to water.

Maelor slid the tray onto a little circular table next to me. Bread, honey, and fruit nestled on the tray next to a teapot. The scent of lavender rose from the spout. "The kitchens were closed when we arrived last night," he said. "I ordered them to bring you food as soon as the sun rose. I know you haven't eaten."

My stomach rumbled as I watched curls of steam rise from the bread. But hungry as I was, I couldn't quite bring myself to eat it. This wasn't food. This was blackmail. "Do you think that if you treat me well enough, I'll do whatever you want?"

I wished I could take the words back. In my fatigue, I'd let too much of my true feelings slip out.

A muscle tensed in his jaw. "You're in Ruefield under the command of the Raven Lord. You'll do whatever I want, no matter how I treat you." The morning light caught in Maelor's pale eyes. "And I know you're starving, so why not eat it?"

"I thought we were supposed to ignore everything our bodies wanted," I said dully.

"You could survive these trials, Elowen." He leaned forward, his gaze piercing. "You were the only one able to escape yesterday. You have skills the others don't."

"And why would you want that?"

He stared at me, narrowing his eyes. "It's not your place to question me."

He had a point. Only my fatigue had loosened my tongue, but I should be keeping my doubts to myself. Better for him to think I was an idiot.

"Of course." I poured some lavender tea. "Aren't you hungry? You haven't eaten. Nor have you slept."

He studied me like he was trying to read me. Something about him was unnervingly still, a wolf crouching motionless before an attack.

After a moment, he raised a dark eyebrow. "You're not worried for yourself, are you? It's the boy you were trying to save."

My stomach plummeted. *Bollocks.* He'd already figured out how to pull my strings. At least he had no idea where Leo was.

I crossed my legs, wearing a bland smile, and I sipped my tea. "That boy? No. We're not related."

"You do remember I said I can tell when people are lying?"

"We *aren't* related," I said. "So your lie-detecting abilities must be broken."

"Maybe not by blood." He rose from the chair and

pulled on his Raven Lord's robe, buttoning it down the front. "Fine. I'll find him."

Panic twined around my heart. "No," I said sharply. "He doesn't belong here, and he doesn't have anything to do with anything. He's just an ordinary boy."

"I won't bring him here." He finished buttoning his robe. "I will only make sure that he's safe so you'll agree to eat. Can he write?"

My heart was racing out of control, and I didn't answer. Surely the Raven Lord would never find him. Not unless Leo went back to the Briarwood manor. But without me there, the Baron would surely turn him away. Not in a million years would I tell the Raven Lord where to find Leo.

"I think he's in the weald," I lied. "Somewhere in the forest."

"If he can write," said Maelor, "I'll bring back a note. You'll recognize his handwriting, I assume. You clearly won't trust me otherwise."

I arched an eyebrow. Did he honestly think I *should* trust him? He must be out of his mind.

He buttoned his stiff black collar. "I will leave him where he is or get him to safety. But if you are unable to focus during the trials, if you are unable to eat or sleep, you're going to die here. And they will either burn you alive or throw your carcass in the fields to rot."

"The weald," I repeated. I wondered if he could hear

the sharp edge of panic in my voice. "And aren't you sweet to care about a little boy?"

He stalked closer and peered down at me. His body went completely still. "Am I sweet? No." His deep voice was unnervingly quiet. "I am a monster. I crave things I should not. I *hunger*, Elowen, like you could never imagine. It's the discipline of the Order that helps me stay in control. It keeps me from indulging in my worst desires. And maybe it was a coincidence that lightning struck your tower after you arrived, but maybe it was a sign. Perhaps you have a greater purpose here, and it's my job to keep you alive."

I stared at him. I had no idea what to believe anymore.

He walked purposefully across the room. With his hand on the doorknob, he called over his shoulder, "You will be locked in here. One of the Silent Sisters will help prepare you for meeting the other Penitents later today." He glanced back at me before opening the door. "Don't try anything stupid while I'm gone."

He closed the door behind him, and I heard the bolt sliding over. His words rolled around in my mind like curses. *A monster.* At least we agreed on something.

I lifted my hand, staring at my fingertips. *I hunger.* Like him, I lusted after the sweet escape of a passionate kiss. But I also craved the creeping shadow of death.

Like him, I was something of a monster, too.

# CHAPTER 15

hree armed Luminari marched in front of me and three behind. At the head of the procession, a woman with a white cloth headdress led the way, draped entirely in thin white fabric. In this part of the castle, the vaulted ceilings dwarfed all of us. I felt tiny under their soaring, peaked arches.

My mind roared with worries for Leo. As I walked, I glanced out the windows, squinting at the bright light that slanted in. The dark mountain loomed in the distance.

What had Leo done all night? There was no way he'd slept in a dark cave in unfamiliar woods.

My jaw tightened. They'd separated me from Leo when he needed me. My anger was a toxin sliding through my veins, threatening to corrode me from the inside out.

After Leo's parents died, I'd been the worst possible

choice to look after him. But then slowly, day by day, I'd grown irrevocably attached to him, and it felt like the Archon had given me a single gift after so much darkness.

The veiled woman stopped before a doorway and motioned for me to enter.

I stepped into a room of white tiles and columns where the sun spilled through windows. In the center, steam coiled from a round bath. A dozen Luminari stood around the perimeter, watching me. The veiled woman stood by the door—she still hadn't said a single word to me.

This all seemed like a great deal of effort just to bathe an accused witch. Supposedly, it served a spiritual purpose. Purification. But I think they were trying to send a message to us. They were forcing us to strip down in front of a group of armed soldiers, to remind us that we had nothing and that they had all the power. Just like Maelor had said, I was here at Ruefield under the control of the Raven Lord, and I would do whatever he wanted.

Then again...

With the right mindset, it could be more uncomfortable for them than for us. The Luminari were warriors *and* monks. Maybe my nakedness would be far worse for their vows of chastity than it would be for me.

I let my cloak drop to the tile floor. I pulled off my shirt, then my trousers. The cold air of the castle whispered over me, and I stripped off my camisole, my underwear.

I took a few steps closer to one of the Luminari—a man with dark eyes and thick eyebrows. His body went completely rigid, eyes locked onto the ceiling. His jaw tightened.

"Something wrong?" I asked. "Are you thinking about the Archon, as you should be? Or are you imagining what it would be like to finally have the touch of a woman?"

They might be armed to the teeth, but all it took was a woman's nipples to scare the life out of these virgins.

The veiled woman stomped on the tiles, and she pointed at the bath emphatically. Barefoot and naked, I crossed over to it. I lowered myself in, feeling my skin heating. The barracks didn't have a bath, and I'd almost never had the luxury of a proper soak in a tub. Instead, the soldiers and I usually washed ourselves in a large metal tin of cool water. This? This was glorious. At this point, I didn't even care if it was all some kind of manipulation.

I dipped down under the warm water, wetting my hair.

The Order taught us that our salvation lay in our minds, our spirits. But they really didn't seem to mind comfort, did they? In here, there was even a mirror that reflected the bright sunlight. I'd only looked in a proper mirror a few times, in the Baron's home.

I rubbed the soap over my skin, inhaling the faint scent of rose. In the heat of the bathwater, the old scars on my wrists turned an angry red.

When I stepped from the bath, water dripped off my body. The veiled woman hurried over with a white linen cloth, eager to stop me from upsetting the Luminari again. As I dried myself off, she slipped away. Wrapped in the linen, I crossed over to the mirror. Polished silver, framed in gold—I'd never seen anything like it.

I stared back at my face.

Father always said I looked like my mother, but I could hardly remember her. I saw only my father— thick, dark eyebrows and eyelashes, a full mouth, sun-kissed olive skin, a beauty mark on my cheekbone. Vanity was a sin, but I thought it would be a shame for this face to burn in the flames of a witchstake.

Behind me, the veiled woman approached. I stared into the mirror while she handed me clothes to dress myself. The black leather trousers surprised me— women in Merthyn almost always wore dresses. But here, I supposed we were to lose our old identities.

I slid into a sleeveless black shirt, the material soft against my skin. A black leather doublet fit tightly over it, almost like a corset. I ran my fingers over the material. This would do nicely as a little bit of armor during the trials, I mused.

The woman handed me long, black gloves, and I

slipped my hands into them. No more using my cursed magic here at Ruefield.

Dressed head to toe in black, I stared at the image of an assassin.

But it seemed I wasn't finished because the woman draped a black hooded cloak over me, then pulled up the cowl over my wet hair. Even if she didn't speak, I understood the message: I was no longer Elowen, only a Penitent.

I stared back at my shadowed face.

I didn't care if Maelor was the Raven Lord. If he harmed Leo in any way, I would end his life.

DRAPED IN BLACK, I followed the woman up a swooping stone stairwell to the entrance of a vast dining hall. As I stepped under the archway, my stomach plummeted at the numbers. In the hall, a legion of other Penitents sat at long tables that stretched from one end to the other. Light from stained glass windows flecked their anonymous black cowls with gold and crimson. My heart sank at the sight of them. Weeks from now, they'd all be dead.

As I stood in the doorway, they turned to stare at me, and the murmurs died down to silence. My gaze landed on the man I'd walked near in the cart—the man with a shaved, tattooed head.

Scowling at me, he mouthed, "Witch."

My fingers curled into fists. So, I definitely had a target on my back. In fact, *everyone* was staring at me. I guess the rumors had spread fast—the stories about the witch who murdered a soldier and escaped on a stolen horse. I suppose they probably never expected me to come back alive.

My gaze flicked to the empty tables in arched alcoves that lined the hall. I desperately wanted to sit alone, except setting myself apart even further didn't seem like a great idea.

While I searched for a place to sit among the others, my gaze locked on Lydia, a wisp of her platinum hair escaping from her hood. I narrowed my eyes at her, feeling the scars on my wrists tingle under my black gloves. She dropped her eyes, hiding in the shadows of her hood.

I recognized another familiar face, though. Without a word, I stalked into the hall and took the seat next to Percival de Montfort. If nothing else, he at least seemed normal.

"You know, I did hope you would make it out alive." His cut-glass accent reminded me of the Baron for just a moment.

"The Ravens are hard to escape," I muttered.

Across from me sat a pale, gaunt-looking man. His dry, flaxen hair hung in front of enormous eyes, and his cheekbones stood out sharply. On his fingers were tattooed the words HARP and BARD.

He smiled at me. "Hello," he rasped. "Your reputation precedes you."

"That's really too bad." In Merthyn, being the center of attention was never a good thing.

A veiled woman slid a plate before me, and I was shocked by how sumptuous it looked: roasted lamb with pumpkin and turnips, and the whole meal flavored with rosemary and thyme. The woman poured me a glass of wine. They really were looking after us here before they killed us. Probably, this was just another way to display their power.

The table had been set with bowls of bread and slices of cheese. I still had no appetite whatsoever, but I did take a piece of bread to gnaw on.

As I did, silence fell over the hall—one that sent chills running over my skin. I turned to watch Sion stride purposefully into the room, his sword slung around his waist. As he passed me, I felt his thrilling power ripple over my skin like the cold sea. His terrifying beauty was like a fist around my throat, choking me.

When he turned to face us, a cold smile flitted over his lips. His energy radiated from him. "Penitents." He spoke quietly, smoothly, because he had our full attention without the need to shout. "I hope you are giving thanks to us for the delicious food we provide in our generosity. The Archon is merciful, and between trials, he wants you well-fed and well-rested. In his infinite mercy, he will choose one of you to survive these trials. The forgiven one will survive a deadly labyrinth tomorrow. Many will lose their way and die of starvation. Others will succumb to the hunger of the wolves. Only those guided by the Archon will make it out alive."

I swallowed hard. I hoped that wasn't true because the Archon and I weren't on great terms.

The colored light streamed through one of the windows, daubing Sion's sharp jawline with scarlet. "In the second trial, you will resist the temptations of the Thornwood Forest. The worthy among you will be able to separate the divine nature of your mind from the animal cravings of your body. You must think clearly to answer our questions correctly." The corner of his full lips twitched, and light glinted from his eyes. "I'm afraid I'll have to kill anyone who fails, and that will likely be many of you." He shrugged, looking serene. "But it's what the Archon demands, and who am I to argue? In your third and final trial, you will enter Tyrenian ruins, haunted by the spirits of the dead from the Anarchy. You will retrieve the Oath Skull. Anyone whose faith betrays him will remain trapped inside the haunted ruins for all eternity."

The way his eyes danced, I felt like this was all a joke to him.

Fear thickened the atmosphere, making it hard to breathe. For a moment, I closed my eyes, trying to imagine myself scaling the outer walls. But they were impossibly high and smooth, without fingerholds or footholds. Legions of Luminari patrolled the battlements, waiting to shoot anyone who tried to escape.

"The small group who remains after those three trials," added Sion, "will be examined by the Pater." He lifted a finger. "One will be forgiven. One alone."

I shuddered.

Sion opened his palms to the ceiling. "The rest will burn in Sootfield to purify our kingdom. It may seem a cruel fate, but it's better to spend an hour on the pyre than an eternity in the torment of the abyss, isn't it? *Deus Invictus, Archon Magne.*"

His final prayer echoed in the hall, and fear roiled in my skull.

When I turned to look behind me, I found the tattooed man staring directly at me.

*A target on my back.*

# CHAPTER 16

*A*s the Magister stalked out of the room, he shot me a long, piercing look that made my pulse race. He'd just enumerated all the terrible ways we could be killed over the next few weeks, and my breath felt shallow, panicked. What were the chances of getting back to Leo now?

"I'm Hugo." The gaunt, blond man across from me interrupted my thoughts. He nodded toward the man beside him and said, "This is Godric. We heard what you did. Quite brave, that daring escape from the procession."

"Thanks." It didn't feel like a great idea to make friends with people I might have to kill in a few days.

"Brave. But we don't approve of magic," said Godric, loudly. "Or witchcraft, in case any Ravens are listening." His cowl had fallen, revealing dark hair pulled up into a loose bun. Wisps trailed down his stubbled cheekbones. He glared at his friend. "We don't need to make friends, Hugo. You won't be able to kill anyone if you like them. You're too nice for that."

*Exactly* what I'd been thinking.

Godric's gaze flicked back to me. "And she's an actual witch, Hugo. She'll kill you in moments, just with her thoughts."

I *wished* I could kill with my thoughts. But at his warning, a shiver rippled up my nape. How many had already decided I was the biggest threat here? I'd be the first target for everyone when it was time to start killing.

"I'm not allowed to use magic," I said emphatically.

"I don't want to kill anyone." Hugo's gaze drifted to the colored windows above. "I'm a poet these days, not a killer. Godric, my slaughtering days are over. The gods speak through my harp."

"*God,*" his friend corrected sharply. "Singular. Remember? Honestly."

"Yes," Hugo agreed. A bead of sweat ran down his temple, and he wiped it off. "That."

"You don't have a choice here, mate," said Percival. A ragged scar ran down the side of his forehead to his temple, and I wondered what had happened to him. "Thanks to the Order, your days of choosing are over. Why do you think they took our clothes from us? We're not *us* anymore. What did you say your name was? Hugo? You're not Hugo anymore; I'm not Percival de Montfort. We're just Penitents. We do what they say. And if they say to kill, we kill."

"Just stick with me as much as you can," muttered Godric to his pale friend.

I swallowed hard as a tiny kernel of an idea began to bloom in my mind. On the one hand, emotional ties were a bad idea. They'd stop us from doing what we needed to do to survive. On the other hand, Godric was clearly going to look after his friend. They were allies. A team. Of course, in the end, only one could win. But it would increase their chances of being that one survivor, wouldn't it?

Loneliness was the Order's greatest weapon. What if we took it away from them?

I glanced over my shoulder and found Lydia staring daggers at me. I swallowed hard. Once, we could have been allies. Not anymore, obviously. She should be lying in bed with Anselm right now, wrapped in his arms.

I turned from her, my gaze flicking between Godric and Hugo. "So, I take it you two are friends."

Hugo nodded. "We used to be soldiers. Now we're troubadours. I live for music. The spirits speak through my harp."

"You don't have a harp here, though, do you?" said Percival. He seemed brutally determined to make everyone face the reality of the situation. "Your harping days are over."

Godric frowned at someone in the distance, and he

blew a strand of black hair out of his eyes. "Guillaume the Dulcet accused us of being Serpent-touched." He glared across the room. "More like Guillaume the Duplicitous." He cupped his hand around his mouth, shouting, "Guillaume the *Deceitful*. Guillaume the *Dolt*! That's right. *Dolt*." His voice echoed over the hall, and a silence followed. Godric folded his arms, glaring. "Guillaume wanted our spot at the Crown and Dagger. Prick. Look where it got him."

Hugo scratched his cheek. "Godric counter-accused him, and now he's here, too. Really, he could have joined our troupe. Because now we're all here. And me, without my medicine." He sighed.

"Nah, he never could have joined us," said Godric. "He can't play the lute to save his life. He's always out of key. Killing that prick would be a favor to anyone with ears. In fact, I can't wait for the trials to start for that reason alone."

Hugo clutched his stomach. "I don't feel so well."

"It's the poppy water, you know that?" said Godric. "I told you to take it easy on that stuff."

Shadows darkened the skin beneath Hugo's bulging eyes. Under his cowl, his platinum hair stuck out in wild curls. "It's made me one with the Archon."

"Oh, *really*?" snapped Godric, pulling up his hood. "You're one with the Archon? Can your almighty omnipotence get us out of here, then, before we all die? Maybe some time before the Trial of the fucking Abyss?"

"What's the Trial of the Abyss?" I interrupted.

Godric's gaze flicked to me, and he pressed his lips into a thin line. "It's the worst one. If we even get that far. People go mad. They eat each other. They smash their own heads against the walls." His sun-kissed skin had paled, and he now looked nearly as sickly as Hugo without his medicine.

"I'm not afraid to die," muttered Hugo. "I will miss my cat, though, if you can miss people when you're dead."

"And you need to get back to Ariel, don't you? He sleeps on your pillow." Godric bit off an enormous chunk of his bread. "Look around the table. Which of these people do you actually think you could kill? Remember when you fought in the Harrowing? You were amazing. Not anymore." Godric narrowed his eyes at me. "How will you last more than a few minutes against a real witch?"

"Don't you know we're all real witches, according to the Order?" Percival snapped.

The way he said it so defensively made me wonder if he had real magic, too.

I twirled my water cup on the table. "Like I said, I'm not allowed to use magic during the trials. They'll kill me right away if I do. I'm not your biggest threat."

I glanced up at the stained glass windows, and my mind churned.

Maybe this meeting was an opportunity. Hugo might not be in the best shape of his life, but he *had* been a trained fighter. Godric was a soldier, too, and the man was the size of an ox.

The thought sparked in my skull, and I leaned forward. "What if the best way to get through this is to form alliances?"

"How would that work when only one person survives?" asked Percival. "At some point, the alliance has to be broken. It's not like we can kill all the Luminari in Ruefield, although…" He trailed off.

I nodded. "True. But I'm just thinking about getting the best chance. And what if our best chance is by keeping each other safe?"

Godric's forehead wrinkled. "And if you can't use your lethal magic, how are you going to help us?"

"I'm not just a witch. I trained as a soldier for Baron Throckmore." I avoided the word *assassin*. "I don't rely on my magic to kill."

Godric slapped the table. "A woman soldier? Well, now I've heard it all."

I sucked in a sharp breath. "All we can do is try to find the best chance of making it to the end."

From my side, a woman leaned forward. She pulled down her hood, showing off her dark hair threaded with glittering jewels and her delicate features. "You will have me as part of your alliance." It wasn't a question, and she spoke with a faint Aquitainian accent. "I will join."

Godric's gaze slid to her. "And what exactly would

you offer? Hugo and I killed hundreds in the Harrowing. Don't tell me you're a woman soldier, too."

She sighed dramatically. "Not a soldier. A healer."

Hugo's eyebrows rose. "Another real witch?"

"No," she said sharply. "Not a real witch. But it angered my parents when I learned peasant skills such as healing, so I did it."

"Sounds like bollocks," grumbled Godric. "No."

Hugo gripped his stomach, and his pale hair hung before his eyes. "Can you help me? I need my medicine."

The woman nodded. "When my father grew poppy-sick, I learned how to heal him. I can help you. If anyone gets injured, you will need me. So, I agree to join."

The fewer people I had trying to kill me at the outset, the better, but I had no idea if this woman was actually good at anything.

"What's your name?" I asked.

Her eyebrows raised with hope. "Sazia de Zallas, daughter of Vicomte Pau de Zallas. And I deeply regret coming to this Archon-forsaken kingdom on the cursed side of the sea."

"Fair enough." Godric rubbed his chin. "What about this? If this Aquitianian woman can actually help Hugo by tomorrow morning, I'll join your little alliance, and I will let her join, too. Because that would be a bloody miracle."

"You won't be able to get poppy water here to wean

yourself off slowly," said Percival. "Whatever Sazia has to offer is probably the best you can do to keep Hugo healthy."

"Good." Godric clapped his frail friend on the back. "We'll get you back into shape, Hugo. Just like you were in the king's army."

My throat tightened. If only that entire army could rise again. But the king had been burned, the maypoles torn down, and the Order had us digging our own graves.

And what could we do about it?

Only take away their greatest weapon—isolation.

# CHAPTER 17

*B*ack in the Raven Lord's room, I'd been sitting on a green silk daybed before a fireplace for hours. Heat from the flames warmed my face and skin as the sun slid lower in the sky. Apart from lunch and dinner with the other Penitents, I'd been alone in here all day, praying to the Archon that Maelor would never find Leo. That he'd actually searched the weald and found nothing.

My mind was a tempest. How many hours had it been since Leo had last eaten? Or slept? At dinner, I'd been a zombie, unable to speak clearly to my new allies. I only knew that Percival de Montfort had joined us, which seemed a good thing. He'd been trained to fight as a knight since he was a little boy.

In here, with only the walls for company, the loneliness made me feel emptied out.

Smoke from the fire curled into my nostrils. The

thing about burning to death was that it was brutally slow, and I'd already had a taste of the excruciating pain. I pulled off my gloves, flexing my fingers. I almost never had the chance to let my scarred skin breathe.

I stared at my wrists where the Baron had burned me. He'd wanted to give me an excuse for wearing the gloves, but he'd also wanted me to understand how truly painful it was to burn. *Don't ever let yourself get caught, Elowen, because the torment awaiting you is like nothing you can imagine.* That had been his lesson.

Sighing, I stared into the fireplace. I shouldn't be quite this worried. Surely Maelor would never find Leo. He didn't know a thing about the Eboria plan or Uncle Hamelin. Maybe Leo had made it all the way to Eboria unharmed.

Restless, I stood and crossed to Maelor's wooden writing desk, which was strewn with parchments, ink, and quills. Some of the papers displayed drawings of flowers, foxgloves and bluebells. Two torn pieces of a drawing lay side by side—a hawthorn tree. Next to the tree, he'd scribbled,

*A grief that may consume my mind*
*The loss of Pearl, two souls untwined*

What was *that* about? A wooden chest sat on his desk, and I opened it to find more drawings—one butterfly sketch after another—stuffed into the box. On some, he'd smeared them with paint. Violent streaks of vermillion, blue, and saffron streaked across the tidy black lines of the wings.

An icy shudder swept over my skin. In the recesses of my thoughts, a buried memory echoed. I'd seen a butterfly carved into a silver amulet...

But just as quickly as the memory had arrived, it was gone again. I was left staring at the oddly agonized art before me. Pain screamed from these vibrant smears of color.

In the corners of the writing desk, where it met the stone wall, I found ashes settled into the cracks. I smudged my fingers over them, turning my fingertips black. When I knelt, I found a large pile of cinders beneath the desk.

Odd. What was he burning in here? I rose, surveying the brightly hued clutter. On a table by the desk, colored pencils lay over a drawing of a landscape —green grass and a tree of bright gold, ripped in two. The words *so surely set in shining gold* were violently scribbled over part of the page.

I picked up a gold pencil to stare at it. I'd never seen anything so pretty in my life. How much would something like this cost?

I stared down at the back of my bare hand and traced gold pencil onto my skin. I drew a little star. With the pencil, I crossed back to the astrolabe, and I stared at my own brown eyes in the reflection. I drew gilded streaks beneath my eyelashes, tracing the sweep of my eye.

As the door creaked open, my heart leapt. I could

hardly breathe as Maelor crossed into the room, his eyes darting to me. I clutched his gold pencil.

He quirked an eyebrow. "What are you doing?"

But I had no interest in talking about the pencils right now. "What happened?"

He gave me a faint smile. "He's fine." As he stalked across the room to me, he pulled a folded piece of paper from his pocket.

With a racing heart, I unfolded it. I exhaled, long and slowly, scanning Leo's familiar handwriting, cramped on the right side where he always ran out of space because he held the pen wrong and smeared the ink at the edges. A few of the letters were backwards, as always.

ELOWEN — THE RAVEN LORD HELPED ME FIND HEMLIN. I WILL AP HELP HIM. HEMLIN.

LOVE

—Leo x

He always signed his name with an elaborate flourish for the *L*.

I traced my fingertips over his signature, imagining him writing it. My gaze flicked up to Maelor. "You helped him find his uncle?"

He nodded. "I found Leo on the road to Eboria. He was starving. I got him some food, and then I brought him to his uncle, who agreed to take Leo in as an apprentice."

"How?" I demanded. "How did you find him?"

He shrugged. "The Archon guided me."

*The Archon, the Archon.* It was the answer for everything here.

I breathed out slowly, and tears stung my eyes. While waiting, my muscles had been coiled tightly as corset laces. With the note in my hands, the tension started melting out of me.

"Thanks," I said simply. A fat teardrop fell from my eyelashes onto the paper, and I turned away, unwilling to cry in front of the Raven Lord. "I want to keep this." I clung to the note. If I died during these trials, this would be the last thing I'd ever hear from him. I slid the note into a pocket in my leather trousers. It would be my talisman. My good luck charm. The most important scrap of paper in the world to me right now.

With my back turned to Maelor, I brushed tears from my cheek.

"He's lucky to have you, you know," said Maelor.

I turned to look at him. I hated that the Raven Lord looked dizzyingly gorgeous in the firelight.

"Well, he doesn't have me now, does he?" I said. "Because you brought me here."

"Maybe the Archon wants you to live." He crossed to me and brushed his thumb over my cheekbone. "You have a streak of ashes on your face."

I didn't explain that I'd been snooping around his things.

I let out a long sigh. "The odds are not great of me returning to Leo. You know that."

"You must just focus on one trial at a time. Will you

be able to sleep now that you know Leo is fine?" asked Maelor. "The labyrinth begins tomorrow. You need to be alert."

"Did he seem welcoming? Leo's Uncle Hamelin?" I couldn't believe I was even asking him this, like I trusted him. He was the bloody Raven Lord.

"Yes. He said he felt bad about not taking him in before, and he regretted it, but he didn't know where to find you. He doesn't have children of his own. His wife died years ago."

I pressed the last of the tears from my eyelashes and waited until I was sure my voice would come out steadily before answering. "Yeah. I'll be able to sleep." Whatever his true motives were, he seemed willing to help me. I might as well use his help as much as possible. "Is there anything you can tell me that will help me get through it alive?"

"I'll tell you what I can, but nothing in the labyrinth is ever certain." He gestured at the green daybed before the fireplace.

His gaze dipped to my lips. The glance was just for a moment, but for some reason, it made my breath catch.

I dropped onto the daybed, feeling all the tension wash out of me. I stared into the writhing flames as Maelor sat beside me. Firelight wavered over his sharp cheekbones, his too-full lips. "Sion will probably tell everyone this tomorrow, but only those who get through the labyrinth by nightfall will survive. The moment the sun sets, the wolves will arrive. They're not ordinary wolves, though. Some say they're monstrous ghosts of pagans from the old days, hungry for the blood of their conquerors. Others say they're the spirits of those who died in the labyrinth, starving for blood, for life. Anyone they catch will be ripped to shreds."

I nodded. "And this is the organization you want to dedicate your life to?"

Ignoring my question, he went on. "The labyrinth is underground but open to the air. Walls will rise up on either side of you. Often, the Penitents grow disoriented and circle around the same part of the maze. You'll smell the dead from the last trial sometimes, and that's a clue that there might be a trap ahead. Their bodies are never recovered. But it can be hard to judge how the labyrinth will behave. The path always changes, almost like it's alive."

"I don't suppose you can draw me a map."

"All I can do is advise that you should get as close to the entrance at the start as possible. Whatever happens, you absolutely have to get out by nightfall."

I nodded. "Okay. I'll get to the front."

"But not the very front. You need others to test the traps for you. Otherwise, move as quickly as possible. There are a number of exits, but they're very hard to find, and they always change." He closed his eyes, rubbing his forehead. "You won't have any weapons unless you can make them in the labyrinth. No one is allowed to use magic."

Even if he was helping me, he was still the enemy, and I could never forget it. In the warmth of the fire-place, he pushed up the sleeves of his black robe. My gaze traced over his forearms—muscled and deeply scarred on his left arm.

"Were you a soldier?" I asked.

He looked at me with surprise. "A long time ago."

"In the Harrowing?"

Instead of answering, he stared into the fire. Shadows jumped and slid over his forearms. I glanced at the scar again, wondering what it would be like to be one of those shadows moving over him. I found myself reaching out to brush the tip of my finger over his arm. Maybe I wished I could hurt him with my touch.

He inhaled sharply, like I'd shocked him, and I pulled my hand away.

"Did that hurt?" I asked.

He shook his head, his blue eyes gleaming with curiosity. "No."

"That's a shame."

A smile ghosted over his lips. The way Maelor reacted to me told me that he didn't spend much time with people.

But of course he didn't. Everyone was terrified of the Raven Lord, and for good reason.

I bit my lip, staring at the bare skin of his arms. As he watched me, I brushed my fingertips over his wrist, and his muscles tensed. My gaze met his again. I felt as if an electric current were moving between my fingertips and his skin.

"Do you feel anything?" I asked.

"Oh, yes." He looked as if he were drinking me in.

The lord was as starved of touch as I was. But he was also a commander of the Order, an instrument of violence and utter destruction. A beautiful man forbidden from enjoying anything—and my enemy.

So why not torture him a little? Why not make him hate himself?

As he watched me, I reached up for his face and stroked his cheek. His eyes closed, and he let out a long sigh that sounded agonized. I brushed my thumb over his high cheekbone. "You still don't feel my magic?"

His skin felt smooth as marble. With his eyes closed, he murmured, "It's a different sort of pain." When he opened his eyes again, he pulled my hand away sharply. "Don't."

It was just as the Baron had taught me—find and exploit the weaknesses of your enemies. I wondered exactly how much it would take for him to lose control completely and betray his precious Order. If he didn't feel repentant for killing the innocent, maybe another sort of guilt could torment him.

He stood. "You should sleep, Elowen. You can take my bed." A line formed between his eyebrows. "That gold looks nice around your eyes."

I hated that a blush spread over my cheeks as he

said that.

I lifted the pencil. "I found your art supplies. This is the most beautiful thing I've ever seen."

"You can keep it, then."

Gifts from the Raven Lord. Was he warming to me already? I arched an eyebrow. "You won't join me in your bed?"

His jaw tensed. "I don't sleep much."

I sighed. "Of course you don't sleep much, because sleeping is enjoyable, and the Archon hates all pleasure." It no longer mattered if I let sacrilege tumble from my lips. What did I have to lose at this point? Maybe as I faced almost certain death, I had a little bit of freedom. But mostly, all I felt was exhaustion sinking into my bones. "If I survive the labyrinth, how much time will there be to rest before the next trial?"

"You'll have one day to recover. After the first trial, the survivors will spend time in the whispering chambers, unburdening yourselves to prepare for the next one."

I arched an eyebrow. "Surely you don't want more names from us."

"No, but you'll confess your sins to us. Cleanse your soul. It's what the Pater wants. Anyone who makes it out of the labyrinth will have blood on their hands."

And we were supposed to feel guilty for killing when they forced us to kill. "And you?" I asked. "Do you have dreams and memories you need to unburden?"

His pale gaze pierced me. "Oh, I have many. And when I'm not committing them, I'm thinking of them. My sins burn in my mind like a fire, Elowen." His gaze brushed down my body, a light stroke. "Right now, I'm thinking of you, and I should not be." He stood, sharply pulling down his sleeves. "I have much to regret. But it's not my role to confess to you, is it?" He waved at his bed. "You take the bed. I'll sleep here, or not at all."

I wondered what kept him up all night, scribbling on paper, then lighting it on fire. I pulled off my cloak, letting my hips swing a little as I walked closer to his bed.

I sighed. "I'll have you know, Maelor, I don't sleep fully clothed." This was an absolute lie. I always slept fully clothed, and with gloves. But if I had a little bit of power, I intended to wield it.

I took a few steps away from him and pulled off my black leather doublet. With my back to him, I tossed it on the ground next to a pile of books by his bed. I couldn't see him, but I could feel his eyes on me, burning like a brand. The air seemed to heat.

I pulled off the leather trousers and my shirt until I stood in nothing but my white undergarments, so thin they were practically sheer. The light undershirt draped over my bare breasts, light and smooth against my skin.

When I cast a look over my shoulder, I found the Raven Lord's beautiful features etched with desperation, fingers curled into tight fists. His pale eyes

seemed to glow in the firelight, and he looked transfixed. As his gaze swept slowly down my body, his eyes
darkened.

And that was all the satisfaction I needed to
contentedly crawl into his bed and wrap myself in his
incense-scented sheets.

Here in Ruefield, I would wring every last ounce of
pleasure that I could from the living world before
death draped its dark pall over me.

MY EYES OPENED. Candlelight wavered over the room,
a writhing gold that mingled with shadows. I sat up,
and the chill of the castle air kissed my bare skin. The
scent of sandalwood swept around me.

Maelor sat at his desk by candlelight, frantically
writing. The air smelled of burned parchment. He'd
taken off his cloak, only wearing the thin white shirt
he'd had on beneath it. He'd again rolled up his sleeves,
and my gaze slid over his muscled forearms.

He turned back to look at me. A muscle flexed in his
jaw, and his pale eyes burned in the dim light. It must
have been a very long time since he'd seen a woman's
bare shoulders or the round outline of breasts under a
chemise. Besides the bath, how long had it been since a
man had seen me naked? With his eyes on me, I felt
acutely aware of every inch of my bare skin, and I
ached to be touched. Because it had been so, so long

since anyone touched me with desire. I loathed the Raven Lord. But I was all twisted up inside, and he was the only one who could touch me. If I pulled the chemise off, I wondered if he would finally snap and break his vows.

"Elowen." His voice sounded husky as he breathed my name.

I let one of the straps of my undershirt fall, exposing the top of my breast. He unbuttoned his white shirt, and I drank in the sight of his muscled body, sculpted by shadows in the firelight. Godlike.

He moved so swiftly across the room that it made my heart race, slipping through the shadows. Evil incarnate—the forbidden fruit—and I wanted a taste.

My heart hammered as he climbed onto the bed, covering me with his body. He slid his fingers into my hair and pulled my head back. The look he gave me was ravenous, uncontrolled. He was losing the tight grip he kept on himself.

"If you're going to act like a harlot, I will treat you like one." Gripping the thin fabric of my chemise, he ripped it off me. The cold castle air raised goosebumps on my skin, and my heart pounded. I shouldn't want this, but molten heat slid through my body. My pulse raced, breath shallowing.

His scorching gaze brushed down my body. As he palmed my breasts, I ached for him. He leaned down, kissing my neck with wicked strokes of his tongue. I shifted my hips up into him, and he groaned.

With an aggressive tug, he pulled the underwear off me, leaving me naked. My bare skin tingled, and the Raven Lord parted my thighs, devouring me with his gaze.

I WOKE FROM MY DREAM, my body glowing with a few beads of sweat. Desire pulsed in my core. Why did my dreams always end at the worst times?

I clenched my eyes shut, mentally cursing myself. I shouldn't have been dreaming about him in the first place.

I could torment him, yes. But I would not torment myself—not over a monster like the Raven Lord. I might be an assassin with a disturbingly high body count, but I did have some moral standards.

I slung an arm over my head. The first milky rays of sunlight streamed in through the windows. When I sat up, I was still catching my breath. I glanced down at my top. Fully intact.

Just as he had in my dream, Maelor sat at his desk in his thin white shirt, sleeves rolled up to the elbows. He turned to look at me, and I pulled up the blankets, covering my chest.

He heaved a sigh. "Elowen, you must get ready to leave. The trial begins soon."

Icy dread slid up the back of my neck, and all the heat drained from my body.

# CHAPTER 18

Draped in dark cowls, nearly a hundred Penitents marched in a grim procession. Beneath ancient stone arches, we stalked closer to the labyrinth entrance. Fear hung in the air, so heavy I could practically taste it. Above the open-air passages, lines of cloaked archers stood ready to pierce us all with a volley of arrows if we tried to escape. Here, the halls had been carved deep into the earth.

As we marched, our alliance of five stayed together. Subtly, I'd been able to maneuver us all to the front. Hugo and Godric flanked me, while Sazia and Percival marched just ahead. Godric's long, dark hair flowed from the side of his cowl, and I knew he must have arranged it that way on purpose. I supposed if I had hair that glorious, I would, too.

Take pleasure where you can get it before you die.

Around us, the air smelled of soil, moss, and damp

rocks. Wind whistled through the rocky corridor. The crumbling stone arches swept overhead, but otherwise, the passage was open to the sky, to the archers. I slid my hand into my pocket, feeling Leo's note. A twinge of joy fluttered through me at the thought that he was safe, even if I wasn't.

"This place is older than the Tyrenians, you know," whispered Hugo. His eyes looked enormous, cheeks hollow. "Built before Emperor Severin arrived from the east. Before anyone here had ever heard of the Archon. Godric and I are masons, but we'll never build anything that lasts so long."

"The Archon does not want us here." In her Aquitanian accent, Sazia dropped the 'H' on "here." She was waving her hand dismissively. "I do not think he gives a shit about any of this. I think we are here because you Merthians have no real culture. I never should have come to this barbaric place."

"We have a culture," said Godric defensively. His eyes darted around. "It's just not…well, it's not the best at the moment, is it?"

"Guess why I was accused? It wasn't because of the herbs," Sazia continued without giving us a chance to answer. "It was because I fell in love with a Merthian woman. And that's not allowed here, is it? So when someone nearly caught us, my lover turned me in as a witch. She said I ensorcelled her. Ridiculous." She tucked her hair behind her cowl. "It would almost be funny if I weren't here."

"I'm sorry," I said.

"It isn't your fault," she said sharply.

When I glanced behind me, my chest tightened at the long line of Penitents marching forward, cowls shading their faces. I wondered how many of us would be alive by midnight.

Not far behind us, the tattooed man glowered at me. "Hello, little witch. Hello to the reason we're all here. Good morning to the cause of all today's innocent deaths. Dark powers like yours are the problem. Did you drain all those bodies of blood, witch, with your wicked magic? With your death powers?"

My breath caught in my throat.

Hugo turned, his eyes wide. "And yet your fate has brought you here. Maybe it was meant to be. Perhaps the Archon, or the old gods—"

"Stop talking, my friend," said Godric, clapping him hard on the back. "There are no old gods here." He shook his head. "Honestly, Hugo. We get on stage at the Raven and Scepter, and you're totally silent. I could hardly hear you singing; do you know how much that threw me off? The poppy water had you half asleep. And now, when I actually need you to be quiet, you can't keep your bloody mouth shut."

Hugo looked bright-eyed this morning. A little bit of color had replaced the pallor, and a smile curled his lips. "I have a good feeling about today." He leaned in closer to me. "They say some passages here were carved by *those gods who we shall not speak of*. They run all the way through the Thornwood to the Kingdom of Bones in the west, where stones rise from the earth, with ancient hymns carved to the moon goddess—"

"Shhh." I put my finger to my lips.

"They say that north of Merthyn, in the black, snow-tipped Sumaire mountains beyond the wall, live creatures called vampires. It's where the region got its name. They can wield shadows, you know. They live forever; they feed off blood. And when they do, the mortals delight in pleasure—"

Godric clamped his hand over Hugo's mouth. "That's enough for today."

Even I didn't want to hear about the old gods and the cursed luck they might bring us. "Are you feeling better, Hugo?"

His answer was muffled by Godric's hand.

"You see? He's better. I'll join the alliance." Sazia turned to face us, and she shrugged. "I gave him a bit of healing herbs. Perfect for energy levels."

Too much, perhaps?

As we marched toward the start of the labyrinth, I clung to the golden thread of relief that twined through me. The little note in my pocket and the thought of Leo sitting at a breakfast table over hot bread with his uncle, who'd never been able to have children. Nothing made me happier than knowing he was safe.

At last, the corridor opened up to a large set of steps. They must have been grand once, but now the steps were half-broken, overgrown with weeds. They led up to a sort of circular stage, its ruined surface covered in moss. Maybe this had once been a temple. Five dark archways led off from the atrium like spokes from a wheel. So *this* would be our start. I led my group around the stone platform, all the way to the other side.

Morning light poured in from the open sky above, and I tilted my head up to it. For some reason, the light reminded me of Maelor. Maybe it was the heat of that dream I'd had. Maybe it was the warmth that I felt at being able to touch someone after so long.

Except he was the Raven Lord, and I mustn't fall under his spell.

When I looked down again, I saw Gwyneth kneeling with another man, praying to the Archon in the Tyrenian language. The boy who stood behind them looked shockingly young, no more than fifteen. I pulled my gaze away from him, trying to erase his full, youthful cheeks from my mind.

*Don't get distracted.*

Across the platform, Sion emerged from another passage, materializing like a ghost out of shadows. When he stepped onto the stage, golden light kissed his tan skin. As he stood in the center of the platform, his hazel eyes slid over the crowd of Penitents, and he turned in a circle to survey us all. Based on the way he held himself, I had the distinct impression that he was enjoying the power that he held over us. Like a god, he craved worship, and his otherworldly beauty only helped the illusion.

He held his arms out. "We bring you down here, among the bones of the earth, to learn who among you is blessed by the Archon. Get through the maze by nightfall, or you will die. I'm afraid we won't recover the bodies. Because you are Serpent-touched, you are condemned to eternal damnation whether or not you're buried in consecrated ground. Only the one forgiven can reach heaven. The rest of you are damned."

A panicked murmur rippled through the crowd. I met Percival's determined gaze. If he was scared, he really wasn't showing it. Maybe, like me, he was simply good at keeping his terror hidden.

"Anyone discovered using magic will be executed immediately," added the Magister. "If you try to climb from the labyrinth, you will be shot by our archers."

Gwyneth's body shook, and her eyes had a manic look. She clasped her hands together, knuckles turning white. "The Archon will protect his most faithful servants." She muttered this again and again, her words growing jumbled.

"Good luck with that," said Percival dryly.

"May the Archon shine his light on you!" Sion's words boomed over the stone. "*Deus Invictus, Archon Magne*. Let the trials begin!"

Chaos erupted around us, and my heart slammed with fear.

I grabbed Percival's arm to slow him just a little. Gwyneth and her pious friend sprinted ahead of us.

"There are traps," I whispered to my group. "Let others go first."

"Archon save us." Sazia's cheeks had already grown pink. We'd barely started, and already, a single bead of sweat trickled down her temple. Her long fingers wiped it away. "If I die today," she said with a sigh, "the Merthian woman's name was Lady Ruthven. The woman who accused me. Make sure everyone knows she's an absolute barbaric monster who barely knows how to read, and that *she* seduced *me*. She sent me a painting of herself nude. Beautiful painting."

Godric's shiny hair flowed behind him as he ran. "If Hugo and I survive, we will avenge you."

Despite everything we'd been told, he didn't seem to entertain the possibility that only one of them would live. It was oddly touching.

Shadows filled the passage, and moss climbed the stone walls. I breathed in air scented of the forest floor, of bones and soil. A sliver of sunlight streaked across the topmost part of the passages to my left.

We were hurtling toward traps, but standing still was just as dangerous. By the time darkness fell, we'd be torn to pieces if we didn't make it out.

Footfalls and heavy breathing echoed off the stone walls as the crowd wheezed and puffed around us. When I glanced behind me, I found the tattooed man staring at me as he ran. That bastard was going to follow me the whole time, wasn't he?

Already, my body glowed with sweat, and I lowered the cowl to let my head breathe. The Order had demanded we keep our cloaks on, but the heavy wool was weighing me down.

Up ahead, Gwyneth and her friend came to a fork in the passage. Two corridors jutted in either direction. The pair hesitated for only a moment, then took off to the right. A group of others went left.

"Which way do we go?" Godric asked through labored breath.

In my mind, I pictured where we'd come from and tried to put together a mental map using the angle of the sun. The path to the right, I thought, would take us back toward the start. I didn't imagine the way out would be right by the entrance.

"Left," I called.

We jogged behind the three strangers into a passage of cobblestones and vine-veiled walls.

When I stole a look behind me, confusion whirled in my skull. Now, *no* crowd hurried behind us. No tattooed man or group of Penitents hustling through narrow passages. Instead, a wall towered over us where the path had just been. It was as if an unseen god had leaned down and silently twisted the passages. I felt unsteady on my feet, as if I'd been dropped into a dream. Panic crackled through my thoughts at the realization that I could no longer trust my senses.

"What in the world?" I breathed.

Maelor had told me the passages might shift, but I hadn't realized it would be this dramatic.

Hugo turned to stare at the new wall with me. "Am I dreaming? Is this all a nightmare?"

Godric whirled around, and he lowered his cowl. Sweat beaded his tan skin. "Bloody hell. Where did that come from? We'll never be able to find our way out if it changes the whole time. And what happened to Guillaume the Dulcet? Because I still want to bash that arrogant prick's head against a wall."

"We keep going." Percival slid his hand behind my back, ushering me forward. "Come on."

"So it's the nobility barking the orders, is it?" Godric grumbled. "Typical."

"I am a knight of the realm," said Percival. "Don't take this the wrong way, but I am more qualified to give orders than drug-addled melody-mongers."

"Question." Sazia jogged next to us, sweat streaking down her temples. "Can you tell me what exactly we are rushing toward if we have no idea where we're going?"

"I don't know, but Percival is right," I said. "We have only one strategy, and we'll lose that if we're too slow. If there are traps, we need to see what triggers them. So let's stay close to the people ahead of us."

"Ah," said Hugo. "So those up ahead are our fodder for the traps."

"I wouldn't phrase it that way, exactly," said Percival. "But yes. We need them to die so we can avoid it. Everything that happens here is because of the Order, so remember that at the end of today. We're not the ones with blood on our hands."

In the stone corridor, we hurried after the trio ahead. With every footfall, I scanned the ground for signs of anything amiss: a tripwire, a flagstone that seemed out of place. I didn't know exactly what I was looking for; I only knew that at any moment, an arrow might shoot out of the walls.

We rounded a corner, and the three men came into view as we raced after them. My footfalls felt uneasy on the rounded cobblestones. The hair rose on the back of my neck as I felt the sense of danger thickening the air.

Not twenty feet from us, a crack rang out, sending a jolt of fear through my body. My arms shot out to stop my allies, and my heart pounded as metal flashed through the air ahead. I stared in horror as a blade carved through the bodies of two of the Penitents, severing them at the waist.

I felt the blood drain from my head.

Now the real carnage had begun.

# CHAPTER 19

*B*lood spilled over the cobbles, sending a primal rush of fear through my veins. One of the Penitents had survived, clipped only along the front of his arm, but the shock of it had robbed him of his senses. He clung to his injured limb, staring down at the wound. His eyes held a wild, animal terror.

Only now did I notice the bleached white bones that lay around the dead bodies.

From its hidden spot in the wall, the blade slid back into place. My breath came hard and fast as I tried to remember its exact location.

But the real question was, which stone had been the trigger?

As my thoughts cleared a little, I realized Sazia was screaming.

I held up a finger to my lips. "Everyone stay still for a moment."

The surviving man turned back to me, pale as a ghost. "They're trying to kill us here," he sobbed, as though it were the first time this idea had occurred to him.

"Yes," said Percival dryly. "That is what they meant when they said only one would survive."

The stranger's pale skin had turned blotchy, and tears streaked down his cheeks to his thick brown beard.

I glanced behind us at another towering wall that had slid into place, trapping us in here.

Hugo turned away from us, doubling over. With a loud, retching gurgle, he vomited his morning's tea onto the stones.

*Oh, Archon.* Right now, we were trapped between a towering stone wall and a guillotine. We'd only just started the day, and Hugo was already falling apart.

"Can you look around you for a trigger?" I asked. "A wire, or a stone that seems different than the others?"

"There's too much blood." His voice cracked. "I can't see…I'm just a baker."

Hugo turned to us, pale as milk. He wiped the back of his hand across his mouth.

"What's your name?" I asked the stranger. Tension had my muscles coiled tightly.

"Reginald." He wiped a hand across his tear-streaked face, leaving a smear of blood across his cheek and beard. "My wife is praying for me. So maybe that's why I'm still standing. Maybe her prayers are working."

"Reginald." Percival pointed at the ground. "Leap back toward us a little. Get out of the way of where the blade came out. See if there's something on the ground. You're next to it right now, and you want to move closer to us. Can you see any slits in the wall where blades might come out?"

Reginald yelped.

"Does it really make sense to help people?" asked Godric. "I thought we wanted their numbers lowered."

I bit my lip. "True, I guess." Letting others die was the logical thing to do, but Reginald seemed like a lost child.

He looked past us and pointed. "There's no way out."

Hugo's bloodshot gaze flicked to the heavens. "I think we all need to accept death at this point. Whether we're in the labyrinth or not, we're all mortal—"

"Not now, Hugo," said Godric. "Write it in a song when we get out."

I scanned the ground around the baker, but I couldn't see anything that caught my eye. It was really hard to tell with the cobbles. "Move a step closer to us, okay?"

He nodded, and he leapt toward us. He was shaking so hard that he nearly fell when he landed, and he broke into a fresh round of sobs. "Okay," he whispered. "I'm okay." He gripped his stomach and leaned over, looking like he was going to be sick. "They're trying to kill us," he repeated. "I don't even know why I'm here."

"I know," I said. "But you are here, and your wife is praying for you, so you'll be okay."

Percival shot me an irritated look, and I shrugged at him. Of course it was a lie, but I usually knew the best thing to say—even if it wasn't true.

Godric crouched down by the wall. "There are some loose rocks we can use to test for the trigger. And, uh… and some human bones." He grimaced. "They really seem gnawed on."

"Perfect." I released a long, shaky breath.

Apart from Reginald, whose mouth was now opening and closing wordlessly, we all gathered bits of rocks in our arms.

Sazia seemed on the edge of madness, too, muttering to herself as she picked up rocks and bones from the edges of the path. "Anon the day with darkness blends. Death by its might makes us decline."

Godric tossed a rock onto a cobble, and we watched as the blade shot out, carving through the air above the corpses.

"I got it!" he shouted. "Did you see that one?"

"Archon help us," muttered Reginald.

"Did you see it?" said Godric, pointing. "The trigger. Just there, by the…by that, uh, that gentleman's torso."

"So, we just avoid that one stone?" said Hugo dubiously. He'd gone pale again, sweat streaking his cheeks.

I shook my head. "What are the chances you'd get it on the first try, though? We need to test for more."

One by one, we tossed our rocks. And for every

stone we hit around the dead bodies, blades shot out of the walls, slicing through the air. The sharp shrieks of blades against the stones made my stomach drop every time.

It wasn't just one stone. It was all of them.

Sazia's brown eyes looked glazed as she said, "Against my will was I exiled from that bright region, fair and fain…"

"Bloody hell," said Godric.

"What if we crawl?" said Percival. "The blades are coming out at waist height. We could crawl beneath them, and they'd carve through the air above us."

"It's not the worst idea," I said.

Percival ran a hand over his close-cropped hair, and he inhaled a long breath. "I'll go first."

"Are you sure?"

"Someone's got to do it," he muttered.

I'd never seen a knight crawl before, but we'd entered an upside-down world. I watched as he got on his hands and knees to shuffle toward the red-soaked cobbles. The blades cut the air above him, but they left him unharmed.

I closed my eyes. "Thank the Archon," I muttered to myself.

I followed, crawling just behind him. My palms pressed into the sticky crimson that coated the stones, and I tried to block out the coppery scent of blood that spilled into my nostrils.

Every time a blade sheared through the air above

me, I felt as if my heart would stop. And with a sharp pang of horror, I realized there really wasn't any guarantee that the blades would stay at the same level, was there?

Still, it was a little late to go back now.

Behind us, Sazia was still chattering wildly, her voice breaking. "I bid my sorrow flee and my fair fortune turn again…"

"When the Luminaries came for us, I was making hot cross buns," said Reginald. "I don't know if anyone ever took them out of the oven. They would have burned. My wife must have found them like charcoal after the Purification. She's not well. She can't run the bakery on her own. She's got a lung sickness. And they want us to die here, don't they? I've done everything they asked, and they want to chop us up and burn us. But my wife is praying. She's praying, so I'll get home to her."

I turned back to look at Reginald, who was following close behind me.

"We're okay," I lied. "Just follow after us." I needed him to stay calm.

Reginald glanced at one of the fallen men's torsos. The corpse's green eyes stared blankly up at the sky, reflecting the passing clouds.

I could see the color draining from Reginald's face. He cringed away from the body. "Oh, Archon save us." He shifted as far away from the body as he could, his path moving off track.

"Reginald, stay just behind me. We know those stones are safe. Try to put pressure on the same ones I do."

His body shook, and his hand slammed down on a stone too far to the right.

The sound of metal against stone sent my pulse roaring.

Pain streaked across the back of my thigh, a searing burst of agony. I froze for a moment, my heart slamming. *No.*

Screams wended through the air around me. With a shaking hand, I reached behind to feel the damage on my thigh. A deep gash had carved through my skin. Fear snapped through my thoughts. What were my chances now of getting out of here alive with this wound?

Shaking, I turned back to look at Reginald. With horror, I realized the baker was no more. The blade had severed him in two, straight through the chest. My heart twisted.

The lacerating pain in my thigh shot through me, making my teeth chatter, and the scent of death hung in the air like a dark cloud.

How many more blades were there? Crawling wasn't safe. *None* of this was safe. My gaze flicked up the wall, and I could just about make out the subtle slits in the walls where blades were shooting out.

"Everyone stop!" I shouted, my voice shaking. "No

one move. Some of the blades are lower than we thought. We can't move."

"What do you recommend we do if we can't move?" asked Godric. "Should we just wait until the wolves arrive?"

"Maybe we should have taken the other path," added Hugo.

"Not very helpful at this point, is it?" Godric shot back.

Percival looked behind at me. "Are you all right, Elowen?"

I felt as if my leg had been ripped in half. "Reginald got the worst of it." The scent of his blood made my stomach turn. "He will not be returning to his wife."

Blood poured from my thigh, and I started to wonder if I would bleed out in the maze, but I tried to think clearly through the haze of pain. My gaze flicked to the walls, where thick vines hung down over the top. As far as we knew, the triggers were only the cobblestones. Could we simply climb on the walls to avoid them? We weren't allowed to go above the wall, or the archers would shoot us. But scaling it…

I closed my eyes for a moment, trying to picture it working. I didn't think the triggers would be in the walls themselves. By the placement of the vines and the slits I could see, it looked as though the blades only cut through the lower half of the wall. The moment we got above that line of vines, we should be in the clear.

I gritted my teeth. "We climb," I said. "Let me show you."

Percival turned to look at me, then up at the vines. They began at around shoulder height, which must be the topmost part that the blades sliced through.

I looked down at the places where my hands and knees had been pressing against the ground. As far as I knew, those were the only safe stones.

Carefully, I rose on shaking legs. Sharp tendrils of dread coiled through me as I reached for the vines above my shoulders, desperate not to slip out of place. I gripped some of the vines above the path and started to pull myself aloft, walking up the rocky wall.

Tiny prickers on the vines bit into my skin. I stared down below me, watching the stream of blood pour from my thigh onto the stones.

I winced as I climbed, pulling myself higher. Above the risk of the blades, I clung to the vines, praying that they wouldn't snap. If I let myself fall, I'd set off more triggers.

As I moved across the top of the wall, my injured leg juddered, and nausea turned in my stomach. I glanced up to find that archers had their arrows trained on me. If I hoisted myself up any higher, they'd shoot me.

My body was shaking uncontrollably, pain mingling with fear.

Percival followed after me, and I looked ahead to the place where the vines dropped all the way to the ground. That was *probably* where the blades stopped, but it was also possible that no one had ever made it that far. When I looked back at the rest of our allies, I found them following Percival.

As I reached the long vines, I scanned the ground for any signs of human bones. I didn't see any here.

My pulse thundered.

I closed my eyes, silently praying to the Archon. And when I'd gathered enough courage, I took a leap off the wall.

I landed hard on the stones, ducking as low as I could in case a blade shot out. Pain ripped through my thigh with the impact of landing, and I clenched my teeth.

But I heard no whoosh of metal through the air. Slowly, I turned to look above me. I sat up to clutch the back of my thigh, and blood spilled through my fingers.

"You're okay," Percival called out. He jumped down next to me, then knelt by my side. "But you're bleeding quite a lot. Sazia?"

"Hang on," said Sazia. She dropped down to the labyrinth floor with a quiet grunt, then flicked her long hair back behind her shoulders. "So much time I spent learning to sew up skin just for moments like this."

I swallowed hard. Part of me wanted to ask her who she'd practiced on, but a greater part of me thought I should just grit my teeth and pretend none of this was happening.

Sazia was still catching her breath as she knelt next to me. She reached into her cloak, and she pulled out a small, cloth package. "They said no weapons. But they didn't say anything about tools."

I winced as she pulled out a needle and thread. She was going to sew me up like a torn rag doll.

She sighed dramatically. "Lie down on your stomach, and we'll get those ugly leather trousers off you, yes? So much leather in this kingdom. The skin of dead animals."

"You're going to be fine, Elowen." Percival cleared his throat. "I mean, until the next trap. Look, just think of happy thoughts. Flowers…whatever women like."

I closed my eyes and tried to imagine Leo reading in a sunlit room. As Sazia went to work piecing together my skin, I blocked out the pain of the needle threading in and out.

But now one question remained—with this torn leg, could I really make it out of here alive?

# CHAPTER 20

With every step I took, a sharp stab of pain shot through my thigh. But really, Sazia had done a beautiful job. She'd cleaned it out, and she'd managed to stop the bleeding. Now, only my trousers were torn open.

We'd been walking for hours. Hunger and thirst slowed us, and I kept imagining how amazing it would be if the sky would open up and unleash a torrent of rain. I could almost taste it…

Using the markers we'd already discovered, we'd been able to avoid traps. Step one: look for bones, bodies, and severed vines. Step two: use the vines to transport ourselves.

But I had no idea if we were actually making progress. Twice, we'd passed the spot where Reginald and his friends lay dead. The labyrinth felt claustrophobic, constantly shifting to keep us mostly on our own, and going in circles.

As we walked, I scanned the surrounding walls, looking for bones. My mouth felt dry as cinders. Up ahead, Hugo was leaning against a wall, vomiting into a corner. His shoulders shook. Whatever herbs he'd taken had clearly worn off.

When we'd started this morning, the sun had been a mere sliver of golden light on the top of the walls. But as pumpkin-orange tinged the afternoon light, my nerves fluttered. The day was stretching on without an exit in sight.

As we rounded a dark corner, the scent of burning wood coiled into the air. Just above the walls, a plume of smoke curled into the blue sky nearby.

I felt my scars tingle beneath my gloves. "Something's on fire."

Percival wiped a bead of sweat off his forehead, and he turned around. "I feel like we might be walking directly toward it."

My mind whirled as I tried to figure out a way for us to orient ourselves. When we'd started, we must have been heading north because of the way the sun hit the western wall. Now, many hours later, we'd turned east. Which way was out? I had no idea.

Ashes floated on the wind, and the scent of burning oak swept past me.

But it wasn't just oak...I sniffed the air, my mind flashing back to the day the Baron had burned me.

I swallowed hard. Some*one* was on fire.

As if answering my thought, agonized screams rang out from the labyrinth, piercing the quiet. Up ahead, in the distance, two figures raced closer from another converging path.

And behind them, I could see what they were running from: a wall of fire that was moving closer. Flames writhed and danced in the passage, rolling like a wave through the labyrinth.

"Obviously the wrong way." Godric grabbed my arm. "Let's go. Now!"

But my eyes were on the two figures because as they ran closer, I recognized them.

Gwyneth's white-blonde hair flowed behind her. And by her side, Lydia ran, her face bright red with the exertion. Smoke billowed into the air behind them.

They were only twenty feet from us now, and I couldn't tear my gaze away. Lydia was the reason I was here—but she'd also once been the most exciting friend I'd ever had. The person who'd convinced me to sneak into taverns and slip behind the bar to steal drinks, or to swim in the ocean under the stars late at night.

"Archon save me!" Gwyneth shrieked. "Archon save me! I am your most faithful—"

As Gwyneth's foot slammed against a stone, arrows shot out of the wall. It all happened in just a moment, the bolts piercing her and Lydia.

Godric tugged my arm again. "Elowen! Let's go."

I stared with dawning horror as each of them staggered forward for a few moments, then slumped to the ground. Behind them, the flames rolled closer. Shafts jutted from Lydia's shoulders and her thigh.

"You go!" I shouted. "I'll catch up."

My breath shallowed. Lydia could heal herself, but someone would need to get the arrows out of her. And if it didn't happen now, she'd burn to death before my eyes.

The smoky wind whipped over me, carrying with it the smell of blood. I sprinted for Lydia, feeling the heat of the fire moving closer. As I ran nearer, my gaze flicked to Gwyneth, her pale eyes staring blankly at the sky. An arrow jutted from her collarbone, and her chest had gone still.

Tears and cinders streaked Lydia's pale skin, and I ripped the arrows from her as fast as I could.

Blood dripped from the corner of her mouth, and she stared at me with an agonized expression as I pulled the last arrow free. Her blood streaked the cobbles. But once I'd ripped out the final shaft, her body was already starting to glow with her healing magic.

If she was lucky, none of the Luminari would notice the forbidden power under the haze of smoke.

"Run!" I screamed at her.

I turned to run, trying to sprint after the others. But as I ran, pain shot through my leg as some of the stitches tore open. I winced, trying to block out the pain to just move.

Above, the darkening sky made my heart thunder. It wasn't just the smoke. Already, night was falling.

Smoke coiled around me as I ran, and I came to a fork in the passage. When I turned to look to the right, I found Hugo running back for me, his blond hair matted with sweat.

"Elowen!" he shouted, skidding to a halt. "Hurry! It's getting dark." He pointed at a giant chasm in the ground. "Look out for the hole!"

He pivoted, running away from me again. As I ran after him, I saw the others in the darkening distance. My heart fluttered as I looked up at the sun disappearing behind the western walls. The growing shadows made my nerve endings snap with rising panic.

Up ahead, the large hole gaped in the passage, taking up most of the way. This was exactly the kind of thing I'd miss completely in the dark.

As I started to edge around it, the sound of footfalls turned my head. I expected to see Lydia coming up behind me, but instead, I found the tattooed man, his lips curled back from his teeth in a snarl.

The moment I looked at him, whispers started echoing in my mind.

*You'll never make it out of here.*

*Give up now.*

*You're all alone.*

The voices grew into screams in my skull, dizzying me. My thoughts whirled with a vortex of confusion. I clamped my hands against my head, stumbling.

*You are the evil we must burn.*

*Leo would've been better off without you.*

*Death flows through your veins.*

*You have no one.*

I gripped my temples, trying to remember who I was, where I was, what I was doing, but anarchy ruled my mind. All I could remember was that I was alone, and that I'd always be alone, and that it was time to give up.

A heel slammed into my back, and a dark wind whipped over me as I fell.

I landed hard, my head banging against a stone. Pain screamed up my legs, up my back, vibrating through my bones. When I brushed my hand over one of my thighs, I felt the bone was jutting out in a place where it did not belong. The stitches had fully ripped open, and I thought I'd broken a bone.

Far above me, a dull, rosy light shone in from the setting sun.

My heart stuttered. I was in no condition to get out of here.

# CHAPTER 21

𝒩ausea climbed up my throat, and I tried to fight it. I was stuck lying on my back, and I didn't need to add lying in vomit to the mix. I swallowed hard, feeling the shadowy ground around me for any clues, any hint of a possible escape. Tempting as it was to give up, that wouldn't get me back to Leo.

By now, most of the whispers had slid from my mind, apart from the one telling me that I was alone. Because that, unfortunately, was true at this point. Alone, and with a bone-shivering pain ripping through my thigh. Right now, it felt exactly as I'd expect it to feel if someone was stabbing me in the thigh repeatedly.

My thoughts flitted back to a few moments ago, before I'd fallen in. That bastard had used magic on me, hadn't he? After all that bollocks about me being a real witch, about how I was the reason we were here…he'd pummeled me with a confusion spell, then kicked me into a hole in the ground.

I breathed in the scent of smoke that coiled in from above. If the fire kept spreading, could I roast in here? Once, Lydia had told me something like that—rumors from the northern kingdom of Sumaire. Apparently, a fire had raged through the capital of Sumaire, burning those who lived in stone tunnels.

Half-delirious, I let my eyes drift shut.

Lydia used to tell me creepy stories in her room. I wasn't supposed to go into the manor house, but the Baron indulged her. She'd even once convinced me it was a good idea to scrawl ghost stories on the walls all over her room in black ink. I remember thinking she was so brave. At the time, I hadn't realized that maybe she was just a spoiled brat, and that it was easy to be daring when you'd never faced a single fucking consequence.

Well, she finally had one.

As the memories faded, I felt the pain shooting through my thigh once more, sharpening my thoughts. Could there possibly be a way out of here?

As my eyes started to adjust to the shadows, I started to make out markings on one of the walls. What *were* they?

"Elowen? Are you there?" Percival's clipped voice floated down to me from above.

At the sound, tears stung my eyes. He'd actually come back for me?

"You've got to get out of here, Percival," I shouted. "It's almost dark. And I'm pretty far down here. Someone used magic on me, just so you know. I didn't just fall in a hole." Even if I was going to die in here, it seemed important for him to know I wasn't stupid. "But you need to get going because I'm in bad shape here, and the wolves are coming for you."

"Give me a second," he said. "We can throw you a vine. The fire is dying down."

I shuddered at the idea of trying to pull myself up on a shattered leg. I called out to him to wait, but he disappeared. A moment later, a vine came tumbling down into the hole—still too high for me to reach, even if my leg didn't feel like it was in twenty-seven pieces.

"Percival?" My voice cracked. "I really appreciate it, but you all should get out of here. I can't climb that. I can't even reach it."

He leaned down into the hole, twenty feet above me, and stretched out his hand. For a moment, I wondered if he was daft enough to think I could reach it. Then I caught a glimpse of a faint golden glow burning in his palm, like an ember. The ember spun in the air, growing larger, until it whirled into a sphere of fiery light.

My breath caught. He was risking his life, using magic to help me.

"What can you see?" he asked.

Percival's firelight slid down, illuminating a wooden door inset into the stone wall. In the center of the door was a wooden wheel carved with symbols. My chest flickered with hope. A way out?

Wincing, I pushed up on my elbows. As I did, jagged agony ran up my thigh, and the noise that came out of me was akin to an animal growl.

When I refocused my attention again, I was staring at what might be a way out. "There's a door! Percival, do you see it?"

Percival's light beamed over carvings in the wheel, which was divided into five sections: a woman in a long dress, a white hound, a key made of bones, a yew tree, and a crescent moon.

I grimaced, reaching up to try to touch the wheel. Pain lanced up my right thigh as I rose, putting my weight on one knee. My head pounded. Wincing, I tried turning the wheel, but the thing wouldn't budge an inch. It was rooted in place on the door.

"What's that on the other side?" Percival asked.

"Give me a minute." Oh, Archon. Could I even get to the other side?

I gritted my teeth and turned to look behind me. There, shapes had been carved into the stone wall. The design was about three feet above the floor, directly opposite the wheel in the door.

The golden light bobbed overhead, illuminating my way. I rolled onto my right side, putting the pain on my good leg. Sharp pain shot through me, and I dragged myself closer to the other side, my body scraping over the ground. I pulled myself closer over the stone, arm over arm. When I was just in front of the carvings, I found four stone pieces laying on the ground, just beneath the carvings.

These were different than the symbols on the door: a bird, a star, an hourglass, and an apple. These pieces matched the carvings in the wall, like a puzzle for children. Except that unlike a puzzle for children, I was pretty sure this one might have deadly consequences. Because nestled between those carvings were slits for blades, just like the ones in the labyrinth.

I struggled to think clearly through the haze of pain. A cold sweat beaded on my forehead.

This couldn't be as simple as matching the shapes, could it?

"I think it's a puzzle!" I called out. One that I very much did not want to get wrong.

Above the carvings, someone had etched words in a language I couldn't even recognize. Something older than Tyrenian. If those were the instructions, I had no idea what they said. My skull throbbed, and I was again repressing the urge to vomit.

I glanced back at the door, taking in the images on the wheel. Was the wheel related to the puzzle?

The images on the wheel were ancient symbols, half-forgotten symbols of the old gods. They lived on in a children's nursery rhyme, one forbidden by the Order.

*Maiden, mother, crone,*
*A yew tree and a bone.*

*The white hounds glower.*

*A crescent moon,*

*Gone too soon,*

*A hunger that devours.*

Pain splintered my leg, making my body shake. My mouth had gone dry.

*Think, Elowen.* It wasn't just a rhyme, though, was it? It was almost like a riddle. Unlike nursery rhymes, this one had an answer. What was the hunger that devoured?

In Merthyn, yew trees meant death. The white hounds, symbols of the old forgotten death god...the maiden transforming into an old crone. Death seemed like the first answer. I, of all people, understood its ravenousness.

But that didn't seem to be an option among these stone pieces. Unless it was a symbol I didn't recognize, I didn't see something that clearly meant death.

Dizziness whirled in my thoughts. With the stabbing pain in my thigh, it was hard to think clearly.

My hand was shaking as I picked up the hourglass. But time...time devoured, didn't it? It withered plants and people. It turned bones into dust, which was very much how one of my bones felt right now.

If I messed this up, I could unleash a volley of arrows or blades. I had to choose something, though, didn't I? At this point, the two most likely options were either a slow death or a fast one.

Swallowing hard, I slotted the hourglass into place.

Immediately, a clicking sound echoed behind me, and I turned to see the wheel shifting slightly on the door. My heart raced faster, and I held the hourglass in its place.

No blades. My chest unclenched.

On the other side of the oubliette, the door groaned open. But the moment I stopped pushing on the hourglass, the door started closing once more.

I glanced back at the hourglass piece. As I pushed it into place again and held it there, the door groaned open once more, revealing a set of stony stairs leading up, washed in twilight hues of violet and peach. Oak leaves littered the stairs. The labyrinth had no oaks…

Freedom lay out there.

I breathed out slowly. There it was—the world outside the labyrinth.

But as I held the key in place, another sort of trap was triggered. While I kept my finger pressed down on the key, water bubbled up from cracks in the floor beneath me. The cracks grew wider, the water rushing fast through the stones. But it didn't seem immediately threatening because it streamed out the open door onto the forest's floor.

My heart fluttered like a hummingbird's wings. "Percival!" My voice echoed off the stone walls. "Tell everyone to come down here. We found the way out."

With my weight on my good leg, I kept my finger depressed on the key, shoving it into place. A cool breeze rushed into the dungeon through the door.

Hope burned in my thoughts even as freezing water poured into the dungeon. Up above, Sazia was sliding down the vine. When she got to the bottom of the rope, she jumped, splashing in the water that welled up around me.

She turned to look at me for just a moment, joy lighting in her eyes. "Is this really it?" Her delighted laughter echoed off the walls. "We made it, Elowen."

"Go!" I shouted.

She crossed outside, and I heard her shout, "We're alive!"

After her, Hugo shuffled down the vine, landing with a splash in the rising water. "Brilliantly done, Elowen."

He looked up, clasping his hands together as he waited for Godric.

Once the two of them were standing in the rising water, they gripped each other's hands. They rushed outside, and I caught a glimpse of them ascending the stairs.

In the back of my mind, a dark thought sang like a dirge. Of course, someone would have to stay behind to keep the door open...

And I wasn't about to ask anyone else to sacrifice their life. What kind of person would I be if I did that?

Percival hurried down fast, a grin lighting up his face. Above, the sound of wolves keened through the darkening night air. As the water rose past my hips, a shiver ran over me. Percival dropped down into the water, and he turned to me. He held out his hand. "Let's go."

I swallowed hard. "You first. I'm right behind you."

He frowned. "Why aren't you moving? Do you want me to carry you?"

"I need to keep my finger on this piece, or the door just closes again."

"Elowen, I'm not leaving you here."

"Then get up the stairs and try to find a big rock or something to keep the door wedged open. It'll give me enough time to crawl over. Can you try it?"

He scrubbed a hand over his jaw, then nodded. He crossed to the stairs, and the frigid water bubbled up around my hips. My throat burned, and I wanted to lean down and drink from it. But Father always said the wrong waters could carry the plague. He said that was how my mother died.

My teeth chattered, and a cool breeze rushed into the dungeon from the stairwell. Maybe that tattooed arsehole had done us a favor by kicking me in here.

It was another minute before Percival returned, grimacing and carrying a broken log. It was the circumference of a large pumpkin. With a loud exhalation, he dropped it between the door and the frame, wedging the door open. For a moment, I wondered if it could be used to press the puzzle piece in place, but it didn't look tall enough.

"There were no big rocks," he said. "But this should work."

I let out a long, slow breath, and I took my finger off the key piece. The moment I did, a banging noise filled the dungeon. The wheel on the door shuddered as heavy oak tried to close itself against the log.

With the wood blocking the water's path, the dungeon was starting to fill quickly. I forced myself onto my knees, and the water rose around my ribs.

Percival peered through the door. "Elowen, let me help." He started to reach inside, offering his hand. But as he did, a great crunch rang out. The door splintered the log into tiny pieces. Percival groaned, trying to force the door to stay open with his arm, but the mechanism of the door was far too strong. He grunted my name, and the door slammed shut with a loud bang, locking him out.

The moment the door clicked shut, it was as though a river burst from the dungeon floor. From the other side, I heard Percival banging and shouting my name, but the icy water rushed in around me, muffling the sound. Panic spun through my mind as I realized I was now trapped in here and unable to fight the rising tide. The cold water lifted me off the floor.

I paddled my arms, trying to keep myself afloat, trying to kick my good leg to stay above the surface. I could hardly swim to begin with, and the weight of the heavy wool cloak was weighing me down. I lowered one arm at a time, letting the thing fall off my shoulders. It drifted to the bottom of the dungeon. I looked up, hoping to see the opening appearing before me, but the water had carried me into a corner. The force of the water slammed me into the ceiling and rushed over me. Frantic now, I kicked my legs, ignoring the surge of pain. At last, my hands brushed against the vine that dangled into the opening to the labyrinth.

Coughing, I hoisted myself out and dragged myself onto the cobbles. I gasped for breath, and the night air seemed to sting my lungs. My cold, wet clothes clung to my body. As I huddled against a wall, my teeth chattered so loudly, I was sure the wolves would hear.

Up here, the air smelled of burned wood and flesh, and the moonlight beamed over me. Dizziness clouded my thoughts. When I looked down, I found that blood was still spilling from my thigh. I was losing too much, too fast. In another twenty minutes, I'd be dead.

In the distance, a wolf howled, turning my stomach into knots of fear.

Now I *was* well and truly alone. The isolation carved through me like a knife.

# CHAPTER 22

*I* leaned back against the stone wall. I didn't feel like I could stand, so I had little chance of fighting a wolf.

I rolled over into the corner of the passage, and the howls rent the night air. Shivering, I hugged my one good knee against my chest. The other stuck straight out onto the stone path, broken and bleeding.

Nearby, a woman screamed. "Help me! Help me!" I shut my eyes tightly, trying to block out the sound of her terror. I was in no position to help anyone right now. Her words blended into wild, agonized shrieks, like the senseless keening of a dying animal. The horror of the sound slid down to my marrow. Was I next?

The pain in my leg had started to numb a little, but I wouldn't be able to stand.

Water glistened on the cobbles around me. I

glanced at the giant hole in the ground, and its liquid surface reflected the shimmering light of the stars. That flooded dungeon was the one way I knew out of here, and there was no going back there now.

The screams had turned guttural.

Had that tattooed bastard made it out of here alive? He'd broken the rules and used magic on me, but I wasn't sure anyone had noticed under the cover of smoke.

Finally, the woman's cries cut out sharply. A dreadful silence settled over the labyrinth.

Should I risk trying to climb out of here? Maybe the archers had left by now.

Except when I glanced at the shadows moving above, I realized they still patrolled the labyrinth. The Luminari moved so silently, it was almost as if spirits were haunting the place. They were going to make sure every last one of us died in here.

The sound of whispering flitted through the air, a ghostly noise that sent shivers up my spine.

A movement caught my eye at the other end of the passage. As the figure moved closer, I realized it was a woman dressed in a black cloak. Her eyes looked wild, and she cradled her arm. But her unhurried pace confused me. Didn't she realize the wolves would tear us to pieces?

When she was only about ten feet from me, I could see there was something off about her—the way her skin glowed with white light, the dazed look on her face. I shuddered at the unnatural sight. When she stood just before me, she stopped, staring at me. Her mouth hung open in a daze, and she held her arm more tightly.

"What am I doing here?" she whispered.

I could hardly breathe. "The Order brought us here. We're on trial."

Grief shone in her eyes. "But my son is waiting for me."

My chest splintered at her words. I knew the feeling, and that she wasn't going home to him. I simply nodded. I didn't think I was going home, either.

She wavered on her feet. "There's something wrong with my arm. And my throat."

When she lifted her chin, I glimpsed the jagged red scar severing her head from her body.

She lowered her head again to look at me. Her eyes glistened. "Am I dead?" Her voice cracked.

Fear rang in my skull. I nodded again. "I think so."

Her expression crumpled, and she turned, slinking off into the darkness. Her black cloak trailed behind her until her figure blended into the night itself.

My throat tightened. In Merthyn, people say that when someone suffers a horrific death, their soul can linger on. With such a sudden, brutal death, she never had time to realize she was dying. She'd wander the same spot, trying to make her way back to her son, night after night. She might never leave.

Fatigue muddled my thoughts, and I slumped against the wall.

I looked down at my hands for a moment, ghostly white and shaking. Could I be dead already, and I just hadn't realized it? Drowned in the dungeon, under the black water...

In the past few years, the Order must have created so many unquiet spirits. All those whose minds couldn't accept the burning or death at the fangs of a wolf. This entire place must be haunted. A legion of the dead swept around me.

Just as that disturbing thought entered my head, a low growl echoed off the stones, raising the damp hair on the back of my neck.

My gaze flicked up to see the pale silver glow of wolf eyes. The world seemed to tilt beneath me. In the moonlight, I could just about make out its form, twice the size of an ordinary wolf. My blood pounded as I realized the creature was carrying a severed arm in its mouth, crimson dripping down the fingers onto the stones.

The wolf dropped the arm and licked its teeth. Its eyes were on me now. This was no ordinary wolf, but something otherworldly. The creature started prowling closer, and I tried to stand. Pain shot up my leg, and my scream died in my throat. My nerve endings sparked with fear.

While I struggled to rise, the wolf lunged into the

air. I'd just caught a glimpse of an opening jaw and sharp teeth when a shadow darted from the darkness. A smudge of night hurtled through the air, and somehow, the shadow slammed into the wolf. As it did, a crack echoed at the impact. The wolf fell silent, its body collapsing on the stones. I stared, stunned. The creature's neck lay twisted at a lethal angle, eyes wide open.

What the hell had just happened?

I felt the cold power of magic skimming over my skin, and I turned to see a cloaked figure looming in the shadows behind me. My breath quickened, and I felt as if death itself was upon me.

When he shifted closer to me, my body tensed. But to my shock, he lifted me into his arms. As his dark cloak billowed around me, he pressed me to his powerful chest.

Darkness whipped around us, but I knew him immediately by his seductive scent. Maelor held me against him as he started racing through the labyrinth passages.

So. The Raven Lord himself—the terror of witches across the kingdom—could wield shadow magic.

Moving swiftly as a maelstrom, inhumanly fast, he cradled me close to him. Somehow, he avoided putting any pressure on my injured leg, and I leaned into his chest. The world was a blur of shadows around me.

Exhaustion washed through me, and I wrapped my arms around him. Why did I feel safe with him?

He radiated the dark, addictive magic of the Serpent.

The wind whipped over me as he turned a sharp corner, then stopped abruptly. He laid me down gently in a small, cave-like space carved into the labyrinth walls. Moss covered the rocks beneath me, and a low, rocky ceiling arched over me. In here, there was hardly enough room for me, let alone him. And yet, he climbed in after me—*over* me. He straddled my thighs, then leaned down and planted his hands on either side of my head.

I stared up at him, the moonlight showing off his high cheekbones. My pulse raced faster, a frantic staccato.

"Why in the Archon's name are you hunting those with magic?" I asked. "I can see what you are."

"What I am is someone trying to help you," he whispered. "But we must stay hidden from the Luminari still patrolling the walls. As long as I move fast enough, they won't see me. If I'm going to heal you, we need to do it out of their eye line."

My chest heaved for breath as I stared up at him. "Why don't we just get out of here?"

"Because I need to stop the blood. Understood?" A razor-sharp edge slid under the low hush of his whisper. For a moment, I thought I saw a flash of a tooth, sharp as a wolf's fang.

"Okay."

"I won't lose control," he said sharply. "But it's the scent of your blood, pumping hot…"

My mind whirled with confusion. *Blood?* Why was he so fixated on that?

"It's not just magic, is it? You're something else," I whispered. In the hollows of my mind, I remembered what Hugo had said earlier: *They say that north of Merthyn, in the black, snow-tipped Sumaire mountains beyond the wall, live creatures called vampires…*

A creature who could live forever. Impervious to my touch. Indestructible.

Maybe those weren't merely drug-addled ramblings. Maybe Hugo actually knew what he was talking about.

I stared up at Maelor's face. His irises, once pale blue, had started to darken.

"What's happening to you?" I asked, breathless. In my thoughts, terror twined with curiosity.

He was a creature of death, like me. And underneath my fear, I only wanted to touch him.

"I won't hurt you." He lowered his mouth to my throat, and his finely carved abs pressed against my hands. "I need to stop the bleeding."

To my shock, his tongue swept over my throat at my pulse, making my body swell with heat.

*Vampires. They live forever, they feed off blood…*

The reason he and Sion were immune to my touch. My heart slammed hard.

"Are you a vampire?" The word evoked something

both alluring and forbidden, like silk running over bare skin. "Are you the reason all those bodies are showing up drained?"

"I don't kill people anymore." He seemed to freeze, his hand tightening around me. "You cannot tell a single person, but I think you need me as an ally. Understood?"

"Why the hell are you the Raven Lord? You're Serpent-cursed."

"You have your magical cravings." His breath warmed my skin as his mouth hovered over my neck. "I have mine. The Order helps me stay in control of myself."

"What happens if you don't stay in control?"

He shifted up to meet my gaze. "I will. With you, I will." Shadows slid through his eyes, and one of his hands slipped under my doublet, smooth against my bare skin. His fingers closed around my ribs. My back arched a little at the contact. By the primal look in his stare, I wasn't even sure he was aware he was touching me. Instead, he was looking at me like I was a meal he needed to devour. And even if it set off alarm bells in my mind, I'd never felt so alive.

"Tell me what happens if you lose control."

A pained expression slid across his features. "I'll forget who you are." Desperation laced his tone. "Forget who I am. Control is the only thing…but the blood makes it hard. So you have to drink mine. To heal you. Trust me."

"What?" I trusted no one, and I particularly didn't trust the Raven Lord. But right now, I didn't have any other choice.

It must be the Serpent in me who delighted in this feeling of vulnerability, who craved the darkness in Maelor. And it was the twisted wickedness of the Serpent who wanted my enemy's hand to move higher up my body, to cup my breast.

Maelor exuded some kind of primal power that drew me in and numbed my pain.

"Drink your blood?" I asked, half in a trance.

"To *heal* you." His voice had turned husky. "Now." He lowered his face closer to mine, his breath warming the side of my jaw.

His voice trailed off, his eyes now pools of black. Fear danced up my spine. I wasn't sure what the darkening eyes meant except that it signaled a primitive, bone-deep warning. I should be getting as far away from him as possible.

And yet...

Why, exactly, did I find those shadow-kissed eyes so beautiful? They were a dangerous, fathomless abyss drawing me in. Like the chasm in the temple, ruination and madness lay in those depths. This close to him, I hardly even felt the pain anymore. My heart pumped harder, blood heating with exhilaration. He was showing me the real version of himself, dark as I was. And it was pure seduction.

In the small space, I found myself pulling off my

gloves. Even if I was near death, I hungered for touch. I was starved of it. *Remember, Elowen. It doesn't matter how pretty he is. He's the enemy. He's the Raven Lord.*

I hated myself for clinging to the thin, black material beneath his cloak, twisting it in my fingers. My knuckles brushed against his bare skin, and I heard him gasp, his eyelids fluttering. I stared as his upper lip rose a little, and sharp fangs shot out from his canines.

He bit into his own wrist, and I froze, hardly daring to breathe. I'd known he was evil, but this was something else.

I stared at the blood running from the wound, transfixed. Under the metallic scent, I breathed in something else. Something sweet and intoxicating that I wanted to run my tongue over...

The blood of a vampire. It must be magic because I should absolutely be recoiling in revulsion at the thought of drinking blood. Instead, I licked my lips, desperate to run my tongue over that claret. *Archon*, I was thirsty.

"Drink." He bent his arm, holding it over my mouth.

My throat was parched from a day without water. I watched as the blood slid down his skin, cherry red.

"Drink, Elowen. Now," he growled.

The word *drink* rang in my thoughts, an echoing command. He didn't seem very well able to explain himself at this point, but that one word was a clarion call I couldn't resist.

I pulled his wrist to my mouth, tasting him—a

sweet wine quenching my thirst. This was all wrong. Unnatural. This evil was an abomination, a crime against the Archon. Surely we'd be cursed again—

It tasted amazing, though, and it slid down my throat, into my chest. I inhaled the spiced scent of him, and a sensual charge pulsed in my core.

Oh, Archon, this *was* dangerous. Drinking from a vampire was like nothing I'd ever experienced. The sweet liquid filled me with warmth. Hot, liquid pleasure swept through my belly. As I drank, every ache, every sharp tear in my body was replaced by a soothing throb through my muscles. I swept my tongue over his skin, and heat swelled in my core.

The only thought in my mind now was what I was made for: running my tongue over this beautiful man. For licking him, and tasting him, and making him gasp, for opening myself to him and letting him fill me whenever he wanted. He was a *god*, and I wanted to serve him.

Touching him, tasting him was the only way out of this jagged loneliness.

If he was death itself, I craved oblivion.

# CHAPTER 23

*I* ached for him, nipples pebbling beneath my shirt. He hovered over me, keeping a few inches between us, but I wanted him on top of me, inside me. I wanted to drag my fingernails down his naked back. I wanted to spread my thighs open and offer myself to him.

With my free hand, I reached under his cloak and ran my fingers over his muscled abs, then stroked over his lower back. Guided by my hand, his hips moved lower, pressing against me. I bent my legs, bringing up my thighs around him. I rolled my hips up into him. There was far too much fabric between us—my wet clothes, his shirt.

When he took his wrist from me, I caught my breath. I licked the sweetness off my lips, craving more. I reached up to cup his cheeks. *More.*

His eyes were pure black as he lowered his head

next to my throat. "You liked it, didn't you?" he whispered, his breath warming my skin. "Vampire blood makes some people feel desire."

But it wasn't *just* desire. My body was vibrating with euphoria, and I wanted to rip his clothes off.

Cupping his cheeks, I brought his face down to mine. I pressed my lips against his, kissing him. A low growl vibrated from his chest, but his kiss was gentle. His lips slanted over mine, then slowly opened. He was tasting me, his tongue twining with mine. A wild need burned in me. It had been so long since I'd kissed anyone…

He tasted faintly of spiced wine.

He slid his hand into my hair, pulling my head back a little as he kissed me, taking control. As his tongue fought against mine, my body hummed with desire.

Under my doublet, his hand roamed higher. His fingertips brushed beneath the fullness of my breast.

With a frustrated groan, he pulled away from the kiss. "No. I can't." His voice was husky now, almost tortured. "Elowen, I can't. You're healed now. And this is just the effect of the blood."

He removed his hand from under my clothes, and I longed for his touch again.

Breathing shallowly, I tried to understand what had just happened. I was still gripping the fabric of his shirt.

"Let's get out of here," he whispered.

"Why are you breaking the rules to save me? You're

the Raven Lord."

His jaw clenched tightly, and one of his hands gripped my waist almost possessively. A little bit of blue returned to the shadows in his eyes. "I know what you did for your friends. You were willing to give your life to save them. There aren't many people who would do that. So, for you, I'm willing to bend the rules a little. But I need to get you out of here quickly. I'm going to carry you as close to the gate as I can."

My chest heaved as I caught my breath. "I can walk now. I can run, even. I feel amazing. Maelor, I feel like a god."

"You still can't run as fast as I can, Elowen."

I hated how much I loved the way it sounded when he said my name.

"I'm going to get you as close as possible to one of the gates. At the other end, the Luminari will be waiting for you. If I had to guess, you're the last left alive. The rest have been eaten by now. And once you're outside those gates, you're finished. The first trial is over."

I smiled at him. "Is this your penance for being on the side of these monsters?"

Ignoring my question, he added, "The Luminari can't know that I helped you. Once I get you near the gate, I'm going to disappear. You'll have to run as fast as you possibly can. Everyone will be waiting for you there. The Pater, Sion, and all the survivors." His eyes searched mine.

I nodded. "Are you trying to redeem yourself by saving me?"

"Maybe." His gaze descended to my lips, and he brushed his thumb over my lower lip almost absent-mindedly. His eyelashes looked long and dark against his pale skin. "You mustn't tell anyone what I am, or I'll be killed. Horrifically. And I still have much to do while I'm here." He met my gaze again. "Let's get you out of here."

He swept me up in his powerful grasp, his cloak billowing around me. I wrapped my arms around his neck, holding on tightly. Maelor took off like a bolt of lightning through the labyrinth, seeming to glide through the air, like he was practically flying.

I'd never heard of a vampire, but he and Sion seemed almost like gods to me. I had a million questions for him, but I wasn't sure he would answer any of them. In Merthyn, we all knew that trusting someone was a risk not worth taking.

His movements started to slow. In the distance, torches flickered like little stars on the other side of open arches. My heart fluttered with joy. The torches meant freedom. They meant another chance to get back to Leo.

Maelor slowed, then stopped. He pulled me back around a corner and set me down gently onto the stones. As he did, a voice rang out from somewhere above. "Traitor!"

Maelor whirled, and I caught a glimpse of a Luminarus with an arrow pointing right at us. The soldier stood on the wall nearby, silvered in the moonlight. We'd been moving so quickly, I hadn't even noticed him until now.

"Traitor!" the Luminarus said again, and loosed the arrow. Maelor darted forward, and his hand shot into the air to catch it in his fingers. As the archer was nocking another arrow, two other soldiers ran for us, readying their bows.

But Maelor was already rushing for them like death incarnate, a streak of midnight racing up the walls. Shadows whirled around the Luminarus, and he screamed for only a moment before they cut his cries short. The soldier's head tumbled into the labyrinth, severed with a jagged tear across his throat. I stared at it, my mouth growing dry. I could kill easily with my touch, but something about Maelor's swift brutality made it feel as if the darkness were about to suck me in.

When I looked up at the wall again, I saw that the two other Luminari were now lying completely still, two horizontal silhouettes under the night sky.

I could hardly breathe. A dark beauty sang in Maelor's destruction.

I pulled on my leather gloves.

From the wall above, Maelor jumped down onto the cobblestones. Blood spattered his high cheekbones, and his pale eyes pierced the dark.

C.N. CRAWFORD

He nodded at the gate. "Run, now. I'm going to clean up the carnage before someone finds it."

My heart was a frantic war drum as I ran for the gates, sprinting for the flickering warmth of the torches on the other side. The night air felt cold against my soaking clothes, and I heard the wild howl of a wolf that must have smelled my scent.

Finally, I made it through the stone arches, my breath ragged in my throat. I fell to my hands and knees, the rocky earth biting into my palms.

"Elowen!" Hugo ran to me, lifting me in an awkward hug. His bony arms jabbed into me. "I knew you'd make it."

I wrapped my damp arms around him. His skin dripped with sweat, and his body shook. From the ground, I surveyed the rest of the crowd over his shoulder. Penitents huddled among the torch-wielding Luminari. And at the far end, the Magister stood eerily still. By his side, the Pater seemed to glow with silver light in his white robes. He wasn't a vampire, too, was he?

Hugo pulled away from the hug, and he vomited onto the earth, making a horrible retching sound. The poor guy desperately needed more poppy tea.

I glanced over at the others in our alliance. Percival nodded at me with a little smile. Sazia and Godric looked exhausted, leaning against each other. As Hugo released me at last, I caught a glimpse of Lydia standing alone in the darkness. She met my gaze, and my chest unclenched with inexplicable relief. Maybe I shouldn't be surprised she'd made it. Deep down, Lydia was always a relentless survivor.

But out of all the Penitents who'd begun, less than half of us remained. I swallowed hard. I relaxed a little when I caught sight of the teenage boy, hugging himself and staring at the ground.

Still, death hung in the air here at Ruefield Castle.

As a trumpet blared, signaling the end of the trial, one of the Luminari started reading out the names of each Penitent who'd survived. As he did, Sion stalked closer to me. His eyes shone with gold from the shadows, catlike. Standing just in front of me, he clasped his hands before him. He leaned down to whisper, "How *exactly* did you make out of there after nightfall?"

The deep timbre of Sion's voice sent a shudder up my nape. "The Archon guided me."

But for reasons I couldn't even begin to understand, my savior tonight was a monster, as Serpent-touched as I was.

"Of course he did." Sarcasm dripped from his whisper.

As Sion stepped away, the Pater Sanctus approached, his eyes locked on me. He wore his cloak open, and the starlight gleamed off his burnished armor, off his silver hair and beard, like he'd stolen the light of the moon itself. As he moved closer, my stomach turned.

"No one survives after nightfall." His voice had a

haunted tone, like the dead lived in him. And he spoke with a distinctly northern accent I hadn't been expecting.

I'd angered him by surviving. And I knew from the Baron not to open my mouth when I'd angered a powerful man.

He gripped my chin tightly, lifting it like he was about to crush it. "No one survives after nightfall."

All I had to do was pull off my gloves and touch his face.

"I'll take care of her." With a dark smile, Sion wrapped his hand around my neck, lifting me into the air. He was crushing my throat, and I kicked him hard in his stomach.

It felt like my boot was meeting a brick wall. Sion threw me to the ground, and I landed on my hands and knees.

"Witch!" My head whipped up, and I caught the tattooed man smirking at me. "She drained those bodies, didn't she?"

I started to push myself up, and Sion gripped me by the bicep, jerking me from the ground. "Come on, little witch. We have some things to discuss, starting with where the fuck is your cloak?"

He shoved me, and I stumbled before him. Anger crackled through my body like hot sparks. I turned, my lip curling as I snarled at him. He was, of course, exactly like Maelor—a blood-drinking immortal vampire with the power of a god.

As he shoved me again, away from the others, it was hard not to scream at the Pater that Sion was as cursed as I was. But if I told them all about Sion's secret, I'd be risking Maelor's life, too. And Maelor seemed to be my most valuable ally right now. So instead, I shot Sion a look of death. Dragging me from the others, he gripped my arm tightly.

He led me through a short path in the forest until the distant golden glow of the castle lights came into view.

With the roughness of his grasp, I really did wish my touch could kill him.

"What exactly do you want to discuss?" I hissed.

Maybe it was the horror of the day snapping at my frayed nerves, but I didn't usually let my anger show so easily—especially not around dangerous people like Sion. The Baron had trained me too well. Around powerful people, the best thing to do was shut your mouth and swallow your pride. But something about him made the words tumble out of me.

He released my arm, leaving me to walk next to him. "I thought you were supposed to be a fearsome assassin. So how did you end up falling into the oubliette?"

I cut him a sharp look. "How did you know that?"

He shrugged. "The Archon tells me things, of course."

Bollocks. He probably used his vampire senses to smell the river water on me. "Someone used a disorientation spell on me. Didn't the Archon tell you? I thought you two were quite close."

Tension sharpened in the air. "Who used the spell?"

I shook my head. "I don't know his name. The man with the tattooed scalp."

"Of course. And I don't need to ask how you got out. You had a little help from a certain Raven Lord, didn't you? Did he look at you with those sorrowful blue eyes and tell you about all the terrible things he regrets doing? All the guilt he feels for the trail of bodies? So depressing. I'm surprised you didn't throw yourself back in the oubliette."

"Why don't you ask the Archon what he told me?"

His eyes glowed amber in the dark. "I must say, I don't think it's a very good idea for you to stay in the same room as him. I can smell him on you, and don't you know that lust is a sin? Honestly. Fornicating with the Raven Lord? Does your shame know no bounds?" His velvety voice had a mocking tone. "The sad thing is, I feel like you're settling for him only because you can't have me. Isn't that right?"

"And you're not exactly what you pretend to be, are you?" *Shut up, Elowen.*

He shifted through the darkness, and suddenly, he was right in front of me, towering over me. The moonlight silvered his high cheekbones, and the wind toyed with a loose strand of his long hair. His masculine scent slid around me and amusement danced in his bright eyes. "You *could* tell everyone what you think you know." A smile ghosted over his lips. "But you know better than to play with fire, don't you? And really, who would believe a Serpent-touched commoner over the Magister himself? The Archon speaks through me, love. Everyone knows that."

Sion could threaten my life, but it wouldn't do him much good. The Baron had dulled the edge of that blade with overuse. Sion didn't know how to *really* get me to jump at his command. Maelor knew my weakness, but I hoped he'd never use it on me.

Meeting Sion's gaze, I shrugged. "I'll do what I must to survive."

His gaze flicked to my hair, and he reached up to pull a piece of grass from it. "If you want to survive, Elowen, you'll stay away from Maelor. And me, of course, but you already knew that." He turned, walking away from me. "You need to get to your new room."

I should feel exhausted, broken. But Maelor's blood still heated my body, and I felt as if I were glowing, like I could take on Sion himself.

His amber eyes slid to me. "I should warn you that there will be dark temptations in the next trial. Try not to get lost in a haze of desire imagining what I look like naked. You'll never make it out of there alive."

"Why are you here, hiding among the Order? Is it some kind of sadistic desire to use their victims as your playthings? Is it because you want to mess with us?"

He shrugged and arched an eyebrow. "Something like that."

# CHAPTER 24

*I* sat on the bed in my new room—a little space with a low, rounded ceiling and walls of rough-hewn stone. A tapestry hung on the wall, one embroidered with an image of a Raven Lord slitting the throat of a bull. *How cozy.*

I leaned back against a pillow, thrilled just to be alive. In my new room, torches in sconces cast dancing light over the stone walls. The door was reinforced with crisscrossing iron bars on one side, a tiny hatch inset into it. Iron bars also crossed over the diamond-paned window frame. Just in case I felt like smashing the glass and leaping to my death, I'd have a hard time of it.

Despite the iron bars and disturbing tapestry, there really was a warmth to the place. And after Sion locked me in here, I'd been delighted to find a pitcher of water waiting on a small wooden desk, along with bread and cheese. I'd gorged myself. Never before had bread and cheese tasted so perfect.

And what's more, the cheese came with a knife. Not a big one, but a knife nonetheless. Sion might think me so harmless he didn't need to worry, but I hid the knife beneath my pillow, saving it for later.

As I lay back on the pillows, I let my eyes drift shut. My muscles had been vibrating with danger all day, and right now, I felt as if I were melting into the bed. The healing power of vampire blood was pure bliss. The Serpent's magic was designed to intoxicate, to keep us coming back for more until the darkness took us over completely.

With my eyes closed, my mind slid back to Maelor, his mouth on my throat. I could almost smell him now, that sandalwood scent enveloping me. He'd told me he wouldn't hurt me.

Did I actually believe him?

The wind whistled through a little crack in the glass that sent a chill into the room.

The door swung wide, and my eyes snapped open. Without another word, Maelor crossed inside, and the door shut behind him. He tugged down his cowl. "There are a few things I should mention."

"About being a vampire?" I whispered.

He stared at me, and the shadows slid through the air around him. "You cannot tell anyone what I am. Do you understand? It will be incredibly dangerous for both of us."

"I'm not sure if you noticed, pretty boy, but my life is already in danger. What I want to know is why did you take such a risk by saving me? And what exactly is your angle in helping me? What do you *want* from me?"

"Because you're the type of person who should be saved." A line formed between his eyebrows, and his eyes shone as he studied my face. "I knew it from the first moment I saw you."

I stared at him, confused. "At the Dome of the Archon?"

He shook his head, and he turned away from me. "Long before that. I heard you in the forest. You were in Briarwood, by the stream. It was such a heart-breaking sound, the crying...a sound of unimaginable loss. Of course, that's how it was when Pearl went..." He trailed off, his gaze on the floor as some private torment seemed to consume him.

I stared at him. "You saw me crying in the forest?" It must have been after Father died.

He glanced at me, as if surprised I'd been listening. "I wanted to reach out to you because your grief seemed so familiar to me. It's my oldest companion. But I didn't. Because I'm not myself anymore, and I haven't been for centuries."

I swallowed hard. I'd seen the name *Pearl* written on his papers. "You said Pearl left. Who was Pearl?"

He took a deep breath. "She was my daughter, a

long time ago. And when the Archon returns and brings souls with him to the heavens, hers will go with him. But I will not. I'm not sure what happens to my kind at the end of time. I'll be here or in the abyss, I imagine." His mournful eyes flickered in the candle-light, and he seemed lost in his own memories.

"What was your life like back then? When you were alive?"

Silence stretched out over the room before he answered at last. "I was a viscount on the Isle of Lirion. Pearl died of the plague when she was only three. We lived a long time ago, before the Harrowing. The war that raged in our kingdom back then was the Anarchy. A battle for the throne." He ran a hand through his hair, staring into the fire. "Pearl was my first great loss. The second was my soul. And the third was my wife, Epona."

The world felt unsteady beneath me as I mentally calculated his age. Long ago, King Ambrosius had died without sons. Ambrosius had named his daughter as his heir, but half of Merthyn was unwilling to accept a woman's rule. A bitter, brutal war had raged across the kingdom for nearly twenty years.

"You're over four hundred years old," I said breath-lessly. "You look like you're thirty."

"Vampires don't age. Something about the loss of our souls keeps us always looking young. But yes, I was alive long enough to fight for Queen Onora's army. The Anarchy erupted after Pearl died, and my loyalty was with the dead king who'd wanted to leave something for his daughter. Because I wished I could have left something for mine."

My eyes stung. "I'm sorry about Pearl. I can't imagine what it would be like to lose a child."

"I still carry the loss, even after all these years. Being a vampire doesn't erase her memory. Sometimes, I wonder if it makes it all worse. Our emotions can be very intense, and I think many vampires find a way to smother it. That's what Sion does."

"How did it happen?" I felt a weight on my chest. "In Lirion, they worshipped the old gods longer than anywhere else in Merthyn. Was that why the Archon cursed you?"

He frowned. "No, that isn't how it works. I don't think there's necessarily any divine reason why anyone is cursed. The vampires were created in the ancient world. It was really by accident, when the Tyrenians first invaded. Merthyn's sorceresses had been trying to create indestructible soldiers to fight the invasion from the east. They used powerful magic, and it worked. We were created to be stronger than mortals. We see better. We hear better. We're as fast as the gods, and we can kill just as swiftly. We can seduce mortals to their deaths and sometimes enthrall them. But magic comes with a cost, doesn't it? And it turned out we were not very good soldiers at all. The newly created vampires lost control on the battlefield; they smelled blood, and they killed their own. It's part of why Merthyn lost to the Tyrenian emperor."

"Why have I never heard of this?"

"After the invasion, the Tyrenian emperor banished most vampires to Sumaire, and he built a wall to keep them from invading Merthyn. Most are now locked in mountainous cities with the wild Pretanni tribes, and only a few vampires remain south of the wall. That's a good thing. In Sumaire, the blood drinking is controlled."

"How?"

"They have thralls. Mortals who enjoy giving their blood to vampires. And they know if they kill all the mortals in their kingdom, they'll die, too."

I stared at him. "The Pretanni enjoy vampires drinking their blood?"

He shrugged slowly. "Many mortals derive an intense sexual pleasure from it, as do vampires."

Heat flushed in my chest as I imagined him drinking from an enthralled woman, both of them lost in the throes of passion. Strangely, jealousy flared at the thought.

"Most of Sumaire functions only at night," he added. "In the day, everything shuts down, except for the mortals."

"Why only at night?"

"We're creatures of shadow, love." His expression shuttered, eyes darkening for a moment.

*Love.* I certainly never expected endearments from the Raven Lord.

Despite everything he'd just revealed about himself, I sensed he was holding back. There was something important he wasn't telling me. Of course—in Merthyn, trusting someone meant death. And if I were Maelor, I wouldn't trust me, either.

But I wondered what he was hiding, and I had a million questions. "I don't really understand. Are you Serpent-touched like I am?"

"No." His eyes gleamed in the torchlight, and he took a long breath. "I don't have a soul anymore at all."

I could hardly breathe. "So that's why my magic doesn't affect you."

"I died, then came back. But changed. I was bleeding out on the battlefield during the Anarchy when someone turned me—a powerful vampire known as the Mormaer. He brought me back to life, and now, every day, my task is to make sure that I stay in control. I don't drink human blood, only animals'. I stay away from temptations like you as much as I can because lust makes me bloodthirsty, and sex makes me lose my mind...and around you, maybe I can feel myself slipping a little. I haven't drunk human blood in years, but..." He trailed off. "Anyway, I'm not going to let my control snap."

I lifted my hand to his face. His skin felt cool to the touch, but it was hard to believe someone so beautiful had once been dead. I associated death with rot and decay, and the man before me was breathtaking. But there was something about the way shadows seemed to stain the air around him, absorbing the light…

When I lowered my hand to his chest, he inhaled sharply. Dizziness whirled in my thoughts when I felt *nothing* beneath his muscles. No heartbeat. Part of my mind was screaming at me that this couldn't be real. But the other part knew there was much more in this world than I understood. After all, I didn't even understand my *own* magic.

And was a vampire really more frightening than someone who killed with a brush of her fingertips? Who was I to call someone a monster?

He pulled my hand from his skin, and his expression looked pained. "When I feel pleasure…it can make it hard for me to control myself. I no longer remember what I'm supposed to be doing or who I am. My thoughts go dark, and I just want to lose myself in the pleasure, to drown in it. It's part of why I stay with the Order. Women are forbidden to Ravens, and the discipline keeps me focused."

"But that's not why Sion is with the Order, is it?" I swallowed hard. "Does he still drink human blood?"

"Yes." He arched an eyebrow. "He takes what he wants, and he always has. The corpses around the kingdom are probably his doing, but he wouldn't tell me."

So what was Sion's weakness? Because when it

came down to it, I always needed to know the best way to end someone's life.

I bit my lip. "And there's no way to kill him?"

A smile flitted over Maelor's lips. "Now why would you want to know that?"

"Because what if he comes after me?"

His jaw clenched. "If you tried to kill a vampire—even if you knew how, even with your training—you'd lose. It doesn't matter that you're an assassin. You're trained to kill mortals, and we're not like you. Our strength is forged from hell itself. From darkness. You're better off not even thinking about killing us, Elowen. You're better off trying to go unnoticed and letting me help you survive the trials. I want to get you back to Leo."

He didn't want me to know how to kill Sion. Or was it that he didn't want me to know how to kill *him*?

He shifted closer to me on the bed, pinning me with his gaze. "You must never tell a single soul about me or Sion. Especially Sion. Do you understand? He's unyieldingly committed to his cause, and he'll kill anyone who gets in his way."

"I won't tell a soul." Unless, of course, Leo's life depended on it. Then all bets were off.

Maybe Maelor and I had an uneasy alliance, but it only went so far.

He stood. "I have to go. But I'll see you in two days for the Unburdening in the whispering chambers."

As he crossed to the door, something sharp tugged

at my chest, that thorny loneliness growing roots in me. "How are you so sure that you don't have a soul?" I asked. *How do I know if I've lost mine?*

He turned back to me, eyebrows rising. "When I used to write my poems, I'd see colors in my mind from the sounds of the words. The letter *I* was red as blood, and *U* the color of pastures, of emerald grass or the raging sea. *O* was the blinding blue-violet of the heavens, of the Archon, *E* like the silver-white of the moon. When I wrote, the world came alive. I could see Pearl's bright blue eyes and imagine lying in the grass with her under the summer sky. But after I became a vampire, it stopped. It's just blank, silent, like my heart has been ripped out of me. I still feel things just as intensely as before. Maybe more so. But I can't create anymore. At least, I don't feel anything when I do. It's all ashes. So I just burn it."

I swallowed hard. "I'm sorry."

His brow furrowed. "I've never told anyone that before."

"Why did you tell me?"

He shrugged, shaking his head. A line formed between his eyebrows. "You make me feel less alone. And the way you try to look after someone you care about…anyway." He ran his hand through his hair. "I'll return tomorrow night, Elowen."

"I thought you weren't supposed to be in here."

He shook his head. "I'm the Raven Lord. No one is really watching what I'm doing. I can help you prepare a little for the next trial. With my help, I'm certain I can get you out of here."

"How exactly will you help me prepare?"

Shadows twined through the air around him. "You'll need to find a way to focus through extreme temptation. And that, love, is my specialty."

# CHAPTER 25

*L*uminari had woken us early, barking at us that consequences must be meted out, that we would reap what we sowed. I had no idea what they were talking about, but I gathered some sort of punishment awaited us before breakfast.

Right now, the surviving Penitents were walking across the courtyard. I was flanked by Hugo and Godric. Coral morning light spread over the long grasses and golden walls surrounding us. Up ahead, Sion led the charge. He wasn't here for the discipline, was he? Not like Maleor. No, Sion was simply ruthless. Maybe he enjoyed the Order because he craved domination. And what better place to fulfill it?

Right now, he was leading us to a large, domed temple across from the central castle. I hadn't completely awakened, and my mind kept sliding back to the spirit of that poor woman I'd seen last night, trying to get home to her son. Maelor wanted me to get back to Leo—but what about her and everyone else?

"Elowen?" Hugo elbowed me. "Are you listening?"

I blinked hard. "What did you ask?"

"You didn't tell us how you survived the wolves. The Pater said no one survives after nightfall."

I smiled blearily. "Some things are just a mystery."

"Right. Best not to ask too many questions," said Godric. "With all the rules they've got here."

It took me a moment to understand what he meant. Godric probably assumed I had killed the wolves with my deadly touch. But he was right about one thing—it was better not to ask questions.

Hugo turned, surveying the surviving prisoners. "More than half of us have died now." His white-blond hair hung before his eyes, and he looked exhausted. "May the dead find their way peacefully to the after-world," he muttered listlessly.

Godric glowered. "But you know who's still alive? Bloody Guillaume."

"What do you think they meant?" asked Hugo. "About you reap what you sow?"

I bit my lip. That particular phrase was never used in a pleasant context, was it? It was never like, *All that time you put into learning the lute has made you a beautiful musician! You reap what you sow.* It was generally something awful. Whatever it was, we'd find out soon enough.

I glanced behind me to find Lydia walking with her

arms folded. She arched an eyebrow at me like a challenge. *I'm still here, old friend.*

If she was thankful that I'd saved her life yesterday, she wasn't showing it.

Percival sidled up and slid an arm around my shoulders for a moment. "I can't tell you how glad I am that you're here with us. I wasn't sure what was going to happen when the Magister took you away."

Up ahead, Sion prowled toward the temple with that languid stride. Towering above everyone, he walked with an easy, catlike gate. His broad shoulders were relaxed, not a care in the world. But I suppose if you had zero morals and the gift of immortality, there wouldn't be much to worry about, would there? A breeze toyed with the loose strands of his dark hair, and he turned back to flash us a half-smile. The morning sunlight illuminated his sharp jawline and golden eyes. Were all vampires blessed with such extreme beauty in exchange for their souls?

By the look on his face, I knew he was looking forward to whatever horror he was about to unleash on us.

I leaned in closer to Hugo, whispering, "You mentioned vampires."

"Ah, yes. In the kingdom of Sumaire—"

I raised my finger to my lips. "Not so loud. Whisper." Then I mouthed, "Is there a way to kill them?"

His forehead wrinkled. "Not that I know of. But there must be. The gods wouldn't allow anything *truly* immortal to survive because then they would be gods, too." He cleared his throat. "If the gods exist."

I nodded. I wasn't sure if Hugo knew what he was talking about, but he'd been right so far.

Up ahead, Sion pushed open the doors of the temple, and we crossed into the dark, damp building. It took a moment for my eyes to adjust inside. Light streamed in from the oculus in the center, casting most of the rest of the temple in shadow. Gargoyles leered from the walls, and the ring of blindfolded torch-bearers held their flickering torches above them.

My heart sped up at the sight of the Pater standing before the torchbearers, dressed in white and clutching his codex. His salt-and-pepper hair hung down on either side of his face, casting dark shadows over his creased features. He was clearly evil enough to be a soulless vampire, too. Except unlike Sion and Maelor, he looked aged.

As I crossed inside, he stared directly at me.

A cold chill rippled over my body. He might be mortal, but the man had immense power, and he seemed more than a *little* annoyed with me.

When all the Penitents stood in the temple, Sion began pacing before us. Did the others notice the way the darkness poured out of him? The cold power emanating from him was palpable.

Sion wore his sword low-slung around his waist, the silver hilt glinting under the light of the oculus. His golden eyes twinkled as he surveyed us. "I do believe I told you all that you'd be killed for using magic in the labyrinth. Didn't I make that clear?"

My nerves crackled. I wanted to look at Percival, but that might give his secret away. So I forced myself to keep my eyes forward.

Sion prowled closer, and his lips curled in a wicked smile. He was staring directly at someone right behind me. He beckoned with a crook of his finger. When I turned, I saw the tattooed man going pale.

"Edric, let's start with you. Why don't you come closer? Have you ever wondered what it might be like to be a torchbearer for the Archon? It's a great honor, you know." Without looking, he reached behind him, grabbing one of the torchbearers by the collar of his robe. He pulled him out of his position and shoved the torchbearer forward. The blindfolded man stumbled with a startled yelp.

Was this allowed in the house of the Archon? I'd never seen a torchbearer shift out of position before.

Sion gestured at the open spot by the chasm. From above, the oculus light streamed in, honey-gold, over the other torchbearers. But the shadows around Sion seemed to swallow that light.

Edric's body shook as he slowly stepped forward. None of us knew exactly what might happen, but I didn't think it was going to be pleasant.

Sion gripped Edric's shoulders, then swung him around to where the torchbearer had stood. He started to draw his sword.

Edric looked as if he wanted to back away, but he'd drop right into the abyss. "I assure you, I have no magic at all. This is all a mistake. I don't see wh—"

His words were cut off by a slash of Sion's sword. So fast. So precise. Edric screamed, his hands flying up to his eye sockets. Blood streamed from them, and his cries continued.

Sion turned back to us, his eyes gleaming with dark delight. He flashed us a crooked smile. "He really *doesn't* see, does he?"

He sheathed his sword once more, then pivoted back to Edric, whose shrieks rent the air. Sion cocked his head, and he reached out to shove Edric into the hollow.

The tattooed man fell backward into the chasm. As his screams grew more distant, my stomach plummeted. Did that chasm ever end, or would he fall forever?

"So noisy, wasn't he?" Sion's eyes flashed wide, and he drew his sword once more. "But I did take out his eyes, so we don't have to worry about him suffering the mind-bending madness of seeing the Archon's face. You do see how merciful I am, yes?"

Edric's blood dripped onto the marble floor, and a disturbed silence spilled out over the temple. I clutched my stomach, trying not to retch.

Sion glanced at the Pater, who stepped forward, holding his book. He pointed at two people—a middle-aged woman with graying red hair and a man with a dark, shaggy beard.

"Come on," said Sion. "Step forward, you two. Let's not make a big scene."

The woman's eyes snapped wide open. "I didn't use magic. I really don't have any."

"I know you didn't use magic, love," said Sion in a surprisingly gentle voice. "But the Pater tells me you two rose above the line of the labyrinth walls to avoid the traps."

Anger heated my veins. "They were just trying to survive." The words shot out of my mouth before I had the chance to stop myself.

Around Sion, it was as if all the Baron's lessons didn't amount to a thing because apparently, my blazing hatred of him burned out all my common sense.

Sion cocked his head as he looked at me, eyes gleaming with gold flecks. "Aw, witchling. You must mistake me for someone with sympathy to spare. If the Pater says they must die, it's not for us to argue, is it?"

His whirled, and his blade carved through the woman's throat.

As her headless body collapsed, Sion pivoted again, swinging his sword through the neck of the man. The man's body slumped to the ground, blood pumping all over the while marble.

My heart thundered so hard, I felt the sound must be echoing off the walls.

Sion sighed loudly. "Honestly, you lot really do need to understand that it's immensely stupid to break our rules. I hope I've made myself clear at this point." He cast a sharp look at me, letting his gaze linger for longer than was comfortable.

Ice rippled over my skin.

Blood continued to spill over the white stone. If Sion was hungry for it, he didn't show it. Maybe he'd already gorged himself outside the castle.

He sheathed his sword. "Go on, and try not to offend our Archon for the rest of the day. Once I get my sword clean, I'd rather not bloody it again today."

My fingers coiled into fists. At all costs, I had to find his weakness. Because if he was going to stand in our way, I needed to know exactly how to take him down.

# CHAPTER 26

In the dining hall, torchlight cast a warm glow over Percival and Sazia as they sat across from me. Storm clouds gathered outside, giving the dining hall a somber look.

Hugo and Godric nestled on either side of me, and I filled everyone's glasses from the bottle of claret on the table. Wine at lunch was usually a bad idea, but I was firmly in my *what do we have to lose* phase.

As I sipped the wine, my gaze trailed over the empty spaces in the hall, chest tightening. This place had been packed not that long ago. Now, everyone had spread out across the dining hall, and no one spoke. Lydia sat alone. So did most people, apart from our little group. Everyone looked dazed, hollowed out. The wine was flowing liberally as the surviving Penitents tried to dull their sorrows.

Across the table, Sazia shuddered. "Did you see the way the Magister blinded that man? Almost looked like he had fun doing it. Honestly, the people in this kingdom…"

I wanted to tell her he wasn't really a person at all, that he was a monster. But I choked down the dark secret, just like Maelor had asked.

I let the wine roll over my tongue. "Not that I'm defending the Magister, but the man he blinded was the reason I ended up in that dungeon."

Percival traced his fingertip around the rim of his glass. "But you'd better believe that if he saw you using magic, he'd do the same to you."

I swallowed hard. As we sat, the Silent Sisters started to bring food to our tables—quail roasted to a perfect golden-brown. They'd been marinated in wine, rosemary, and cloves.

Even if death hung in the air over Ruefield Castle, my appetite had come roaring back. Maybe *because* death hung in the air…I remembered Lydia once saying that death had a way of making people hungry and horny at the same time because we clung to life when it was most in danger of disappearing.

My mouth watered. And as if that weren't enough, the Sisters also brought a vegetable and mutton stew. Steam from the richly scented soup coiled into the air, and my stomach rumbled.

I picked up my spoon, frowning at the food. "Is it

just me, or do the meals keep getting *more* extravagant?"

Hugo slurped his stew. "We skipped breakfast today. Maybe they're making up for it."

"But…why?" I asked. "They quite clearly don't care what happens to us. Didn't one of you say you had a theory about it?"

Godric ripped a quail's leg free. "To show off their power. To try to make us feel grateful for their mercy. Maybe? You know what, I don't really give a toss."

Percival frowned at me over his wine glass. "I do have a theory. Because yes, they could be keeping us in windowless dungeons with only stale bread and rats to eat. The Magister said we were supposed to appreciate the mercy of the Archon. But what if someone gave him that idea? What if someone manipulated him?"

"He doesn't seem like the type who's easily manipulated," I said.

He shrugged. "The Pater, then. We can all see he's unhinged."

Sazia narrowed her eyes. "Tell me, what do you mean? I'm not following."

"There are rumors," Percival whispered, "about a resistance within the Luminari at Ruefield Castle. I've heard they're secretly working against both the Pater and the Magister. Maybe the resistance helped us to get more comfortable living conditions."

The stew was already warming my belly. "I'm still

not sure I follow. Why would they care if we had deli-cious roasted quail when they're letting us get murdered by wolves?"

He leaned over his stew, and the steam coiled before his face. "Because maybe they're working on something big. A rebellion against the Order. Maybe it's not ready yet, and all they can do for us is try to make our lives more comfortable before we die. Before they unleash their big plan. But if you want to know the truth, the rebellion is the entire reason I'm here."

Hugo blinked. "What do you mean, the *reason* you're here?"

Percival slid his gaze to the center of the dining hall, checking to see that no one was near. "I told them I was Serpent-touched. I wanted to come here."

"Are you out of your mind?" snarled Godric, nearly spilling his wine. "Are you bloody daft? Did that crack to your skull rob you of your senses?"

Percival pointed to the jagged scar at his temple. "In a way, yes. I nearly died after a jousting match, and I was unconscious for four days. When I recovered, I started wondering what the point of it all was. I was risking my life just to show off before a bunch of nobles. I could die at any moment, and for what? For the entertainment of other aristocrats? One day soon, I'd be bleeding out on the list field, having accom-plished exactly fuck all. But if I join the resistance? At least when I die, my life will have had a purpose. In theory. If I can find them."

Hugo whistled. "Well, I'm impressed."

"Don't be." Percival sighed and leaned back, not touching his food. "I've made zero progress so far in identifying the rebel Luminari. It's not like we have many chances to speak to them."

I breathed in deeply. "What do you think they're working on, if they do exist?"

He shook his head. "If they exist, I think they're trying to find out more about how to bring down the Order. Searching for weaknesses, information about the best time to rise up." He leaned back further, his shoulders slumping. "Or I've cocked it all up, and there is no resistance, and I've sacrificed my life for nothing."

My mind churned. "I don't know that we can take on the Order. I don't know how to find the rebels. But do you think we could at least find a way out?"

"How?" asked Godric. "You've seen the walls, with archers at the top. We can't scale them, and even if we could, we'd be shot before we got over."

My thoughts flicked back to the books I'd read in Maelor's room. "Hugo, you mentioned tunnels in the lands around here. The labyrinth was part of that, yes? They were tombs from long before the Tyrenians invaded. So what if there's more? What if there is a way out through the tunnels?"

Percival scrubbed a hand over his mouth. "How would we get to them? It's not like we can explore."

"I've spent some time with the Raven Lord," I whispered. "What if I can get information out of him during the unburdening?"

Sazia smirked. "Let me guess, do your methods involve him being celibate and extremely sexually frustrated? Use your tongue skillfully to loosen his, yes?"

Percival met my gaze. "You can't mention the resistance to him. If he doesn't yet know it exists, he'll report it to the Pater. It could ruin the entire rebellion and cost them their lives. You can't give him *any* information. Just find out what you can from him."

I nodded. "Of course. I won't mention it."

At this point, I was keeping secrets from everyone. I wasn't telling my allies about the vampires, and I wouldn't be telling the Raven Lord about the resistance. "Maybe I can find something else. An escape route."

"Just be careful." Godric's brow furrowed. "And if you can, ask him about the Trial of the Abyss. Ask him if it's real. I've heard things...terrible things. I've heard that most in the final trial will end their own lives out of sheer horror. I've heard they kill the other Penitents with their teeth—"

Sazia slammed her cup down on the table. "We get it, Godric. But we don't need to feel that terror now, do we? Can we just try to enjoy our meal a little bit? Honestly, the food is the only good thing here."

"She's right," said Percival, scrubbing his hand over his jaw. "We still have another trial before we even get to that one, yeah?" He plucked his wine glass from the table. "And in the meantime, we can think about a plan for escape and keep our eyes open for signs of the resistance. We won't go to our deaths like sheep. We will fight back. It's the only thing that can give my life a purpose at this point."

# CHAPTER 27

*B*etween every meal and every trial, we were escorted back to our rooms and locked inside. And that time gave me a very solid understanding of why the prisoners in the Maubergeonne tower had put so much effort into carving their names in the walls. There was fuck all else to do here.

I'd only just come back from dinner, but I'd already changed into my white nightgown. I'd fall asleep as soon as I could.

I did have a nice view of the courtyard, though. The maze of hedges snaked across the landscape, and its shadows grew long in the evening light. It was a vast landscape of budding plants and golden stones. Above some of the hedges, I could see the arcs of water from a fountain spraying into the air, catching in the light of the setting sun like honey drops.

I bit my lip, imagining what this place could be like

if anyone ever managed to extract it from the crushing grip of the Order. In the old days, maybe music played here, and young women met their lovers among the thorn fences. Maybe, once, people danced among the statues and fountains like in the tapestry the Baron loved so much.

I walked back to the bed, plucking the gold pencil off the table—my little glittering gift from Maelor. In the reflection of the pewter mug, I traced gold beneath my eyelashes. Out there, I had to go unnoticed. But in here, what difference did it make? Eyeliner or not, I was already the center of attention.

I lifted the pewter cup and blinked at my reflection. Leo would be delighted if he saw this on me. A pang splintered my chest at the thought of him, and I dropped the cup.

Sighing, I lay back on the bed.

When a knock sounded on the door, I rolled onto my side. "Yes? You know I can't open it."

I heard the sound of a key clicking in the lock, and the door creaked open. Maelor stepped inside. A lock of his dark hair fell down by his sharp cheek-bones. His mouth quirked in a half-smile. I truly hated how much I liked seeing him, and how my heart started beating faster just at the sight of his beautiful face.

The door closed behind him, and he lifted a little bottle of blue liquid. "We're going to practice for the next trial."

I sat cross-legged on the bed. "You're very much breaking the rules, Raven Lord."

"The Archon guides me."

*Sure he does.* "You could help all of us, not just me."

"When I said vampires are powerful, Elowen, I didn't mean I could single-handedly take down the entire Luminari army."

I bit my lip. "Okay, fair enough. But is this really what you want to dedicate your life to? Is the Order your life's purpose? Because I'm not the only one with a little boy waiting for me. Last night, I met a woman's ghost right after she died. She was just like me, trying to get home to a kid who needed her."

He pulled out the chair from my desk, sitting close to me. He took a deep breath, looking at me from under those long, dark eyelashes. "I just need you to try to trust me as much as you can for now."

A tiny fleck of hope sparked in my chest.

I took a deep breath. "Fine. I'll trust you, then."

His dark eyebrows pressed together. "Then believe me when I say there's no easy way out of here. Passing the trials is the best thing you can do, and only one of you will live."

I arched an eyebrow. "So I don't suppose there are any tunnels that I could use to get out?"

"There are ancient catacombs, but they're not an escape. The foundations of the walls would block your way, and even I couldn't break through those." For a moment, his gaze dipped to my lips. "If I could get you out of here, I would."

I desperately wished I had Maelor's uncanny ability to tell when someone was lying. "What do you know about the Trial of the Abyss?"

He brushed a strand of hair out of my eyes. "One trial at a time, Elowen. I'll tell you about that later. But first, you have the Trial of the Temptation to get through." He lifted the bottle. "I need you to drink this, and then I'm going to tie you up."

I blinked. "You're going to what?"

The candlelight sculpted his cheekbones with shadows. "The potion will make you overcome with temptations, and I need you tied up to make sure you don't do anything you'd regret."

My cheeks heated. "Are you worried I'm going to try to seduce you?"

A smile flitted over his lips, but it was gone in an instant. "Yes. And the moment I get turned on, I completely forget myself. I'll turn into a beast of pure instinct. I'll kill or fuck or take what I want. If I lose control of myself, I'll do anything for pleasure. No one wants that." As he said this, a shadow swept through the air in front of him, and his magic brushed past me. It was a dark caress that sent goosebumps over my skin.

I could so clearly imagine what he'd look like without those black robes on because I'd felt his powerful body when his arms had wrapped around me on the horse, when I'd reached behind me. Under the fabric, he was all muscle. If he really lost control of himself and ripped off those clothes, if he grabbed me in my nightgown...

My breath quickened.

"No one wants that," I repeated. I wondered if he could see the blush creeping over my cheeks. "How do you do that? With the shadows?"

"I wasn't doing that on purpose, but sometimes, if I lose focus, the shadows have a will of their own." The corner of his mouth twitched. "It's just vampire magic. And that means it's another thing you can't tell anyone about." He uncorked the bottle and handed it to me. "After I bind your wrists, your job will be to answer questions. Just simple math questions. The whole purpose of what we're going to do is about focus."

"I'm terrible at math."

"I promise to make it easy. The difficult thing will be mastering your own desires."

"And what's your secret for doing that?"

"You appeal to the power of the Archon. Just repeat after me. *Deus Invictus, Archon Magne.* Drown out your own thoughts with holy words. The Archon will help you focus on what's right."

"*Deus Invictus, Archon Magne,*" I repeated.

I took the bottle from him, breathing in a heavy herbal scent. I looked at Maelor over the rim of the bottle. "What if I drink this and I'm overcome with

244

visions of killing people with my touch? What if *that's* my true heart's desire?"

He shrugged, giving me a mischievous smile. "I'm not here to judge you. But there's only one way to find out. Drink."

I took a sip, and it tasted of anise and bitter herbs, sweetened with honey. It stung my throat, making me cough a little. I licked it off my lips.

Maelor pulled it from me, and the warmth of the drink spilled down my throat.

My eyelids fluttered closed for a moment, then opened again just in time to see wisps of shadow snaking through the air, which slid around my arms in a tingling touch. His magic thrummed over my skin, tightening around my wrists. The shadows pulled my arms together behind my back, and the magic sent vibrations along my biceps. Tendrils of magic slid up to my shoulders, stroking me. But my wrists? His magic bound those tightly, and it felt silky against my skin, buzzing slightly with a strange power.

I lay down on my side. "All tied up."

As I breathed in the alluring scent of him so close to me in my room, my heart raced. Every stroke of his shadows sent a warm shiver of pleasure through me. Was that the elixir working already or something else? Was it my addiction to dark magic?

With my arms tied, he stood over me, peering down at me. "You must be feeling something now."

Dizziness swept through my mind, and I rolled

onto my back, hands beneath my hips. I bent my knees, and the nightgown fell up around my thighs. With my arms wrenched back, I felt as if my nipples were straining against the delicate material of my night-gown. And it was a strangely pleasurable feeling...

Maybe I liked being vulnerable with someone as powerful as Maelor...

My pulse raced, and I opened my eyes to find him watching me with curiosity. "Give me the math."

He moved closer, and my breath grew shallow. The mattress depressed as he lay next to me on the bed, propping up his head. He reached down to one of my exposed thighs, fingers stroking me, languid and teasing.

"Why are you always trying to tempt me with your body?" His voice was a low purr. The slow brush of his fingers over my skin made me want to clench my thighs around his hand. His dark eyelashes lowered as his gaze slid down my body. "I'm here to test you, but now I feel as if the Archon is testing me."

"You're distracting me," I said. "You were supposed to give me a question."

"How about this for a question: are you aware that you drive me crazy? Your skin looks like honey, and I want to taste it."

He lowered his mouth to my breast, over the thin fabric of my nightgown. His mouth closed around one of my nipples. Through the fabric, the wet heat of his tongue made my back arch, and his hand slid further up my thigh, brushing against my sex. A light touch—too light. I wanted to writhe against him. Right now, I'd do anything he asked.

"You're not focusing, are you?" His deep voice ripped me out of the fantasy.

My heart hammered hard as I realized Maelor wasn't actually next to me on the bed, but rather sitting upright. He was sitting on the edge of it, by my thighs. And right now, I was thankful my hands were tied because I knew *exactly* where they'd be if they weren't.

I took a shaky breath. "*Deus Invictus, Archon Magne.*"

He arched an eyebrow, eyes transfixed on me. "You didn't hear my question at all, did you?"

"What was the question?"

"A merchant is riding from Ebeline. Twenty miles on day one, and fifteen on day two."

He reached down, grabbing my hips, and rolled me onto my front. I turned my head to the side on my pillow, still trying to catch my breath. I was flushed, breathing fast, and I had the mortifying feeling he knew exactly how turned on I was.

"Focus, Elowen. How many more miles must he travel to arrive in Shalem if it's forty miles from Ebeline?"

He raised the hem of my nightgown to my waist, then pulled my hips up, so I was kneeling. My bound wrists lay against my hips behind my back. With my arse in the air, exposing my underwear, I tried to remember the question.

"What are you doing?"

"Honestly, Elowen. If you're going to act like a shameless whore, I think you might need some discipline. Don't you?"

My core clenched, my body humming with need. He yanked down my underwear to my knees, exposing me completely. The cool castle air slid over my bare skin, between my thighs. He could see all of me, now, and I wanted him to.

My pulse raced as I realized he'd know exactly how aroused I was. Why was I so desperate for the Raven Lord?

"Now," he murmured. "Why don't you try answering the question?"

Before I could get the words out, his hand came down on my backside. *Hard.* So hard I was sure he'd leave a red mark. And to my horror, pleasure rippled through me at the strike. Against the cotton nightgown, my nipples felt exquisitely sensitive.

My mind flared with depraved images of everything I'd like him to do to me.

*I'll fuck or take what I want. If I lose control of myself, I'll do anything for pleasure.*

Archon, how I wanted that.

I could no longer remember exactly what I was supposed to be doing because all I could think about was the aching need for him to fill me hard and fast. He was the Raven Lord himself, and I was desperate for him to fuck me hard.

He smacked me again and again, each time, his hand moved lower. "Do you have an answer, or do I have to keep doing this all night? I can feel your arousal, Elowen." His fingers slid down between my thighs—then stopped. I needed more friction, and he was denying me. He was in complete control here, showing me just how hungry I was for him.

I didn't care how shameless it was anymore. I moved against his hand, desperate.

"If you're going to act like a harlot, Elowen, I will treat you like one…" He trailed off, his voice deep and husky. "Perhaps this is why the Archon cursed you."

The Archon. Yes! That is what I was supposed to be doing.

"*Deus Invictus, Archon Magne*," I muttered. "*Deus Invictus, Archon Magne!*"

I was on my back again, fully clothed, as the vision disappeared. My blood roared, body humming with desire. My heart pounded, and Maelor waited for my answer. My entire body felt flushed, glowing. The ache between my thighs hadn't subsided.

"Five miles," I said through labored breaths.

"Good girl," he said softly. "But next time, start the chanting sooner. It really took you a while."

I swallowed hard. "Weird."

Curiosity sparked in his eyes. "What were your visions like?"

My chest heaved as I tried to catch my breath. I

swallowed hard. "Just killing people. Total massacre. So much…so much carnage."

He frowned. "Oh. One more time, Elowen. Tomorrow night will be harder. And if you mess that up, you die."

I nodded. Archon, I wanted him.

But this time, as I envisioned him bending down to claim my mouth with his, I had the words already on my tongue.

*Deus Invictus, Archon Magne.* These words would be my salvation.

# CHAPTER 28

*P*ercival stood by my side in a row of Penitents. As we waited to give our confessions, torchlight cast flickering silhouettes over the dark mahogany booths. Muted voices carried through the latticed wood windows, the quiet hum of unburdening.

A metallic scent floated through the air under the smell of incense. In the temple's marble atrium, we weren't far from the dome where Sion had slaughtered three people just yesterday.

Percival leaned down, whispering to me, "Are you ready?"

I nodded, distracted. Even with the cloak on, the cool temple air washed my skin with a chill, raising goosebumps. The thing was, I didn't have anything *under* the cloak except a damp chemise and my underwear. That was all part of my plan.

Maelor was very clear that when his dark side came out, he lost control. He was also very clear that women were his weakness. I just had to make sure I got into the right booth; he was the Raven in the last whispering chamber on the left. Then, I'd pull off my robe and loosen his tongue.

Sion's words sang in my mind. *A Raven who thinks of nothing but forbidden touch, and a witch who can kill if she does.*

One of the chamber doors creaked open, and Sazia stumbled out, tears streaking her cheeks. She didn't meet my gaze as she walked past us, shoulders slumped. What were they saying to people in there?

Percival nodded at me. It wasn't the Raven Lord's booth, so he took my spot, and he crossed over to the open door. I waited, rocking a little on my heels, until Maelor's door creaked open.

Lydia sauntered out, smiling serenely. She was starting to look a bit like herself again. With a dewy flush in her cheeks, she radiated self-assuredness. Now *that* was the Lydia I knew.

She flashed me a little smile, then fluttered her fingers at me in a wave. "Do you know what, old friend? I think the Raven Lord likes me."

I stared at her as she walked away. How had I never realized how much she was like her father?

I took a deep breath and crossed over to Maelor's chamber.

As I stepped inside, his eyebrows knitted together.

In here, the shadows seemed to caress his sharp cheek-bones and jawline, and his black eyelashes were a stark contrast to his pale eyes. "It's you."

I took the seat across from him. It was so cramped in here that our knees touched. "I'm here for my unburdening."

He wasn't wearing a full wool cloak, but rather a lighter robe of cotton that buttoned up to his throat. The fabric looked rich and soft to the touch.

With his eyes on me, he stood. "Excuse me a moment."

He pushed the door open, leaving me alone.

While I waited, I surveyed the little booth. Sinuous carvings snaked across the dark wood over-head, etchings of twisting vines and ripe fruit. The armrests of my chair, too, had been ornately carved into the form of human arms wrapped with coiled serpents. The burnished wooden hands caressed the snake's head at the end of the armrests. In the dark mahogany of this booth, it was almost as if the Order wanted to make sure we never forgot the sensual allure of the Serpent.

I stroked a fingertip over the serpentine carving, feeling the smooth surface.

From the atrium outside, the scent of incense coiled in through the latticed window at the top. A long time ago, people had some anonymity in these places, with screens to shield the penitent and the confessor. But that had changed after the Harrowing. Of course, the

Ravens wanted to know who *exactly* was delivering information to them.

Apart from killing Rufus, I'd never been in one of these before.

I pulled my cloak tightly around me, wondering if Maelor even planned to return. When the door groaned open at last, my chest unclenched.

It was now or never.

Under the wool, I crossed my bare legs. "What am I supposed to say in here, Maelor?"

He shrugged. "The Order wants you to unburden your guilt after the first trial. You might find that it's freeing." He shrugged slowly. "Or you could tell me about your visions of carnage. The ones you referenced last night."

*Did* I feel guilty for anything? I didn't feel guilty for what I was about to do, but neither was I ready to launch right into a seduction. Yes, my visions last night had been purely sensual, but that hadn't been real. It was merely a product of my own fantasies. In real life? I had an inkling of how he might react, but I couldn't know for sure.

What I did know was that it used to drive Anselm wild with desire to see me swim in the sea in my underwear. It was the way the white fabric went transparent and clung to my body, showing off the curves of my breasts. I think he loved the way it concealed and revealed at the same time. That's why I'd wetted my chemise with water before coming in here.

Still, the thought of taking my cloak off right now sent my heart racing. What if he reacted with horror? Called the Luminari?

*When I'm turned on, I'll do anything for pleasure.*

"Something on your mind?" he asked quietly.

"My curse." I was stalling.

"What about it?"

"You asked about guilt." I swallowed hard, closing my eyes. "I knew we weren't supposed to give offerings to the old gods. I'd heard the Archon might curse those who gave offerings to the forest gods, but I did it anyway. I was sure at the time that one of the old gods lived in the weald that bordered the manor, but I no longer have any idea why I thought that." I opened my eyes. "I'd been warned, and I broke the rules, and I ruined everything. The Archon cursed me, and the curse hurt everyone around me. I nearly killed Anselm when I touched him. There was a servant I killed by accident, a woman named Mary. And Lydia wasn't around to heal her…"

My throat felt tight. None of this was going to plan, but Maelor was right. In a world where I always kept my real self hidden, maybe it did feel good to unburden myself. This was like lifting a weight off my chest. "Leo's father was a gardener, like mine. His parents were both accused of being Serpent-touched, and I wonder if that was because of me. Because they found Mary's body, and everyone knew someone at the manor was a witch. But it wasn't me who went through the trials. It was Leo's parents. Someone accused them. They survived the trials, but they burned on the pyre. So the Order left another boy at home, waiting for his parents who never returned."

"But you weren't the one who accused them," said Maelor.

"I know. But then, somehow, it got even worse. Someone murdered my father, and I can't even remember it happening. For all I know, it could have been me. And maybe I won't let myself remember because sometimes, I like killing…" The words felt torn out of me as I realized I'd never admitted it before, not even to myself. "Sometimes, the Serpent himself commands me, and I can't tell his thoughts from my own."

Maelor's eyes seemed to burn as he looked at me, and he leaned forward, taking my hands. "Elowen, it wasn't you."

"How do you know that?"

"I just know. I can tell when people are lying to me, and I can tell when they are lying to themselves."

I leaned closer to him, breathing in his spiced scent, feeling a thrum of shadow power ripple off him. "You don't think I'm capable of killing?" If that's what he thought, he didn't know me very well at all.

He arched an eyebrow. "I know you're capable of killing. But I also know you will do anything to protect those you love because I watched you slaughter a

Luminarus and steal a horse to get back to that boy. And he's not even your own flesh and blood."

My eyes stung, and I pulled my hands away from him. I was losing control of the situation. I was supposed to be subverting this confession, getting information from him. Not the other way around.

With a deep breath, I rested my hands on the carved mahogany snakes. I slid my fingers over the hard, smooth wood, turning over in my mind how to approach this.

I blinked, clearing the haze from my eyes. "What about you, Maelor? What kind of guilt eats at you?"

He still leaned in, resting his forearms on his knees. "More than you could possibly imagine."

"How about allowing the Pater to live?" I whispered. "Do you feel guilty for that? You could kill him and maybe even get out of here alive before anyone even noticed. There's a kid in these trials, you know. He looks like he's fifteen, maybe younger."

He put a finger to his lips, his pale eyes blazing in warning. "And you need to put that kid out of your mind, just like I have."

My nostrils flared. "No."

I felt his dark power skimming over my skin beneath my cloak like a caress.

I shifted forward, my lips near his ear. "Someone like you could take the Pater down if they wanted. What stops you from ending it all? If this is what the

Archon truly wants…" Even I couldn't bring myself to finish the sentence, the ultimate heresy.

*If this is what the Archon wants, maybe the Archon is as twisted as the Serpent.*

"Elowen." His breath warmed the shell of my ear. "Talking about this is dangerous."

I'd laugh if it weren't so depressing. Was there anything in Ruefield Castle that *wasn't* dangerous? Because I'd spent at least one day this week hauling my broken body above flying blades.

Even Maelor's shocking blue-eyed beauty was dangerous. I felt at risk of falling under his vampiric spell if I wasn't careful.

I reached for his face and brushed my fingertip over his full lower lip. "So why not end the danger for everyone?"

His expression darkened. "Because it's not that simple."

What seemed simple to me right now was that I just saw two people executed yesterday simply for trying to stay alive. "Not that simple?"

He shifted back from me abruptly and dragged his hand through his dark hair. "If you're finished, Elowen, I must move on to the next Penitent. You're supposed to be unburdening, not interrogating me."

My heart started to race. I hadn't achieved what I'd come for yet.

I crossed my legs, this time letting the cloak fall open to reveal a completely bare thigh. Just as I'd hoped it would, his gaze dipped, eyes darkening. Heat spread along my cheekbones, my chest flushing.

He scrubbed a hand over his mouth, his eyebrows drawing together. He stared at my thighs, and my pulse raced.

"Elowen, did you come in here half-naked?" His voice had gone husky, sensual. His gaze flicked up to me, heat burning in that pale blue. "What am I going to do with you?"

# CHAPTER 29

$\mathcal{M}$y heart fluttered, breath turning shallow.

I thought I had him where I wanted him. "I'm sorry. This cloak is making me feel very hot. I don't know why they have us wear them." I started to unbutton it, and his eyes slid down to follow the movement of my fingers.

He stared, entranced, as I opened it up before him, showing him the transparent fabric that clung to my peaked breasts. The cool air of the whispering chamber kissed my bare skin, raising goosebumps. My naked thighs clenched as he looked at me like he was hypnotized.

His hand moved for my waist before he drew it back again. With a tightening jaw, he forced his eyes up, but his gaze didn't get farther than my nipples. He'd stopped moving, and shadows slid through his eyes.

That darkening of the blue felt like a warning. Like a message to mortals, telling us to run.

Yet here I was, offering my bare body to the vampire.

"This is a bad idea," he murmured. "Because I want you more than anything, Elowen. And that is a very dangerous thing."

As with Sion, I now heard the faint tinge of a Lirion accent in Maelor's voice, a roll of his *R*s. Maelor had just been better at hiding it. It was an accent transported through time, the lilt of a language that died out a century ago.

My heart thundered, blood heating.

I let one strap of the chemise fall down. I leaned forward, stroking my hands up his thighs. "Would you ever be disloyal to the Order?"

He gripped his armrests, eyes dark as night. "How much more evidence do you need?" he hissed. "For you, yes. You've seen me be disloyal over and over. But Elowen, if I lose control…I can be lethal."

My heart raced faster, but it wasn't just my life on the line. I still needed more from him. Despite all his warnings, I needed him to lose control. "There's something else I need to unburden, I'm afraid." I bit my lip. "It wasn't really carnage that I fantasized about, Maelor. I saw you stripping off my clothes, touching me. Lust is a sin, isn't it? Is it a sin to imagine you tying me up and fucking me hard?"

His fists clenched, knuckles going white, and he

tore his gaze from my breasts. "You're playing a dangerous game with me."

"None of this is a game. Not how much I miss being able to touch someone. I thought I'd never kiss another person again, and then you came along. You risked your life for me, and I felt your lips on me and your tongue against mine. I can still feel where you touched my ribs like a warm, delicious brand. I feel like I'll die if I don't have more."

His chest rose and fell, and he leaned forward. Now, instead of gripping his own armrests, he was gripping my waist. "The Archon is watching us." His voice had grown deeper, the accent even thicker.

And his words sent a warm shudder through me.

I'd shifted so close to him, now, I could practically kiss him. "Aren't you hot?" I whispered.

Maelor's eyes looked heavy as I started unbuttoning his robe. While I opened the buttons, he closed his eyes as if he were giving in. Beneath the robe, he was wearing black trousers and a simple dark shirt. Already, I wanted to climb into his lap, to feel the steel of his muscles beneath me.

He muttered a prayer to himself in Tyrenian—then a sharp curse in what I assumed was Lirion.

His eyes snapped open again once I pulled at the final button, just by his lap. The darkening blue in his irises lured me in. "Don't have any idea what you're unleashing," he rasped. I felt as if the real Maelor was arriving at last. "The things I would do to you." Now his fangs had emerged—sharp ivory daggers, warning signs.

My heart skipped a beat, and my gaze swept down over his exposed chest. Pure, carved muscle, just as I'd imagined.

"And the trials are dangerous, and yet here we are. Maelor, I need to unburden, don't I? Because my vision was of you," I whispered. "Your eyes went dark, and I liked it. Because I like the real you. You told me if I was going to act like a whore, you'd treat me like one. You ripped my clothes off me, and you could see exactly how much I wanted you. You spread my thighs open, and you fucked me hard until I screamed your name. And last night, when I fell asleep, I had to pleasure myself while I was thinking of you."

It wasn't even a lie.

A quiet growl rose from his chest, and the sound alone had molten heat pooling in my core. Something in him must have snapped completely because he pulled me into his lap. "Do you know what you're doing to me?" One of his hands slid up into my hair, gripping it in his fist.

His fathomless eyes, black as a moonless sky. His hand slid into my damp undershirt, caressing my bare skin. Under the wet cotton, my nipples peaked with sensitivity, already aching for his touch. My pulse was racing, and heat lit up my body.

As I straddled him, I could feel the length of him

straining against his trousers. I rocked my hips against it.

"Maelor, is there really no way out for any of us?"

He ran his hand over my stomach, my hips. "If there were, I would tell you."

As I lowered my lips above his, hovering close to him, I tried to remind myself that this was an interrogation. "The Pater—is he a vampire, too?"

"No. But don't even think about trying. You'll be killed...so fast."

I rocked my hips into him, and his fingers slid up, cupping my breast. He tugged lightly at my hair. "You stay away from him, Elowen."

Maelor would be disloyal to the Order, but Sion? He was standing in my way. "And what about the Magister?" I whispered. "Is he always loyal, or might he break the rules like you?"

"Unwavering and brutal loyalty to his cause. He and I are not the same." One of his hands reached down to cup my arse. "And he is the last person I want to think of right now."

My breath quickened. If Sion was going to stand in my way at some point, I needed to know if I could end his life.

I brushed my lips against Maelor's. "Why do vampires only go out at night in Sumaire?"

He inhaled sharply, then ran his tongue over his fangs. "We burn in light." His words were a husky exhalation. "Creatures of the night. Of shadow magic."

"In the light of the Archon," I whispered, "you incinerate."

"The Archon shuns us…and we are monsters, love, because I could kill you at any moment, but that's not what I want from you right now." He pulled me down to kiss him, lips slanting against mine.

Every wicked, sensual lick of his tongue built a wild ache inside me. This wasn't the kiss of a cleric but the deeply sensual kiss of an experienced lover. Despite the vow of celibacy, this man knew *exactly* what he was doing. Pleasure rolled through my body. My nipples had gone hard against the cold fabric of my top, and I wanted to pull it off.

I forced myself to pull away from the kiss. "But you don't burn."

He palmed my breast over the damp fabric, staring in a dark-eyed trance as he ran his thumb over my hard nipple. "I burn."

I could hardly catch my breath. *Deus Invictus, Archon Magne.*

"I mean in the sun. You can walk in the light. I've seen it." I lowered my lips to his, hovering just out of reach.

"Pendant. It's magic."

My mind flashed with a memory of a silver pendant etched like a butterfly.

"Sunlight." I gasped. "Is that the only way to kill a vampire?"

His hand slid deeper into my underwear, touching

me where I was wet. I gasped, moving against him. He spread me open, and the erotic ache grew.

"Wooden stake to the heart." The words were practically a moan, and he pulled my hips down against his.

The ache inside me made it almost impossible to think now, and I rocked my hips against him. He lowered his mouth to my throat, kissing me with languorous whorls of his tongue. He might not have a soul, but the man knew how to use his mouth.

A very dim part of my mind wondered what kind of trouble I'd be in if someone opened the door and found me half-naked, riding the Raven Lord. But I also didn't really care right now.

When I felt his fangs slide over my throat, my heart skipped a beat. I was completely vulnerable to him now, but I *craved* that danger.

With a hand gripping my hair, he tilted back my head. I slid my fingers into his hair. He grazed his fangs over my skin. At the same time, he was cupping me between my thighs, feeling my arousal. "I want you as mine to command, Elowen. I want to fuck you night and day."

*Deus Invictus, Archon Magne.*

"You really think I couldn't kill the Pater," I murmured.

With a sudden jolt, he pulled his mouth from my throat. "No!" He gripped me by the biceps, his eyes pure shadows. "You can't kill him." His eyes shifted to an agonized expression. "I can't do this."

He shoved me off him, and I fell back into my chair, gasping for breath. Pain etched his features, and his eyes had darkened to pitch. "Elowen, you need to leave. *Now*. I know what you're doing."

I missed the warmth of him, the feel of him already.

Forcing myself to focus, I snatched my cloak from the chair. I still wanted more of him, and a traitorous part of me wished I could have kept it going longer. But he was the Raven Lord, and I'd come here for information.

I pulled my cloak around myself and stepped from the whispering chamber, a warm glow lighting up my body. I hadn't learned anything about the next trial, but I'd still gained some information.

As much as I loathed the man, the Baron had taught me well. So why did I feel an emptiness carving through my chest?

# CHAPTER 30

Twilight spread its silvery veil over the kingdom, tinging the mist with indigo. Sion led us over a winding path of broken cobbles to a remote part of the sprawling castle bailey, an enclosed area with walls as high as the battlements.

A cold breeze whipped over the grounds, rushing into my hood. We'd all been handed tapers, but no one had yet explained why. So we walked in a silent procession toward the next trial, holding unlit candles.

Crooked graves lined the path, and the mist shifted around them.

Up ahead, towering walls loomed before us, stretching out of the fog toward the darkening sky. Moss and sinewy tendrils of ivy snaked over the walls. The sight of them made a shiver run over my skin. The grandiose size of everything here boasted of the Order's power.

We'd been whittled down to just under fifty people now, and a heavy sense of dread hung in the air.

Sazia shivered as she walked next to me. "Any idea what the bloody candles are for?"

I shook my head. I'd been able to tell them about Maelor's strategy—stay focused by chanting to the Archon. But I didn't know anything more than that.

"You remember the chant?" I whispered.

She nodded.

Clutching my taper, I looked around me, wondering who would be left by the end of the trial. My gaze landed on Lydia, who stared back at me with an unreadable expression.

I glanced ahead. As the mist thinned a little, I could see through the gates to what the walls enclosed: a cloistered garden of overgrown plants, gnarled and wild. Light and shadows writhed from torches fixed in iron sconces at the gate's entrance.

Maelor stepped from the garden, the firelight caressing his beautiful face for just a moment. He cradled a brass chalice, and his cold blue gaze slid to mine. For a moment, I thought I read anger in his eyes. Apparently, Maelor did not appreciate being used for information…

My heart started racing at the sight of him, and I nearly missed the fact that Sion had already started speaking, or that the Pater stood behind him, draped in white. A silent phantom.

"I hope you're thankful for all we've done for you so

269

far." Sion's gold eyes twinkled with a violence that made me want to run the other way. "The food, the soft beds from the Order. We've given you a chance to survive, even if we should have burned you all by now."

I let out a long sigh. I didn't care if he looked like a god; his arrogance made my stomach turn. Shadows seemed to slide from his dark, velvety robe, mingling with the mist. Did anyone else notice?

He stalked closer to us, graceful as a cat. "If you want to live the rest of the night, you must find your way out of the garden before your candle goes out. If your flame dies, you will, too. All you must do to get out is answer three riddles, and you can walk free from the garden." A faint smile flitted over his lips, and cold power radiated off his body. "But this is a trial. Before you enter our cloister garden, you'll sip from the nectar of temptation." Those rich gold eyes flicked to me. "When you do, all your forbidden desires will stir in the darkest parts of your mind. And as temptations cloud your thoughts, you won't remember why you need to get out of the garden. All you'll remember is the need to taste forbidden fruit." He was gazing directly at me as he said, "Don't let your wanton lust take over your mind."

My heart fluttered.

Sion pulled his gaze away again, his expression growing bored. He sighed. "So do try to stay focused, and keep that candle lit."

Maelor stalked closer to us, and he offered the

chalice to Hugo. Hugo looked a little *too* eager to drink from the mind-altering elixir.

Dressed in white, the Pater glided forward, looking like a spirit from another world. My heart skipped a beat when I realized he was staring directly at me, a sharp line between his eyebrows. As Maelor went from one Penitent to another, lifting the chalice to their lips, the Pater walked closer to me.

He stopped directly in front of me, and revulsion skittered over my body. "Magister. Did you interrogate her thoroughly?"

Sion smirked. "Do you doubt my brutality?"

"It's just that I don't see any marks," snapped the Pater.

Sion arched an eyebrow. "The worst scars aren't always visible, are they?" A sharp edge undercut his deep, velvety tone.

I took a sharp breath. Was Sion trying to help me or just save his own skin?

The Pater's lip curled. "When I was a boy, King Ambrosius V created a famine in the north." He turned to me. With a leather-gloved hand, he gripped my chin. "Did you know that, little witch?"

I was pretty sure that was a rhetorical question, so I kept my mouth shut.

The Pater dropped my chin again with a look of disgust. He pivoted away from me, and he began pacing before the crowd. He folded his hands behind his back. "Ambrosius V said we didn't pay enough tax.

What he really wanted to do was to starve us all to death. He took everything we grew."

Maelor stood before Percival, raising the chalice to his lips.

The Pater pivoted again, marching before us, his eyes on the ground. "In the north, Ambrosius turned the living into the dead, and a garden of bones stretched from Eboria to the cursed walls of Sumaire. He wanted to make room for the wealthy farmers from the south." His deep, haunted voice sent a chill down to my marrow.

He was staring at me again. "You probably don't learn about that on your rich southern coast, do you? About the peasants in the north? The living skeletons who tried to fill their bellies with soil and tree bark? You didn't learn about the parents watching their children's cheeks grow hollow as empty graves." His voice rose to a shout, spittle flying from his lips. "And you didn't learn what it means to feast on the dead as they fall, to feel the horror of devouring what's left of your loved ones. To become a ravening animal instead of a man. That was the work of the Serpent. You may think our trials are brutal. But you don't know true cruelty, little witch. That comes from the dark touch of the abyss. The Serpent's evil infected Ambrosius, as it infects you." His voice rumbled over the horizon like thunder.

I held my breath, certain I was supposed to keep my mouth shut.

"Because you never crawled through a barren field, chewing on moss, knowing that death was stalking closer. You never considered what it would be like to kill a man for a rotten crust of bread. And you never watched your sister die, then considered…" He trailed off, then blinked. "Nor were you ever saved by the Archon himself. Chosen by him to lead us out of that darkness. You never saw his light, so blinding and pure, or heard his voice in your mind. You only hear the voice of the Serpent. I know that, witch, because I can see the darkness in you. The Archon never blessed you with a blazing certainty that your life's one purpose, your one mission, was to rid the world of evil. It was *me* he chose." His eyes burned. "The Archon chose me." It sounded as if sorrow sang in his haunted voice, and it rumbled through my gut. "I am his messenger, appointed by him to carry out his will on earth. He spared me from the famine so that I would not fail him. Do you understand, you Serpent-touched whore?"

I simply stared at him. He'd worked himself into a fervor, and whatever was coming next would not be pleasant.

He seemed to snap out of a trance, and he let out a sigh. "Good. Now you all understand my mission. You know why I don't lie in a grave with the rest of my family. I was chosen." He darted closer to me, shaking. "So how about we see those hidden scars right now? And please don't plead modesty because we all know what you truly are."

Sion's gaze moved slowly to mine. His body was still as stone.

My heart was racing as I tugged at the fingertips of my leather gloves, and I pulled them off. Gripping the gloves in one hand and the candle in the other, I turned over my wrists. In the dusky light, the Pater stared at my pink, warped skin. A cold breeze slid over my bare flesh.

It would be so easy to simply reach out and touch his face…

But then I'd never seen Leo again.

"Good," the Pater whispered as he stared at my scars.

A sharp snap of cold iced the air, and I met Sion's gaze. His jaw muscles flexed, eyes narrowing at me. Darkness bloomed around him, billowing like smoke in the mist.

The Pater kept staring at my disfigured wrists. "The Serpent lives in this one. Only pain will bring an animal to heel. Put the gloves back on."

Sion's cold gaze was still locked on me, his eyes glinting with shards of gold. I pulled the leather gloves on again.

Maelor stood before me, his eyes downcast as he lifted the chalice to my lips. His long eyelashes cast shadows against his cheekbones.

My chest ached. I'd used him for information, and now he didn't even want to look at me.

The moment I sipped from the chalice, my thoughts

started to cloud. An intoxicating, ghostly music swelled in the air around me, but I knew I was imagining it. There were no instruments anywhere in sight.

I turned, catching Godric's eye. "I hear the most beautiful music," I whispered.

He smiled at me, his eyes bright. "So do I. I'm writing this down when we get out of the trials. A dream song of light and dark…" His voice trailed off.

As if from a distance, I heard Sion give us the order to light our candles as we crossed inside the garden.

I followed behind Percival, watching as he touched his candle's wick to the wavering torch. Fear coiled through my chest as I lit mine. The moment the flame snuffed out, so would my life.

I cupped my hand around the flickering candle, shielding it from the breeze. As I stepped into the garden, I took in the wild, untamed beauty. Pinpricks of white light meandered around the paths as the Penitents held their candles, wandering in a daze.

I could see that once, this cloister garden must have been glorious. Vast and rambling, it stretched between distant stone walls. Gnarled trees twisted into the air, and crumbling statues stood faceless, fingerless among the briars. This garden was like a labyrinth of its own, one of overgrown paths and faded grandeur.

And soon, many of us would be lying dead among the thorn bushes. Still, the potion was warming me up from the inside, and I didn't feel as much dread as I should have.

I glanced at Godric. From under his cowl, he giggled at me. He wandered off, shielding his candle from the breeze.

Moss had grown over the rocky paths, softening their edges, blending them into the green. From between the stones, grass and weeds straggled into the air.

My gaze flicked to an armed Luminarus lurking in one of the shadows. A cold blade of clarity pierced me for a moment. The Luminarus had nocked an arrow in his bow, ready to shoot down the first person who let their candle die.

I backed up into a curved, stony alcove by one of the garden's edges—a good spot to shield my candle. I should be scared, but bliss dulled my fear. I was alive, wasn't I? In a daze, I stared at a crumbling fountain nearby, the basin full of rainwater and fallen leaves.

We were supposed to be doing something here... riddles. Where, exactly, did the riddles come from?

The garden's scent coiled around me—the musky soil, swollen with rain, and the delicate perfume of violets and primroses. My body felt soft and heavy. I leaned back against the curved stone wall, and the dew from the leaves dampened my hair. I let my eyes close. I was at one with the garden.

When I opened them again, the world beamed with buttery light around me. Ripe fruits hung from the trees—scarlet pomegranates made my mouth water, bright and round as blood drops. My eyes closed again, and this time, when they opened, night had fallen. Above, stars glittered in the sky, and a perfumed scent wrapped around me.

*The candle.*

Were those the temptations? I could resist a little fruit.

But in the next heartbeat, Maelor emerged from the darkness, as if formed from the shadows.

Ah. *There* was the temptation.

# CHAPTER 31

Shadows slid over him, and his eyes glinted with desire. Already, my body was heating with the memory of his hands on me. The way he told me he wanted me as his to command…

His gaze slid down to my mouth, and he brushed his thumb over my lower lip.

Warmth crept over my cheeks, and my breath shallowed. "Something making you nervous?" Maelor murmured. "Do you finally understand what I am?"

My heartbeat pounded so hard, I was sure he could hear it. I kissed his thumb, and his eyes darkened. Heat radiated through the air. Just being this close to him made my skin feel alive, craving his touch. His dark shadows were licking at my skin under the cloak.

When I looked up at him, I felt like he could see right into my soul. He could read in my eyes how much

I wanted him. Maelor's seductive beauty was a sharp blade, ready to carve me open.

I wanted the heavy cloak off me.

I licked my lips. "*Deus Invictus, Archon Magne.*"

"I need you to answer something for me." He leaned in closer, whispering, "What sister of the sun rules the night?"

He leaned down, and he wrapped his palm around the back of my neck. Cold, perfumed air whispered over my bare skin…what happened to my cloak? I'd dropped it down to my feet, along with the rest of my clothes. I'd just stripped, right here in the garden. I was in my underwear again, nothing else. He was dangerous, yes, but I also wanted to wrap my naked body around his, to feel our bodies glow with heat.

Maelor's mouth lowered, just over mine. He smelled like sin.

As my pulse raced, I tried to slow my breathing. Maelor's darkening gaze brushed down over my bare shoulders, and his hand slid under the strap of my camisole. He pulled it down, and his thumb brushed over the top of my breast.

A small, sensual smile curled his lips, and liquid heat spilled between my thighs. His lips slid over mine at last in a light, teasing kiss. It was over too fast.

"What sister of the sun rules the night?" I repeated. Just as I was about to say *moon*, Maelor stopped me with a deeper kiss. My lips opened against his, and his body pressed against mine. Behind me, the damp rocks cooled my back. His tongue brushed against mine, gently teasing me. I threaded my fingers into his dark hair.

*He could kill you, Elowen.*

His hand moved down over my hips, leaving a trail of heat in its wake. As he cupped my arse, I moaned into his mouth.

He finished the kiss with a sensual nip to my lower lip. I whispered the chant, trying to remember the riddle.

Maelor pulled away.

"What sister of the sun rules the night?" I repeated.

His mouth hovered above my throat. "Her tears fall from fire and wavering light. And when her final tears are shed…" A wicked stroke of his tongue on my neck had me arching my back. Maelor's knee pressed between my thighs, rooting me in place against the ivy-covered wall. His fangs raked over my jugular, and my thighs clenched around him.

With the cool night air caressing my skin, I tried to remember the danger I was in.

*Deus Invictus…*

"What was it?" I asked through heavy breaths. "When her final tears are shed?"

He raised his head and met my gaze. A dark smile curled his lips, and his eyes were pools of night. "As she dies," he murmured, "they cut off her head."

My heart started to race. I was going to fucking die here. *Deus Invictus, Archon Magne.*

When my candle went out...

"A candle!" I shouted. It was another moment before I realized I'd answered the riddle.

Shadows consumed Maelor, and I glanced down at the candle in my hand. I let out a long exhalation as I took in the flickering flame. Still here. Still alive.

The wax was spilling over my fingers, hot on my skin. How much time had passed already? Nearly a third of the candle had burned down, and darkness cloaked the night sky. Through the tree branches, I had a view of twinkling stars and a sliver of moon.

Maelor was gone now, but I was still half naked. I wondered if I should pull the cloak on again, but I had to stay focused on the candle. I shielded it from the breeze, staring at the little flames.

The sylvan perfume of aged wood floated through the air, mingling with lavender.

I closed my eyes and smelled sandalwood coiling around me. Maelor's shadows brushed over me, thrumming along my bare skin.

I looked up to see him standing before me once again. Only now, he wasn't wearing a shirt, either. In the moonlight, his finely cut abs and chest were sculpted with silver and shadow.

*Deus Invictus, Archon Magne.*

"Do you have another question for me?" I asked. "The second riddle."

His gaze slid down me like he wanted to devour me. He bared his fangs, then flicked his tongue over the white points. He stood before me now, his magic humming over my skin.

"What a creature," he murmured. He prowled forward, a faint smile on his lips. "You will be the ruin of me."

"The riddle."

Maelor traced his hands down my arms from my shoulders to my wrists. As he did, heat slid through my blood. When he reached my fingertips, he gripped my wrists and held them above my head.

Hadn't I been holding something? I wasn't now. He pinned me against the rock, my hands pressed into the wet stone.

His mouth hovered over mine. "The thing about vampires, my love, is that we take what we want. We fuck and kill and drink, and even if I ended your life, you would die enraptured with such exquisite pleasure that it would all be worth it. You would die dragging your nails down my back and moaning my name."

My legs were turning to liquid.

*Focus, Elowen.* I muttered the phrase again to myself. My breath hitched. "What's the riddle?"

The dew on the leaves dampened my skin, and Maelor pressed his muscled body against mine. He leaned down, his breath warming my throat. "What creature, when it moves, speaks every tongue?" His fangs grazed my skin. At the touch, heat swept through my body. Slowly, he trailed kisses over my throat, over my jawline.

As he kissed me, visions flitted through my mind—Maelor writing feverishly at a desk as bright colors stained the air around him. He kissed me deeply.

When he pulled away from the kiss, he loosened his grip on my wrists. His hands trailed down my arms again, leaving heat in their wake. "Elowen," he whispered, "you have awakened something in me that should have stayed at rest."

"The rest of the riddle," I whispered.

"What creature, when it moves, speaks every tongue…" He grabbed my arse, lifting me up against the wall. His hands held me up under my thighs, and his hips pressed into mine. He bit his lip, and his dark, heated gaze raked down my body. "Its mouth spews poison, the innocent are hung. When still it stands, it makes no sound at all."

My arms draped over his bare shoulders, and I felt the muscles moving in his back. "Mouth spews poison," I repeated. "The innocent are hung." Sounded familiar. Slander was a common currency here…

"It hears no words, no poor man's call," added Maelor.

My thighs were wrapped around his waist, and he started to move his hips into me.

"A pen," I gasped.

He practically dropped me, and I slammed into the ground. "Good. Now try to stay focused for the last one, will you? You're running out of time."

"You were the one distracting me," I hissed.

I looked down at the candle in my hand. Somehow, I was still holding it.

"You're running out of time." His words echoed off the stones, but when I looked up again, he was gone.

Now, the white wax had spilled down over my wrist, and the wick had burned down near the bottom. Only an inch or so of candle was left, and my blood roared. Bollocks. Was I actually going to make it out of here in time? I needed the next bloody riddle, now.

"Maelor?" I whispered.

This time, when he emerged from the shadows, his eyes danced with mischief, and a sensual smile curled his lips. When his gaze slid down my half-naked body, mockery danced in his eyes. "Did you really need to seduce me for information, or was that just something you wanted to do?"

My lip curled. "What's the riddle?"

"Turn around."

I arched an eyebrow. "That's the riddle?"

"No, that's me telling you to turn around."

I did as he asked. The garden breeze washed over me, and I could feel his eyes on me.

Maelor came up behind me and threaded his fingers into my hair, tugging it a little. From behind, he pressed against me. As he pulled my hair back a little more, his fangs found the delicate skin of my throat. His other hand cupped my breast, and my nipple went hard against his palm. "Don't you know how dangerous it is to repress your desires, Elowen?

Because I know that if you were left alone in a room with me for twenty minutes, I could have you begging me to fuck you." His accent had shifted, pure Lirion now.

"The riddle." I hated the way I felt my thighs opening, almost against my will. Molten heat spilled through my core as his hand slid down from my breast, over my belly, and over the top of my underwear. *Deus Invictus, Archon Magne.* "Get on with it," I breathed.

"What's the point?" His hand trailed over my wet heat.

He still gripped my hair lightly, my neck fully exposed. Right now, I was under his complete control. His fangs started to pierce the skin, just a little. Pleasure surged through my body, and he licked my skin just where he'd pierced it. "Delicious, my love."

"Give me the riddle."

"I want to consume you like a mouthless devourer consumes beasts," he purred.

My pulse raced. "You…what?" *Deus…something…*

He was toying with me, making my hips shift back into him. At the same time, he murmured against my throat, "The devourer eats forests like bread. It thrives and grows when well-fed. But give it water, you'll find it dead."

His fingers glided over the spot just where I needed him, but it wasn't enough pressure.

And when my gaze flicked back to look at him, I found that it wasn't Maelor at all.

It was Sion palming my breast, touching me between my thighs.

"Didn't I tell you?" he purred. "I'm the one you really want. I know your body better than you do."

"Fire," I whispered.

A sharp smack across my cheek made me gasp. I opened my eyes to find myself clutching a nearly dead candle and staring at Lydia.

"Snap out of it, Elowen," she snarled. She was clutching one of my gloves in her hand. "You're about to die."

"Fire." I repeated the answer to the riddle.

The light from her candle lit up her face, shadows wavering beneath her hollow cheekbones. "I know. I already finished."

I glanced down at the candle in my hand—nearly dead.

"Get your cloak on," she snapped. "We need to get out of here before they shoot us."

I blinked, then hurried to pull my cloak over myself, one arm at a time, holding that little flickering candle in the air. I looked up, surprised to find Lydia waiting for me. She shielded her own candle, then walked just in front of me to the gates, like she was leading the way for me.

My body still buzzed from the elixir, and I tried to slow my breathing as we crossed closer to the gates. Just at the exit, I turned around to see the dead lying scattered in the ruined garden. And all the euphoria of that elixir drained out of me, leaving me shaking.

Bodies littered the earth—Guillaume the Dulcet among them, an arrow jutting from his throat. His pale eyes stared up at the sky. There were a dozen more. I shuddered, staring at them. It could have been worse, I supposed.

A gentle hand on my right bicep pulled my attention away from the macabre scene, and I turned back to see Maelor.

"I knew you'd make it."

"I nearly didn't."

For just a moment, he leaned in and whispered, "You'll live through this."

But it wasn't just me anymore.

Because now, I wanted them all out.

# CHAPTER 32

*I* sat at my table, pouring myself a cup of tea with shaking hands. A fire crackled softly in the little hearth, and the reflected orange flames wavered over my pewter cup.

One more trial behind me.

But now, I had no intention of cutting down the competition. Now, I wanted to find a way to break all of us out.

True, no one had ever breached the Ruefield walls, not in their thousand years of history. But there was a first time for everything, wasn't there?

I sat on my bed, and my gaze flicked outside to the moonlit castle landscape. A cool breeze whistled through the window. At night, when everyone was asleep, the wind seemed to fill the room with an eerie keening.

I stared through the iron bars. In the glass's reflection, I saw my own gold-lined eyes reflected back at me over my mug. As the door slammed open, I nearly dropped it. A few drops of hot tea splashed on to my fingers, and I turned to see Sion looming in the doorway.

My stomach dropped. I'd *really* been hoping for a visit from Maelor. Sadly, I had a feeling he'd be avoiding me from now on.

I looked up at Sion through the steam of my tea. "What do you want?"

"Is that any way to greet the Magister Solaris?" He closed the door behind him and pulled out the chair from the desk. He dropped into it, leaning back against the desk and folding his arms. He looked perfectly at ease in here. Of course, someone like him probably felt comfortable anywhere. Someone who could kill literally anyone he encountered and didn't feel an ounce of guilt about it.

His dark amber gaze flicked down to my wrists. "Tell me exactly how you got the scars that I did not give you."

"Are you going to kill me if I don't?"

"I might."

The heat from the tea warmed my face, steam coiling into the air. "I'll take that chance."

He sighed, looking bored with the conversation already. "Baron Throckmore, was it? The man you worked for before you came here."

"How exactly is this your concern?"

He sat up, leaning closer, and pulled the cup of tea from my hands. He set it on the desk, then grabbed both of my wrists, turning them over to see the damage. "It's just that it looks very intentional to me, as if someone held your arms above a flame. You're burned in exactly the same spot on both sides. That left me with some questions."

I shrugged. "Just a freak accident. I was cooking."

"Was it?" Malice danced in his eyes. "That's funny. That's not what the Baron said when he spilled his guts."

My stomach plummeted. "You spoke to him?"

He dropped my wrists. "Harboring a witch is a grievous crime." He shrugged slowly. "And he was harboring two. I had to investigate what he was up to."

My heart slammed fast. I couldn't imagine what kind of torture the Baron had endured to give up that information. And while I didn't have a huge well of sympathy for him, he couldn't be murdered. Not if I wanted Leo to stay safe. The Baron's men could find him in Eboria.

My mind started to whirl with panic. "I don't know why he said that. But I'm assuming he was in a great deal of pain when he told you that he burned me. You must know that torture doesn't yield reliable information, don't you? He didn't know a thing about my magic."

His eyes glittered in the firelight. "I didn't tell you

that he said he burned you. But of course, he did offer that up. He wanted you to feel the pain of fire, didn't he? And it gave you a pretext for wearing the gloves. He was helping you hide your magic."

My throat had gone dry. "Please let him go." I didn't give a fuck about the Baron. But if he was killed, his soldiers might come after Leo.

A lock of his dark hair fell down before his eyes, hanging beneath his square jawline. "You're protecting a man who maimed you." A faint smile flitted over his lips. "I have heard of women falling for their captors and tormentors. Since you're so keen on the Raven Lord, perhaps you're exactly that sort."

Anger flickered through my chest, simmering hot.

The way I saw it, I had two options. I could hope for the best. Maybe no one would find Leo in Eboria. Maybe if the Order executed the Baron, his last will would be null and void. I didn't have the laws memorized.

Or I could find a wooden stake and kill Sion.

I stood, staring directly into his eyes. They sparkled, the deep amber of whiskey.

I pressed my hand over his heart. Nothing. No warmth, no heartbeat. Just a solid wall of still muscle.

"What are you doing?" His voice was a low murmur, accent thickening. "If you think you can seduce me like you did my old friend, it won't work. I kill who I want, Elowen, and I enjoy it."

He smelled of spiced wine and old books, with the faintest hint of leather. Light and shadow danced over his square jawline, his perfect features. His terrible beauty felt like a weapon, designed to confuse and seduce. Was that a vampire thing?

I pulled my hand away and met his gaze. "If you kill the Baron, there might be consequences."

He arched an eyebrow. "Why don't you illuminate me, then?"

I clenched my jaw. "Maybe I'll tell the world about your secret."

"You'd risk your life to protect that filth? Did you fall for your tormentor?" A wicked smile curled his lips. "And Maelor, too. Is there any end to your sinning, dark one?"

"You have no idea what you're talking about."

He stared down at me, then brushed a lock of hair from my eyes. With the brush of his fingertips, a shiver ran through me. "Gold. Now that is enchanting." He sighed. "Ah, yes. It reminds me of myself. Is that why you drew the gold on your eyes?"

I blinked, shocked at the turn in conversation. "Why are you here if you already know everything you need to know?"

The iron-crossed door opened, slamming into Sion's muscular shoulder. It was like the sound of heavy metal hammering against stone, a boom that echoed off the wall.

Sion's shoulder dented the metal slightly.

*Archon above.* These guys were stronger than the castle walls.

Maelor shoved the door all the way open, his expression dark. A chill spread through the room. "What the fuck are you doing in here, Sion?"

And here I was, trapped in a small room with two vampires.

Sion gave a slow shrug. "Just visiting our old friend."

*Our old friend?*

Maelor's eyes had darkened to midnight, and he flashed his fangs. In the next heartbeat, he was standing before me protectively. "Stay away from Elowen."

Maelor was like a wall, strong and impenetrable. From the other side of him, I heard a low, animal snarl from Sion. The primal sound made a shiver hiss over my skin. "Have you stopped writing poetry long enough to actually pay attention to another person?"

"After all these centuries, I've finally found someone worth talking to." Maelor's arms widened, and the air crackled with tension. "Now get the fuck out."

"Enjoy the night, lovebirds. Just try to make sure it doesn't end in a pool of blood."

He slammed the door closed behind him, the sound echoing in the room. When Maelor turned to me, his eyes were the dark blue of a midnight ocean.

I frowned at him. "Is he going to tell anyone that you're here?"

He cut me a sharp look. "Don't worry about him."

I took a deep breath, trying to sort through the tempest of my thoughts. I dropped down onto the bed. How much did I trust Maelor at this point?

I could tell he was still furious with me. But I was also desperate for an ally to keep Leo safe.

He sat down next to me on the bed, and I touched his arm. "Sion has Baron Throckmore, the man I used to work for."

"That man let you take his place in the trials."

I nodded. "The problem is that the Baron has set something in his will. If he's murdered or executed, his soldiers are supposed to kill Leo. Leo's killer gets the gold."

Shadows stained the air around Maelor. "That's how he controlled you?"

I nodded. "I don't want Sion to know anything about Leo. But can you persuade him not to kill the Baron?"

"I think I can." His eyes shone again with a pale blue. "I'll try to get the Baron out, or whatever's left of him. The man would probably rather be dead at this point."

"He can kill himself, then." I let out a long, slow breath. "Leo is fine as long as no one executes or murders the Baron."

Maelor narrowed his eyes. "I can't stay here long and risk you trying to seduce me again." A hint of steel undercut his velvety voice.

I arched an eyebrow. "The first thing you told me when I got here was to look out for myself, that I had no friends. That I should trust no one. Why are you surprised?"

"So you preyed on my weakness." He reached into his robe and pulled out a small silver flask. He took a sip, and I smelled the faint scent of whiskey in the air. He didn't offer me any. "It's really very vampiric of you."

My chest tightened. "The Baron trained me to find people's weaknesses. Yours wasn't hard. Sion told me that from the beginning."

He frowned at me. "And you wanted to know how to kill me?" He might be hundreds of years old, but in that moment, he looked young. Innocent, almost. "The wooden stake."

My heart fluttered. "No, Maelor. Not you. I wanted to know how to kill Sion."

"So, tell me." He reached for a strand of my hair and twirled it around his finger. Then curiosity flickered in his expression as he searched my face. "Is that the only reason you wanted to seduce me? For information?"

I wavered for a moment between the impulse to tell him everything and keeping my cards close to my chest. The truth was, I could drown in his otherworldly beauty. I felt safe with him, despite what he was. "No, it wasn't the only reason. I want you, and that's real."

At those words, shadows flared in his eyes, and his

eyelids lowered. He leaned closer, pressing his hands on the stone wall behind me. As he did, his sandalwood scent wrapped around me. An agonized expression etched his gorgeous features. He sighed. "Ah, but you are forbidden."

I reached up to slide my palm against the side of his face. He pressed his lips against mine, kissing me hungrily, desperately. His tongue swept against mine, and heat swooped through my body. I opened my mouth to his and wrapped my arms around his neck. My back arched, hips moving against him.

His kiss tasted faintly of a sweet whiskey. I stroked my thumb over his high cheekbone.

He pulled away, eyes dark with desire. Still searching mine, like he was trying to read the mysteries of the heavens in my face. He slid his tongue over a fang. As he did, he let out a soft noise, a low, tormented moan. "I have to go before I lose myself, Elowen. And I'm already forgetting why I came." His voice was a harsh sigh. "I have to tell you about tomorrow. It will be the most difficult trial of them all. The Trial of the Abyss."

I inhaled deeply. "What is it?"

He flicked his tongue over one of his fangs again, like he was still considering piercing my throat with them. "It's different to the other trials. None of the Luminari will be watching this one. It's too dangerous, even for them. Last time, we drugged you with temptations. This time? It will be terror."

I closed my eyes, sighing. "Wonderful. I really needed more terror in my life."

"The fear itself is not lethal, of course. But usually, during this trial, many of the contestants beat each other to death while suffering horrific hallucinations."

I cleared my throat. "Is there any way to, I don't know, switch the potions?"

He shook his head. "It won't be a potion this time. It's a toxic mist that will fill the dungeon. And I won't be able to interfere with any of it because the Pater is more paranoid than ever right now."

"Why?"

"Never mind that. Listen, tomorrow, the terror might make people violent. You'll all be trapped in the dungeon together. But the Luminari won't be there to see if you kill anyone. Pull off your gloves, and keep yourself safe."

I shook my head. "I don't want to kill these people."

He ran a hand through his hair and sighed. "Just stay alive. And this time, you can try to stay in reality by focusing on the feeling of the stones beneath your feet. Take off your boots and stockings, feel the cold of the stones. Use it to anchor yourself to reality. And look for shadows. The apparitions, the visions…they won't have normal shadows. It's how you can tell reality from the illusions."

I nodded, my stomach already growing tight with tension. "Okay."

"You'll want to run into the tunnels, but don't.

That's where the mist will come from. It will only get worse there." He brushed his thumb over my lower lip. "You must get through tomorrow, Elowen. Kill whoever you need to. Please do whatever it takes to come back to me because I cannot take another death. I cannot take any more."

# CHAPTER 33

Dawn light pierced the window, and I sat up in bed to stare through the thick window-panes. I rubbed my eyes, trying to shake off the fog of sleep. Immediately after breakfast, we would go to the dungeon for the Trial of the Abyss.

Some people might not know their worst fears, but mine was always in the forefront of my thoughts. My fears were as known to me as the feel of the wind against my skin. Because I'd had the nightmares a thousand times, and a thousand times, I'd jumped out of bed to make sure Leo was still breathing. In the dead of night, I always had to check that I hadn't actually killed him with my touch while he slept.

Through the window, I felt the chill of a breeze slip-ping through the cracks, howling. It was cold for spring today.

As I stared out at the courtyard, a door opened at

the ground level of one of the stone towers. I caught a glimpse of two figures, one of them tall, dressed in black. When I squinted, I could just about make it out as Maelor. He was practically dragging the other man along—a broken-looking figure, his head lolling forward. The man's feet dragged over the cobbles.

The man had a shorn head, just like the Baron's. For a moment, he lifted his face, and I could have sworn he was looking directly at me, green eyes piercing in the morning sun. A shiver rippled up my spine. The rest of his face was hardly recognizable, bruised and swollen, his jaw hanging open to reveal missing teeth. The man would be eating soup for the rest of his life. It didn't matter how formidable he'd been before. Like everyone else, he'd meet his end gasping and terrified.

He and I could both be cruelly calculating, vicious. But that little flicker of pity I felt was what set me apart from him.

Right now, the Baron would think me weak.

And maybe I was. Because I'd been asking Maelor why he wouldn't kill the Pater if he had the chance. But why didn't I? Why not make the ultimate sacrifice? If I had the chance to simply brush my fingertips across the Pater's cheeks, would I take it?

After all, what greater gift could someone have than a life that served a purpose?

\* \* \*

I STOOD IN THE DUNGEON, nestled between Godric and Percival. As usual, I'd told my allies everything I could over breakfast. But this morning, we'd hardly eaten.

Fear hung in the air, so sharp I almost felt it raking at my skin. Down here in the dungeon, the smell of damp and decay slid off the stones.

We were in a sort of large central hall, with tunnels jutting off like spokes of a wheel. Torches lined the walls, the orange light dancing over dark, sweating rock.

I turned, surveying what was left of the Penitents. Now, less than half remained, all with cowls pulled up as if they hoped the shadows would consume them. I'd been thinking of them so much as my adversaries before, I'd hardly bothered to look at them.

Some of them looked older, their skin lined, faces gaunt. I was frankly surprised they'd made it this far. But a lot of them looked so young, it made my heart twist. A beautiful woman who couldn't be more than nineteen stood nearby, wide-eyed, arms folded. Her hair was a pale flaxen color, and she had a delicate beauty that men often loved. It hadn't helped keep her out of here, though.

My gaze landed on the boy who looked about fifteen, and my breath caught. I could read it so easily in his expression—he was terrified, but he was trying to hide it with a resolute expression and a clenched jaw. His lower lip jutted out. With that look on his face, he reminded me of Leo when he was upset.

I let out a long, steady breath.

If I did what Maelor wanted—if I made it out of here alive and let the rest die—what kind of life would that really be? A broken one.

It wasn't just about my alliance anymore. I wanted all these people out of here. I wanted the chaos that would unfold from cutting off the head of the Order. I wanted to watch the man draw his final breath, blue veins racing under his pale skin. I *craved* it.

Lydia leaned against the wall, her chin held high. She thought she'd be the chosen one, didn't she? And why wouldn't she? She'd always gotten everything she wanted. Except, perhaps, Anselm's heart. No wonder she lost her mind.

She flicked her blonde hair over her shoulder, then narrowed her eyes at me. "*What?*"

Through the door, the sound of raised voices turned my head. Shouts pierced the thick wood, though I couldn't quite make out what the voices were saying. I rushed toward the door and pressed my ear against it.

"The Archon grows angry with me," the Pater shouted.

My breath caught. His harsh shout made the hairs raise on the back of my neck.

"Tell me what's happening, Magister! Why are so many of them alive?"

Through the wood, I couldn't quite make out what

Sion was saying in response, just the deep tone of his voice.

"I'll tell you what it is!" shouted the Pater. "I have allowed the Serpent to thrive here at Ruefield. Because a traitor lives in our midst. Did you know that?" His voice rumbled through the wood.

My heart pattered, and I shot Percival a nervous look. I whispered, "He's talking about a traitor."

Had the Pater learned about the resistance? Or did he know that Maelor had helped me?

Even before he entered the room, the Pater's anger was like a dark miasma clouding the dungeon air, making my skin prickle with fear. Who needed toxic, mind-bending mist when we had his rage?

"The Archon calls on me," he went on. "I am his most devoted and fervent soldier. He calls on me to cleanse this land of the Serpent's magic. But evil has breached our holy army's defenses. It spreads so quickly. One moment, you are a person. The next, you gnaw on tree bark. A ravening animal. One day, you lie in your father's arms. The next, you wonder if you could really..." His voice grew quieter, and I missed what he said for a few sentences. Then his voice rose to a shout again. "I need you to find out who warned Eboria! Why was the city prepared for our attack?"

Fear slid through my bones. The Pater was trying to conquer Eboria?

"The Archon knows we allow witches to live in Eboria. That den of iniquity!" he screamed. "As the

Archon's most loyal soldier, I must do as he commands. How is it that they knew we were coming? How is it that they closed the city gates so far in advance and prepared their archers? They had warning!" His voice rattled the door. "Perhaps I will retaliate against the Serpent by killing more of them today. Them, the Serpent's wickedest soldiers. I shouldn't allow a single one among them to live. Because what have they done to help the Order?"

The moment I heard the iron bar shifting outside the door, I leapt back. I shifted into place with the others just in time for the Pater marching into the room, his fists balled. His nose was slightly scrunched in disgust.

Sion sauntered in behind him. In contrast to the Pater, Sion looked relaxed, almost bored. He walked with a languorous pace, then leaned against a wall. He folded his arms, staring disinterestedly into the torch flames.

Normally, half a legion of Luminari followed everywhere the Pater went. But down here in the dungeon, he had only Sion for protection. And Sion seemed half-asleep.

The Pater stared at us and steepled his fingers. He looked as if he were mentally devising some sort of horrific torments for us.

A cold thread of fear coiled through me. He wanted to conquer Eboria? The one last refuge in Merthyn.

Leo's safe haven...the northern city had *always* been independent, even in the times of the kings.

My fingers twitched. It was almost as if fate were screaming my name.

In the depths of my chest, the Serpent whispered to me: *Don't you want another taste? Drink from the death of someone truly powerful.*

My magic thrummed beneath my skin. Without the Pater, the Order would be in chaos.

*End it all now.* The rattling whisper of the Serpent rang in my skull.

If I caused enough chaos by killing the Pater, would the others be able to hide in the tunnels? Either way, this was bigger than just us now. This was all of Eboria, a teeming and ancient city. A free city.

The Pater's cold gaze slid to me. "Your son was marked by the Order, yes?"

I could hardly hear over the roar of my blood. A red-hot current of rage had my legs shaking. I breathed slowly, making sure my voice wouldn't shake when I answered. "Who?"

"Your *son*. The boy."

"I have no son." Just like the Baron had taught me, I stared down at my gloved fingers as though I were inspecting for dust. I wore a mask of boredom. "I have no family at all." I sighed, glancing at him. "Someone gave you bad information."

The Pater's mouth twitched. "Your ward, then.

Marked by the Order. Shall we bring him here, see how he'll do in the trials?"

My heart thundered. "I have no idea what you're talking about." The best way to keep the shake out of a voice was to make it go deeper, husky.

How had he suddenly learned about Leo? My gaze flicked to Sion. He'd seen him, hadn't he? They day of the witch-finding.

The Pater stared at us, unmoving. "Let's find the boy."

Red-hot wrath spilled through me.

The Pater must die.

# CHAPTER 34

*I* stared at the Pater, envisioning exactly how amazing it would feel to kill him.

But after his threats about Leo, he'd already seemed to lose interest.

A small smile tugged at the corner of his lips. "My Penitents, my work with you is not yet finished. Through the destruction and utter degradation of the Serpent's soldiers, the evil one despairs in his defeat. I want the Serpent to feel his loss through your misery. If his evil lives among us, I want him to know my boot is on his neck."

I lifted my hand, my heart racing wildly. Slowly, subtly, I started tugging on the fingers, loosening the glove on my right hand. Sion's eyes looked half-lidded as he stared into the torchlight. Sleepy, unbothered.

The Pater closed his eyes and held out his hands to

the heavens. "*Deus Invictus, Archon Magne.* In the light of our glory, Merthyn grows strong."

I pulled off the glove, and it slid off my wrist—

The reaction was *instant.* From nowhere, Sion's hand was clenched around my throat, choking me. Lifting me in the air, his fingers crushed my windpipe. "You forget yourself, witch. Your gloves must always remain on." He dropped me to the ground in a heap, and he stared down at me. "Scatterbrained, aren't you?"

I touched my throat, feeling the tender muscle. I rasped for breath.

Sion glanced back to the Pater. "What are we waiting for? Let's leave the rats to die down here." He glanced back at me, eyes sparking gold in the torchlight. "You're all alone down here. In normal times, only a dozen ragged and bloodied witches return from here. But today? I can't promise it will be that easy."

He turned, ushering the Pater out of the room to safety.

My mind was a raging storm. The Order would keep trying to take down Eboria until they succeeded. Either the great northern city would give up their independence or they'd starve to death after a long siege. The Pater might lament his own childhood of eating soil, but he had no problem imposing the same fate on others.

Slowly, I stood, dusting myself off.

"What the hell was that?" whispered Percival.

I touched my throat, wincing. "The best chance I

had at killing him. They're going to invade Eboria, the last refuge. All I need to do is get close enough to stop him."

Godric stared at me. "You're lucky the Magister didn't kill you."

"They're going to kill us all if we don't stop him," I gasped. "He'll just keep going and going, more trials, more death."

*He's going to bring Leo here...*

From the stone wall, Lydia clapped her hands slowly. "All hail the martyr. So sweet and giving, isn't she?"

I curled my lip at her before restraining myself. "We're all about to drown in a toxic mist that will choke us all with terror. We're going to attack each other. Why don't we leave the bitter sarcasm for that?"

Sazia stared at the door, wide-eyed. "Did you see how fast the Magister moved? What *was* that?"

Such touching devotion to his leader…

I breathed in, already smelling the pungent scent of wormwood roiling into the room, along with the musky smell of burning henbane. I coughed as it swelled in my lungs. Belladonna, too, acrid and poisonous.

"You need to be ready for what's going to happen." My voice rang off the damp stones. "We are going to see visions. Terrifying visions of the worst things you can imagine. And we're going to get confused and try to kill each other."

"But there's a way to avoid it," added Percival.

"How, exactly?" asked a woman with long gray hair.

I tried to think clearly through the panic in my thoughts. "We need to work together. All of us, now." The floor started to feel unsteady beneath my feet. Already, my heart was racing and a cold sweat had broken out on my forehead. I swallowed hard. I wanted to tell them exactly what I meant, but I didn't have time to form a whole coherent argument. "Take off your boots. Right now, take off your boots."

"Who put you in charge?" asked Lydia.

"Just do it!" I snapped.

Lydia was grinding down the last shreds of my patience at this point. Or was that the mist bringing out my rage? I leaned down, untying my boots. "If you're barefoot, you can try to anchor yourself with the floor, yeah? Feel the stone beneath you. Connect to it, feel how solid it is."

My heart was a drumroll pattering against my ribs.

"Elowen?" Leo's voice called to me from one of the tunnels, and my blood turned glacial.

Oh, Archon no. The Pater had found him already. I staggered back, dizzy.

There in the tunnels, Leo was calling to me, his voice clear as a bell.

"Do you hear that?" My voice cracked as I shouted.

Percival was staring at one of the tunnels, and he nodded. "My brother is here."

I grabbed Percival's arm. "It's not real. It's not real! Whatever you're seeing now, it isn't real."

Percival whipped back around to the others, some of them already speaking to their invisible friends. "Look at the shadows!" he shouted. "Your visions won't have shadows in the torchlight."

Screams erupted around us.

I stood, barefoot on the stones, feeling the cold spread beneath my soles. When I turned back to the tunnel entrance, I saw Leo shuffling closer, dressed in tattered and mud-spattered rags. "Elowen?"

Where a dark shadow should have spread over the stones behind him, I saw only gray stone.

I closed my eyes, slowing my breathing. I shifted my toes against the cool rock. An agonized cry rang out, and I opened my eyes to see a woman grip the boy, her hands around his throat. His eyes bulged as she pressed him against the wall. I lunged forward and grabbed her arm, pulling her off him. She swatted at me with her free hand, and I twisted her arm behind her back. She struggled against me, still trying to get back to the boy.

A low, growling noise rose from one of the tunnels, sending shivers over my skin. Then a distant, eerie howling followed.

A man with shaggy red hair staggered forward, his eyes wild. I was still gripping the woman by her arm while she screamed at me. I let go of her just as the man reached for me. I punched one of his arms away, but he grabbed me by the face with his other hand.

The effect was instant, his body seizing up with the touch of my bare skin. Just as dark veins shot through his face, his appearance changed, growing younger and sweeter. It was no longer a stranger, but Leo dying on the floor at my feet. Even if I knew it wasn't real, I felt my stomach plummet all the same.

I closed my eyes, feeling the cold stone beneath my feet. "It's not real." Then, louder. "Everyone stay still! Don't move. Nothing you see happening is real. Just stop moving."

Howling from the tunnels rose, louder now. It sent shivers over my skin, sparking a primal need to run. But just like all the other horrors in here, it was all in my head.

"Nothing you're seeing is real!" Percival echoed my words.

The growling grew louder, and my heart skipped a beat as an enormous wolf careened from the tunnel into the round dungeon—exactly like the creatures from the labyrinth.

"It's not real." I chanted my new mantra, closing my eyes. And soon, the others joined in with me, until we were all chanting together.

An agonized scream interrupted us, but I kept my eyes closed. "It's not real," we chanted.

When I opened my eyes again, my stomach plummeted. I was still seeing a vision of the wolf, rampaging around the dungeon. A man lay dead, his face half ripped off, throat torn out. With a ferocious growl, the wolf leapt onto the flaxen-haired woman. She screamed, but it was cut short as the wolf ripped her apart with a snarl.

My heart pounded as my gaze slid down to the stone floor.

The fucking wolf had a shadow.

I couldn't breathe. "It's real!" I shouted.

I had no idea if my touch could kill an animal, but I had to try. While the wolf feasted on the woman's body, I pulled my glove off. I lunged forward, swiping my hand across the wolf's head, stroking the inside of its ear.

The wolf yelped, and it unlocked its jaw from the woman's throat. He'd practically severed her head, and I shuddered. As the wolf staggered back, he turned, stumbling back into the tunnel.

Lydia ran to the woman, touching her forehead. Her body glowed with her healing magic, but it was too late. The woman lay still, mouth agape in horror.

Percival grabbed my covered arm, and I turned to see his brow furrowed, eyes darting around the tunnels. "What's happening?"

My mouth had gone dry. "That wolf was real. They're sending…" My voice trailed off. What if they sent more?

The scent of blood hung heavy in the air, and I pivoted to peer down the tunnel the wolf had gone into. Fear vibrated through my bones as I saw four more wolves charging through. I turned again. My blood roared at the sight of another wolf running from the opposite direction.

The stones felt unsteady beneath my feet. "Percival, I can't kill them all." I couldn't breathe.

"Everyone stand away from the tunnels," Percival boomed. "Now."

I had no idea what he had planned, but I did my best to shove everyone into the center. As I did, I felt a blast of hot, dry heat behind me. I turned to see Percival hurling an enormous ball of fire down the tunnel toward the wolves. Flames raced from his hands like ink, spilling along the perimeter of the dungeon and flowing into the tunnels.

Holy *Archon*, he was powerful.

Smoke billowed around us, and we huddled together, coughing. The stones heated beneath our feet.

"Percival?" I shouted over the roar of flames. "Can you put the fires out?"

He turned to me, his face lit by dancing orange flames. Fear etched his features. "No. And I created too much. I panicked."

So maybe this was how we were going to burn. Not on the pyre, but trapped beneath the earth.

# CHAPTER 35

Smoke curled into my lungs, and I coughed deeply. Even though I knew coughing would only pull the smoke deeper into me, I couldn't help it. I wasn't like the vampires. I had only one supernatural strength, and that was killing with my touch. I'd burn in a fire; I'd bleed with a blade. So, as the soot coiled into my nostrils and throat, spots darkened my vision. My eyes streamed with tears, and I looked up to see Percival panicking in the dancing firelight. I glanced back at the door. I knew how these dungeon doors were made—vertical and horizontal wood nailed against each other with iron studs, nearly impossible to break through.

The stones felt warm beneath me. The fire wasn't spreading, but the heat was. Around me, everyone was pulling off their cloaks. Sweat streaked down my temples, and I pulled off my own. Coughing, I also loosened the doublet around my waist.

The smoke had one silver lining—as fatigue sapped our strength and muddled our thoughts, none of us had the energy to attack each other. The deranged, mind-bending hallucinations had started to wane. Maybe the fire had burned out all the toxic mist. Coughing, I leaned against someone's shoulder. She leaned against me, her blonde hair trailing against my shoulder. I'd recognize Lydia's smell anywhere— perfumed like primrose, even in here.

The stones burned beneath us, and it was hard not to think of the story she'd told me about the stone cities burning in Sumaire, the victims roasting as they'd tried to shelter in the tunnels beneath the earth.

We'd both loved Anselm. Was that what led us here to these burning stones? A love that dragged us to ruin? Anselm's face flickered in my memory, a kind-eyed ghost.

*Elowen, meet me by the pear trees so that I can taste you—*

Now, he was lost to us. My head was hammering, thundering.

No, it was a great pounding on the door, and I turned, teary-eyed, to see the wood splintering above us. It looked like someone was taking a battering ram to the great dungeon door. Was I imagining this?

Lydia yanked me up by my elbow, and I stood, huddled against her. A fist shot through the thick wood, blood streaking his knuckles and wrist. Brutally, someone was tearing at the door from the outside until nothing remained of it and the door came off its hinges.

Through the puff of smoke, I saw Maelor. His robe hung open, and blood poured down the front of him. His shirt lay torn, ripped open where he'd been stabbed. His piercing, pale eyes took in the scene, and screams erupted in the dungeon. To them, Maelor looked terrifying right now—a man standing when he should be dead. A man capable of tearing through a fortified door with his bare hands.

"The trial is over," he bellowed. "Get back to your rooms. Take the stairs up to the courtyard and find your way back. The Magister Solaris will make sure you end up locked in your rooms again, so don't try to run."

He was here to save us, but he looked so inhuman now, still standing despite his horrible wound.

I staggered to my feet. "Come on! We need to get out of here. Do as the Raven Lord says. The trial is over."

Maelor slipped back out into the torchlit corridor, and I found him there, leaning against the stone wall, clutching his chest. I sidled up to him, grabbing him around the waist to help support him. But dizziness was swirling in my thoughts, too. Neither of us was in great shape.

As the other Penitents slipped past us, I huddled

against him, coughing. "Maelor, what the hell is happening?"

"I'm ending the trial."

We were the last ones left, hobbling along. Down here, it was a network of dark tunnels spiderwebbing beneath the castle, and he led me into a narrow passage. There were no torches in here, and I couldn't see a thing.

"Should I return to my room like the others?" Coughs racked my chest, and I doubled over. I gripped my stomach. "I feel sick." My head throbbed, and I wheezed with every breath.

"You sucked in too much smoke."

Nausea climbed up my throat, and I stumbled. Maelor scooped me up, pulling me against his chest.

My lungs weren't working properly, and my breathing rasped. "Are you all right?"

"Don't worry about me," he said quietly. "You were right, love. You need to find a way out. This is all my fault."

My eyes were drifting closed. "Why would it be yours?"

"The Pater hates you. He suspects someone helped you after the first trial. He won't kill you yet, though. But the failure in Eboria set him off. He knows someone at a high level sent warnings to the independent city. And now he knows I'm a vampire."

I laid my head against his chest. He smelled intoxicating. Even injured as he was, he still made me feel safe with his powerful arms wrapped around me.

He walked only a few feet before he stopped in his tracks. He muttered something in Lirion, and his muscles tensed.

"What's wrong?" I asked.

"I hear Luminari coming. The Pater is trying to kill me, and I'll need to hide somewhere for a few minutes."

My mouth felt watery. "What happened?"

He turned down another narrow tunnel, carrying me swiftly through the darkness. "He's upset about Eboria. He suspected I was a traitor, and that was confirmed fifteen minutes ago when I slaughtered twenty of his Luminari to get down to you." Under the soft velvet of his voice, I could hear the strain in his throat.

We stopped in front of a heavy wooden door, and he glanced behind him. He gently let me down, and I leaned against a stone wall as he opened the door. As it groaned open, orange light beamed out.

I followed him into a stone room of flickering torchlight. It was a small underground temple with a row of whispering chambers.

Maelor turned, quietly dropping the iron bar over the door to lock anyone else out.

I wavered on my feet, surveying the space. Instead of an oculus and torchbearers, a round chandelier hung from the ceiling, flickering with lit torches. A pit in the center sheared down deep into the earth. It seemed the maddening face of the Archon dwelled even in the dungeons.

Dizzy, I dropped to the floor, lying flat on my back. The flagstones chilled my skin through my thin shirt. Standing above me, Maelor pulled off his cloak and laid it on the ground next to me. He scooped me up again, shifting me onto his soft, sandalwood-scented cloak.

"Do you think they saw us?" My speech sounded slow, confused.

"No." The torchlight danced over his high cheek-bones, his full mouth. A lock of wavy dark hair hung before his fathomless eyes. He brushed a strand of hair off my face. "I can help you recover before you go back to your room. You inhaled too much smoke, and it's poisoning you."

My mouth felt watery, my thoughts dulled and confused. "Were you stabbed in the heart, Maelor?"

His fangs flashed above me. He bit into his wrist, and I stared at the scarlet drops that spilled down his skin. "Only with steel, so I should heal. It's just taking a long time. I haven't drunk human blood in years, so some of my vampiric strength has diminished."

He held out his wrist to me, and I licked my lips, feeling parched.

"Drink from me, now." His deeply sexy, commanding voice had my lips parting.

A drop spilled onto my tongue, sweet and rich. I

pulled his wrist closer, and I licked his skin, drinking from him.

Blood shouldn't taste this good, a burst of sensual pleasure that lit me up from the inside out. As I drank from him, heat slid through me. Moments ago, I'd felt hardly aware of what was happening around me. Now, I felt acutely in tune with my body. Unrestrained, the silky shirt dragged against my sensitive skin, teasing me. Under the thin fabric, my breasts rose. Maelor's magic flowed into me, filling me with his strength. He was imbuing me with his essence—his heartbreaking beauty and that jagged sense of loss he carried with him. Colors slid through my mind: bloodred, grass green, the blinding blue of the heavens, and the silver-white of the moon. And as it did, desire coursed through me.

An erotic charge ignited in me with every sweet drop that spilled into my mouth. When I opened my eyes to see Maelor's beautiful face, I knew he was the only one who could quench the building fire. I was vaguely aware that I'd tangled my legs around his. The truth was, every inch of my body demanded to be kissed, licked, and stroked by him. And he must have felt it, too, because his free hand slid beneath the fabric of my shirt and held my waist.

When he pulled his wrist away, I sighed deeply and licked my lips. His eyes had darkened to midnight, and he pressed his hands down on either side of my head. "Elowen, I can feel how much you like it." His voice had gone husky, rolling his *R*s. "I can hear your heart racing. I even heard you moan faintly." He seemed on the edge of losing control. "You have no idea how much I want you."

And the truth was, I needed more. I cupped his perfect face and pulled him down to me. He kissed me deeply, claiming my mouth with his. In ecstasy, he brought my quiet soul alive.

His hand roamed under my shirt, and he palmed my breast as his tongue stroked mine. "Right now, you are my world." When he gripped my shirt in his fist, I felt as if something in him were about to snap.

My leather trousers, my thin shirt—I wanted it off. In fact, I wanted every inch of fabric between us gone. He was a new world I needed to explore, to map out the fine topography of his muscled body. Except he was still injured.

I sat up, tangling my fingers in the rich fabric of his shirt. I wanted to pull it off him.

He'd warned me about what would happen if he drank human blood. Maybe I just felt desperate to heal him, or maybe I craved that knife's edge of danger, but I wanted him to drink from me. "I want to heal you," I murmured.

He lowered his mouth to my throat, and he trailed kisses over my neck. Then lower, over my breasts. Over the light material of my shirt, he closed his mouth, biting just a little. His tongue flicked over the fabric, dampening it.

He intended to toy with me—and I intended to move him along. My hands were on my own shirt, unbuttoning it as a desperate, sexual need coiled tight inside me. I ached for his mouth on my bare skin. I pulled open the last buttons of my shirt, and I slid it off.

In the cold dungeon air, my nipples had tightened to sensitive peaks, my nerves craving his touch. As he took in the sight of me, he let out a low growl that thrummed over me. Shadows coiled off his body like smoke and brushed over my skin.

His midnight eyes pierced me, his dark lashes lowered. His expression was sensual, hungry. "Elowen, I haven't stopped thinking about you since the moment I first saw you." He kissed my throat. "And then that first night when you stayed in my room here, and you slipped into my bed wearing those thin scraps of fabric on your perfect body—" He kissed me, his tongue swirling over my throat. "It was the most excruciating torment. An image I shall never forget as long as I live —same as this moment."

I slid my fingers into his hair. "Drink from me. I want to heal you."

His body went rigid for a moment, and then I felt the sharp prick of his fangs against my throat. "Is that really what you want from me?" His deep, throaty voice vibrated through my belly.

"Yes." A sensual spark heated the air between us.

"My control is slipping." His fangs flashed, and he

licked one of them. "Elowen." Despair laced his hoarse tone. "I'll never be able to resist you. You have no idea how much I want… "

Without finishing his thought, he enveloped me in an embrace, one arm curled behind my back. He cupped my head, and then his fingers threaded into my hair. Gently, he pulled back my head, arching my throat to him, making me completely vulnerable. His breath warmed my neck. As the tips of his fangs skimmed my skin, my muscles went tense. Just for an instant, fear fluttered through me. As if sensing my nerves, his lips brushed over my skin, and he kissed me once more on my neck. "It will only hurt for a moment," he murmured.

Such a tender embrace, then a sharp, piercing pain as he struck deeply. He punctured my throat. The pain only lasted for a heartbeat, and then desire flooded me, an aching need I'd never known before. I let out a moan as he drank from me. Hot shivers raked over my body.

Every inch of my skin felt sensitive, tight with want. I craved more of his touch, more of his tongue. As his shadow magic stroked my skin, my hips moved up against him. He drank deeper, groaning a little. A scorching need coursed through me, and I wanted my body naked beneath his.

I reached for his shirt, only half aware that I was tearing it off him, shredding the fabric. His tongue swirled over my arched neck, sending waves of molten pleasure pulsing through me. I ran my hand up his chest. Already, his skin had healed, and his steely muscles flexed beneath my fingers. His body was magnificent, and as he pressed against me, sheer pleasure rocked through me. My hands moved up again, feeling the muscles shift slightly in his back.

I gripped his hair hard, arching my neck to give more of myself to him. I wanted him to keep going, to drink deeper—but the languorous strokes of his tongue felt as if they were already healing the bite. When his tongue healed my throat, he finally pulled away with a soft, warm kiss to my skin.

He pushed back. His hair fell before his eyes, and his dark, agonized expression bored into me. He looked drugged with pleasure. "You will be the ruin of me, Elowen." He stroked his fingertips down over my ribs, so lightly. He left a trail of hot shivers in the wake of his touch.

He reached for the waistband of my trousers, then pulled them down off my hips, to my thighs, and off completely. Warmth surged under my skin, and I wanted to see all of him, too—every gloriously etched muscle. I leaned forward to unbutton his trousers. Shadows whipped the air around him as I unleashed his rock-hard erection. With a half-smile, I met his gaze. I licked my lips, running my finger up the glorious length.

He growled quietly. "If you're going to toy with me,

you'd better be prepared for me to return the favor. Vampires like to dominate."

He reached for my underwear, smoothly tugging it off. As he did, shadows slid through the air around him, and he brushed a dark, scorching gaze down my body.

Like silk, his shadowy magic slid around my arms, and it bound my wrists up over my head. Gently, he cupped his hand behind my head as he used his magic to tug me down to his cloak again.

He pressed his palms on either side of me, taking my nipple in his mouth. He caressed me with his tongue while he touched me excruciatingly lightly between my thighs. A brush of his thumb on my wet heat, a whisper of a stroke where I was exquisitely sensitive. My hips bucked, desperate for more contact, for more friction. For him to fill me with his hard length. On instinct, my thighs spread wider, like I was offering myself up to him. Trying to tempt him into me.

He would not be rushed. He released my nipple, then trailed heated kisses down my body. Slowly, his tongue whirled over my waist, my hip bones. He was taking his time tasting me, exploring.

As he moved down to my thighs, pleasure fluttered through me. His kisses were agonizingly slow, lazy swirls of his tongue. I wanted to scream his name, to beg him to fuck me, but he seemed in no hurry. A warm glow lit me up, beads of dew on my skin. He licked me deeper, possessively.

He lifted his mouth from me, and I ached for his touch again.

"I adore your perfect body," he murmured. "Every inch of it. You were made for me."

As tendrils of his shadow magic licked at my skin, my bones turned liquid. I gritted my teeth. I was trying not to cry out, to risk altering the Luminari.

Finally, he kissed me where I was wet, and my thighs clenched around him. I let out a soft cry, and my fingers curled into his hair. My hips rolled, and I moved against his mouth.

He raised his face. "You were made for me," he purred again.

I flexed my wrists, bound in his magic. He'd brought me just to the edge, and I wanted to pull him into me. My hips rolled. "Then fill me."

His low growl skittered over my bare skin, and he moved up my body again. "So impatient. But how can I deny a command from our Lady of Death? The way you smell, the way you taste, is intoxicating."

He paused at the heat of my entrance, then slowly slid in. As he pushed deeper into me, he pierced me with that dark gaze until his eyes closed.

As my body adjusted to him, a soft moan escaped my throat. The warmth of sunlight spilled onto my skin like honey.

He lowered his body over mine as he thrust fully into me, and his teeth grazed my throat. Bone-deep pleasure gripped my mind as he moved in and out of me, excruciatingly slowly. He groaned as my body coiled tightly, pulling around him. I was gasping his name as he kissed my neck, moving my hips in time with his.

My mind burst with the colors he so loved, the violet of the Archon, the green of pastures stretching under white clouds…

As I let out a cry, he claimed my mouth. My tongue tangled with his as he slammed into me. His magic released my hands, and I raked my nails down his back. Ecstasy rippled through me, shattering me into a million pieces. I turned limp, liquid, and he pulled me against him, folding me into his arms.

He leaned his forehead against my throat, murmuring, "I could see the world alive again. Just then. Just for a moment."

"I saw it, too."

My heart still slammed in my chest, and he brushed the damp hair off my face. "We have to get you back to your room, love."

\* \* \*

MILES

*I* crossed into the dining hall, my cowl raised. I'd spent a full day locked in my room with only a few cups of water, but the hunger didn't affect me. The thrill of vampire blood still pulsed hot through my body.

I scanned the dining hall until I found my allies huddled around a table. Their grim expressions made my stomach tighten. We were running out of time, and I had no idea if Maelor would be able to help us again.

As I drew closer, my gaze landed on the meager offerings on the table. Tonight, there was no wine or quail or rich stew. Instead, my friends sat before crusts of bread and pale brown glasses of water.

I took a seat next to Sazia, frowning at the bread crusts. "So, it seems our benefactor is gone."

Godric raised his eyebrows. "Speaking of benefactors, are you going to tell us about the Raven Lord letting us out of the dungeon?"

Hugo's eyes brightened. "I told you all about vampires, didn't I? Did you see what his chest looked like? He didn't die from that, only because he's already dead."

Sazia flicked her hair behind her shoulder. "I have a little question for you. Is he part of the resistance? Or did you seduce him so thoroughly that he's now under your spell?"

I leaned forward, glancing at Percival. "He was the one who saved Eboria." Everyone leaned closer as I whispered. "The Raven Lord was working against the Order. He warned Eboria. He killed a dozen Luminari yesterday. And yes, he might be why we used to have good food. Now, he's in hiding. The Pater is furious that so many of us have survived, and he blames Maelor for that, too. He knows someone passed along warnings. He's in a complete fury."

Godric's face blanched. "What do you think he'll do next?"

"He's going to kill us all." I took a deep breath, picking up a stale piece of bread. "We have only two options: we find a way out, or we kill the Pater."

"Or, of course, the third option, where we all die," said Hugo.

I winced. "Let's avoid that one. But the Pater won't be easy to kill, and Sion is standing in the way." Might as well let it all out now. "Look, Sion is a vampire, too.

But he's committed to the Order. Maelor said he's unfailingly loyal to his cause—or something like that. So he won't help us."

"But…why?" asked Hugo. "Is he a true believer?"

"I don't know," I said. "But I think he's here because he's a sadist and enjoys death."

"What did Maelor say about killing the Pater?" asked Percival.

"Not to try it. That I'd be dead within moments. And maybe he's right. It's a last resort." With a pang, I realized Maelor still wasn't telling me much about the resistance.

Hugo stared at me. "What did it feel like when he drank your blood?"

Sazia's mouth dropped open. "You did *not* let him… did you?"

"Never mind that," I said sharply.

She chewed her bread thoughtfully. "Do you know what, darling? I saw a dead Luminarus with his throat torn out in the courtyard from my window. Drained of blood. Looked like something a vampire would do. Maybe he can kill all of them."

My stomach swooped as dread fluttered through me. I'd never mourn a dead Luminarus, but *was* he losing his grip on his control? All those warnings Maelor had given me…he'd been perfectly restrained until I'd shown up.

I pushed those thoughts out of my mind. "Let's think of a plan." I glanced at Percival. "As far as I know, we're the only ones left who have actual magic, right? And Lydia."

Percival nodded. "I think so. If anyone else had useful magic, it probably would have come out during the last trial when I nearly murdered everyone."

"You didn't murder us. You saved us," I said emphatically. "The wolves would have killed everyone."

Godric frowned, his gaze flicking to Percival. "Your fire power...I know you can't put a fire out if you start it, but do you think you could keep it at a steady temperature for a long time? A steady, very hot temperature?"

"Yes," said Percival. "As long as I'm not completely panicking, I can also keep it from getting too big. It was just with the wolves—"

"No one blames you," said Sazia. "We're all fine. I mean, apart from that woman killed by the wolf."

Godric and Hugo exchanged a look.

Hugo raised a finger. "You're thinking of that forge near Sootfield, aren't you?"

"What are you talking about?" I asked.

"It was a repair job we did as masons," Godric said. "You know, troubadour life doesn't pay all the bills. So with the right level of heat, over a long enough time—"

"You could make the walls swell and crack," Hugo added. "It wouldn't break them completely, but they'd be weakened. But it might take...well, it would take a very long time."

Godric leaned back, folding his arms. "Intense heat

in the right places can weaken a wall. If it's done correctly, the stone expands and contracts. It will weaken the foundation. You'd need one of us to guide you, and it would take hours. You'd have to stress the stones at the right points. And we'd still need something to smash through it. A battering ram or something."

I raised my hand. "There's also a giant wooden door," I said. "Might be easier to burn wood than try to melt rocks."

Percival raised his eyebrows. "It all sounds like a good idea, but there's also the issue of archers shooting us to death. They're patrolling above every wall in Ruefield."

"Excellent point," I said.

Hugo raised his water glass. "There are catacombs beneath all of Ruefield. All sealed off. Ancient hymns to the ancestors, the earth's quiet tombs…"

"They're sealed off," I repeated.

Godric leaned forward. "What if we destroy the wall from underneath, where no one can see us?"

Sazia shrugged. "It sounds like a good idea to me— but there is the little problem where you might end up crushed beneath the rocks of collapsing tunnels. Yes?"

"Right," said Godric. "Sod that. We'll keep thinking."

But before we could continue, a hush fell over the hall. I turned to see the Magister crossing into the room, darkness billowing around him. The temperature seemed to drop, and the candles flickered.

He turned slowly, taking us all in. "The Pater knows that you have had help figuring out how to evade death in the trials." His footfalls echoed off the flagstones, his dark cloak blending into the shadows around him. "The Pater knows that the traitor, Maelor, passed along advice to you all. Rest assured, our Luminari are hunting for this demon. Maelor is Serpent-touched. A monster. And he will burn on the pyre."

I gripped the wooden table, staring at him. I wanted to scream that he was worse—a vampire who actually delighted in death instead of trying to control it. But the Pater wasn't here, and it didn't matter what the rest of us thought.

Torchlight from the chandeliers above wavered over his eerie golden eyes, terrible and beautiful at once.

"You will no longer meet with each other here in the dining hall. The Pater has realized you could use this time to conspire. He believes you have been passing along secrets and tricks about how to survive. Did you think it would work? That we'd let you live?" A wicked smile curled his lips. "Until the next trial, you will remain locked in your rooms. And the next trial, I'm afraid, isn't much of a trial. From your windows, you may see us setting up pyres in the courtyard. You will all burn along with the traitor, and we shall restore ourselves in the glorious light of the Archon once more."

The world tilted beneath me. We were out of time.

We wouldn't have a chance to figure out how to deconstruct thousand-year-old walls. We didn't have the luxury of experimentation.

Maybe the others still wanted an escape plan.

But me? I'd been trained to kill.

First the Magister.

Then the Pater.

# CHAPTER 37

*I* sat on the stone floor of my room, legs splayed. Hunger squeezed my stomach, but I was ignoring that. I was only focused on the wood in my hands, the knife in my grip. Late that night, after Sion had told us about the pyres, I'd broken the chair legs. I'd started carefully carving the end of one of the legs to a point. I considered making a few of them, but then I couldn't imagine a scenario where I'd need more than one. Either I'd kill Sion in one single strike or he'd rip my head off in the next breath.

When you strike a vampire, you'd better not miss.

The knife had been useful for making a stake holster, now hidden in my cloak, too. It had taken ages, but I had nothing but time in here. Several days with nothing to do but cut strips from my bedding with the serrated edge of the blade. I threaded the strips through small holes in the cloak, making a little pocket.

As I sat on the cold stones, I held up my stake. I touched the sharpened tip, and it pricked my finger. A little drop of blood beaded on the tip, shimmering like a crimson jewel in the candlelight. I popped it in my mouth, sucking on it to stop the bleeding.

Looks like I had a weapon.

The problem, of course, was that I'd been locked in here, without any chance to get anywhere near the Pater or Sion. I just had to assume he'd attend the burning.

I slid my new stake into the cloak pocket and hung it on the wall. As I climbed onto the bed, a cold wind whistled in through the glass. Shivering, I peered out into the darkened courtyard. Torchlight danced on the vast, overgrown courtyard. It cast ghostly shadows of the pyres that made my skin crawl. Over the past few days, they'd set up the pyres there on purpose. Right outside our windows. They wanted us to watch through the glass as they raised one stake after another. They wanted us to tremble with dread as we imagined what it would feel like to burn.

Eight rows rose up over enormous piles of kindling. They'd even built the stairs for us to climb to our deaths. From the torchlight, shadows danced over the heaps of wood.

My breath clouded the glass, and my stomach churned at the sight of them.

At least no one had found Maelor yet. I knew this for two reasons. One, I'd discovered a note from him in my room, left on my pillow. Which was…unnerving. It was hard for me to believe I could sleep through someone opening the door and crossing inside, but I guess I did. I'd woken up to a piece of parchment that said:

*"I must keep my distance from you. I'm blood-hungry. But I'm working on a way to get you out of here, mapping ancient paths beneath the tunnels. I'm sorry I cannot take more than you, but it's simply not possible. It would attract far too much attention. Please burn this note immediately."*

As soon as I'd read it, I'd dropped the note into the fire, watching the smoke curl into the room.

The problem was, his plan of leaving the others behind to burn wasn't good enough for me.

I pressed my forehead against the cool glass.

Besides the note, there was another reason I knew Maelor was still out there. Once or twice a day, I'd see Luminari carrying one of their own, their necks ripped to shreds. One time, I saw the blur of shadows through the courtyard. Through the window, a scream had pierced the glass—cut short.

Out there, Maelor was ravenous.

A creak sounded in the room, and I turned to see the metal hatch sliding.

My eyebrows flicked up. They'd already delivered my dinner of stale bread and water.

I crossed to the door and stood on my tiptoes. I

pressed my hand against the iron bars and peered through the hatch.

At the sight of the Pater standing just before my door, my veins crackled with quiet fury. Warm light glinted off his armored chest, and his white cloak draped over his shoulders. In the darkened hall, he stood eerily still.

He steepled his gloved fingers. "Hello, Mother of Death."

*Drain him of life*, the Serpent rasped in my skull.

My fingers twitched. "Do you want to come in?"

A small smile curled his lips, and he shook his head. "Ah, no. I don't need your lethal touch, thank you. I merely want to know where Maelor is. You and he seem…close." His eyes narrowed. "You let the Serpent feed on you, didn't you?"

If only Maelor would rip *his* throat out. "How would I know where he is? I've been locked in here for days."

"I think he still comes to see you."

"Don't be ridiculous." My fingers curled around the iron bars. "He's probably long gone from Ruefield."

He tapped his index fingers together. "You wouldn't want your son to burn, would you?"

The stone seemed to slip away beneath my feet, and I had to grip the bars to hold myself steady. My blood roared in my head.

As I worked to keep my face a mask of calm, I

relaxed the muscles around my mouth and eyes. "I told you, he's not my son."

The Pater glanced to his right. "We have not conquered Eboria fully, but of course, I have contacts there. Influence. People willing to serve the Archon. I could bring Leo here easily. We can put him next to you, yes? Tomorrow morning, when we purify you both in our flames. Leo will find it a comfort to be so close to you, I'm sure." His gaze darted back to me. "Unless you can remember where Maelor is. If you have useful information for me, perhaps we can spare the boy when we kill you tomorrow. Send me information tonight when your thoughts are clearer."

My mouth had gone dry. "How am I supposed to send you information?"

His silver hair hung before his face, and shadows darkened his gaunt cheeks. "Examine your soul. One of my soldiers will return at midnight. My soldier will bring the message to me in the temple. If we find Maelor by morning, little Leo will be spared." He arched an eyebrow. "I trust you will make the right decision for that child, if not for the kingdom. I have been told that you care for him a great deal."

*Who told you?* Fury hummed through my marrow.

As the metal gate slid closed, I found myself left alone in my room. Nausea climbed up my throat, and cold anger rattled through my bones.

Did the Pater actually have Leo? He might. After all, if Maelor could find him so easily, I'm sure Sion could, too. I wasn't exactly in a position to demand proof. And in any case, I'd already made up my mind.

I wasn't going to wait any longer.

I turned and crawled onto my bed. With a hammering heart, I inched over to the window. The wind whistled in through a crack.

Vampires had excellent hearing.

"Maelor!" I called into the night wind. Three times, shouting his name into the rushing breeze. I sat back on my bed, breathing rapidly.

Would he ever forgive me for what I was going to do next?

Right now, my body was coiled tightly with desperation. No matter what, I had to keep Leo safe.

I glanced down at the leather doublet wrapped around my shirt. It skimmed down over the waistband of my leather trousers. I was wearing too much, wasn't I? If I was going to truly distract him, some of this would have to go.

I stood and pulled off everything except my underwear. With shaking hands, I frantically laced the doublet back up again. And it worked, I think. Without the shirt underneath, it showed off the curve of my breasts.

I laid my shirt and trousers on the floor before the fireplace, and I poured out my cup of water on them. Half-naked, I pulled on the cloak, just over my shoulders. This outfit made no sense at all. It was the costume choice of a madwoman. But it was utilitarian in its own way. Bare thighs and cleavage to distract the vampire, and the cloak to hide my tools.

A tiny click in the keyhole heralded his arrival. The door swung open, and his piercing gaze landed on me. As he stared, the blue of his eyes blended to shadows.

The firelight washed over his perfect features, and he closed the door quietly behind him. My throat tightened.

His gaze swept down my body, lingering at my breasts, then brushing down over my bare thighs. "What on earth are you doing?"

"I spilled water on my clothes."

My gaze tracked every one of his movements as he slid his key into a pocket inside his cloak, just on the left side.

"What's wrong?" he said. "I told you it's dangerous for me to be near you. Why did you call me here?"

"We're out of time. The Pater says that he's going to burn us all in the morning."

If I told Maelor my plan, he'd tell me to hide underground. He'd tell me to let the others burn while I saved only myself.

It wasn't good enough anymore.

I walked closer to him and touched the side of his face. Already, my heart was racing. Really, it wasn't hard to seduce someone you already wanted. "I couldn't stop thinking of you while I was locked in here."

It wasn't a lie.

He covered my hand with his, then pulled my palm before his face. His gaze narrowed on the tiny drop of blood on my fingertip, and he licked it. He sucked my finger into his mouth, eyes closing as his tongue moved against it.

He released my finger, piercing me with a heated gaze. "Elowen." His voice had gone deep and husky. "I can't stop thinking—"

I tilted back my head and pulled his face down closer to mine. I brushed my lips against his. He let out an agonized sigh, and his eyes went fully dark. His hand slid up behind me, and he cupped my head. Then he whirled me around, pressing my back against the wall. He claimed my mouth with his, kissing me deeply. As he gripped my hair, one of his knees slid between my thighs.

I rolled my hips, moaning into his mouth. My fingers slipped into his cloak pocket and wrapped around his keys. As I kissed him back, I gripped the metal and tucked them into the sleeve of my cloak.

Maelor pulled away from the kiss, his eyes searching mine. The bittersweet loss of his touch pierced me. Would I ever kiss those beautiful lips again?

A pained expression etched his perfect face, and he pressed his hands against the wall behind me. A lock of his dark hair fell before his shadow-stained eyes. His control was slipping again. He looked like he wanted to fuck me hard against the wall right now.

"Need to get out of here," he whispered.

"I need to go with you." Nerves fluttered through my chest. "What if we try to get everyone out? I can't leave them all behind."

"Absolutely not. It's not possible, and you'll just end up risking your own life. I told you when you first got here, you can't have emotional ties. You're alone here."

My throat tightened. "Apart from you."

"I'm trying to get you back to Leo, which would practically be a miracle at this point."

I narrowed my eyes. "What if I tried to save them anyway?"

"I'm afraid I would stop you, darling." A muscle flickered in his jaw. "I'm going to hide you."

It was exactly as I'd thought.

He flashed his fangs, licking one of them. "And after I get you to safety, I must keep my distance, Elowen. The number of people I've killed in the past few days..." He trailed off, scrubbing a hand over his mouth.

I knelt down and picked up the damp trousers from the hearth. I slipped into them, ignoring how cold they felt against my skin.

I pulled on my boots. The moment I was fully dressed, I said, "Let's go. Are the halls well patrolled right now?"

He reached for the door handle. "Not many people. A few Luminari, but almost all of them are outside, looking for me." He turned back. "I can't carry you this time. Being close to you right now is not a good idea." His Lirion accent rolled through his words. "Just try to move as quickly as you can, and I will guide you to safety."

I nodded. He opened the door and looked in both directions.

My heart slammed wildly as I followed after him, a thrill charging my body. In the hall, I turned to him, gasping. I opened my eyes wide and pressed my palm against his chest. "The note," I said. "I didn't want to burn it because it was all I had from you. But I left it in there."

He cursed under his breath in the rolling *R*s of Lirion, and he pulled the door back open. He crossed inside, and my nerves sparked with anticipation.

With shaking hands, I slammed the door shut. I brought down the iron bar, trapping him inside.

"Elowen!" His voice pierced the wood, and my chest went tight. Guilt twisted through me.

"I'm sorry," I whispered.

I'd either be around to let him out after I killed the Pater, or the Luminari would. In a fight between him and mortals, all my money was on the vampire. Maelor's growl echoed through the iron and wood, but he couldn't risk being too loud—not with half the castle looking for him.

"I'm sorry," I said a little louder. My eyes stung.

This was what the Order did. It turned you against those you loved. Because none of us could fully trust each other with the truth, could we? The Order was the hollowness that lived in our chests.

I whirled away and hurried through the darkened hall.

With a racing pulse, I pulled open one hatch after another until I found the person I was looking for. Percival sat on his bed, his head in his hands.

Trembling, I unlocked his door with the stolen key. I pulled up the iron bar and pushed open the wood into his room.

Percival's face lifted to mine, and shock lit up his countenance. "How in the Archon's name..."

I lifted my hand, gripping the keys I'd stolen. "I don't have time to explain. Your job is to let the others out. Keep them hidden in the tunnels, and I will try to find you. The Pater means to execute us tomorrow, and I'm not letting it happen." I tossed the keys to him and turned to run.

Just one story down, I ran into the first Luminari.

# CHAPTER 38

*I*n death's dark shadow, I stalked closer to the soldiers.

They faced the other way, hands on their pommels, bodies alert. I crept up behind them, silent as the night sky.

*Ring their funeral bells. I will inscribe their epitaphs with my touch...*

They must have felt my breath because one of them whipped around, trying to draw his sword. But it was too late for him. My hand had already brushed against the back of his neck.

*I am death.*

Just as the deep purple started to creep under his skin, I pivoted. The other Luminarus's eyes had opened wide. I brought my hand across his face in a sharp slap. *I am darkness, death. I am things which are not.*

Rot began to spread under his skin. The elegant lines of decay...

The Serpent was hungry tonight, and I would be feeding him.

And yet, I had to stay sane. I reached down, pulling one of the scabbards off the bodies. Better to use a sword than my curse.

I tightened the leather scabbard around my waist, under my cloak. Quickly, I reached for their daggers. I tucked those tightly into the pocket of my cloak next to the stake.

Fully armed, I ran through the hallway, keeping my footfalls light. I turned into a narrow stairwell and charged down.

At the bottom of the stairs, I slowed, moving silently. From the shadows, I peered around the corner. Two Luminari stood on the landing. Just beyond them was the door to the courtyard.

Drawing the sword, I rushed forward. As they turned, I aimed for the throat. I severed the first man's head from his body. Lightning-fast, I pivoted to parry the second man's blade swinging for me. My sword clashed with his once, twice. I had to end this quickly before he alerted anyone else.

I struck hard, and when his sword clattered to the floor, my blade found its mark in his throat. Blood spilled over the stone, and I pushed through the door. In the shadows of the courtyard, my gaze flicked over the stakes. They jutted from gnarled tangles of kindling like dead, inverted trees.

I crept through the shadows and stalked into the old hedge maze. Here, under the shadows of yews and hedges, no one would see me. I breathed in the scent of violets and bluebells that grew wild all over the courtyard. Such a pretty, perfumed breeze on a gruesome night like this…

If I let the Pater's plan unfold, the only thing people would breathe in tomorrow would be the scent of burning flesh.

My quickening heartbeat seemed to throb in my skull. As I stalked farther across the courtyard, the landscape changed. The air no longer smelled as fragrant now. Here, the plants were jagged and dark— hawthorn trees with prickled branches, blackthorn that reached to my waist.

*Pater, ready yourself for fate's final call. I'll deliver you to eternal silence.*

As the temple came into view, cold sweat dampened my skin. A few narrow windows let out warm light onto the tangled, overgrown gardens. On a moonless night, I could hardly see a thing here. Which was good, because it meant the Luminari wouldn't see me, either.

My breath came quickly and sharply as battle fury hummed through my body.

Somehow, I felt as if the earth withered around me with every footfall. As I moved closer to the temple, I caught sight of two Luminari guarding the door. Crouching behind a blackthorn, I stared at them. Two narrow windows flanked the temple door, and the warm light highlighted their shoulders, the sides of their heads. I couldn't quite see their throats, but I had a good sense of where their necks were, and where I might hit the vital blood vessels that ran down either side of their throats. I cocked my head. A vampire would know this part of the throat well—there, on the sides, were the arteries that carried life-giving blood from the heart to the head. A pulse beneath the skin. Sever that, and a person would die.

I reached into the pocket of my cloak and pulled out the two daggers, one in each hand. My heart beat like a war drum against my ribs. Narrowing my eyes, I focused on my aim. I'd done this so many times with the Baron, practicing for hours at a time until blisters had formed on my fingers where I'd gripped the daggers. When I'd failed, he'd slapped me hard with the back of his hand, drawing blood from my lips.

I held my breath, then threw the first one. Just as one soldier started to slump down, I threw the second dagger. The soft thud meant I'd hit my mark.

Reaching for my sword, I raced toward the door. I didn't know if I'd hit them in the right place until I was standing over them. Then my chest unclenched as I took in their slumped, lifeless forms sliding down the wood of the door. Dark blood spilled out from their throats onto the stones. I let out a long, slow breath.

Gritting my teeth, I pulled the bodies out of the way.

In the shadows outside the temple door, I peered through a narrow window. It was no great surprise to see Sion in the temple, sword slung around his waist. He leaned against a pillar, relaxed, arms folded.

Light wavered over the stones as the torchbearers held their flames aloft. Shadows crawled across the stone floor, over my heart.

*The stroke of death nears...*

Behind Sion, the Pater held out his hands, his lips moving in prayer. Did he always spend all night in this temple?

Of course Sion was here, protecting his master. My blood went cold as my gaze flicked to him again. The Pater knew all about Leo now. How much I cared for him...Sion must have seen him that day in Briarvale. He must have hunted him down. And of course, a vampire would see *everything*. Hear everything. The crowd screaming about the boy...he'd stored it all up to use later on.

Ice ran through my veins. Maelor wouldn't have told him...

Would he?

Through the window, I watched as Sion's jaw went tight. His nostrils flared, and his golden gaze flicked toward the window. Judging by how rigid his body went, I could only assume he smelled the blood.

My mouth went dry, and I pulled the stake from the pocket.

My heart was a wild beast.

It wouldn't be an easy thing, forcing a wooden stake into someone's chest. The stake was sharp as a blade, but I would need an immense amount of strength and speed behind it. As Sion stalked closer to the door, I gripped the stake in my right hand, cupping the left around its base. I shifted my weight onto my back leg. My blood roared.

When he opened the door, his golden eyes landed on me for just a moment.

I felt time slow down, the night breeze toying with a strand of his long hair.

With all the force I had, I drove the stake upward, under his ribs and right into his heart.

# CHAPTER 39

*H*is eyes widened with shock, and a drop of blood spilled from the corner of his mouth. "Elowen," he whispered.

It wasn't like killing someone with a sword or dagger. This stake had a lot more resistance, and I *felt* it going in, cutting through his flesh.

His face was so close to mine, his golden eyes blending to black. He smelled of cloves and old leather-bound books—a strangely homey smell that didn't fit with him at all.

When I pulled my hands from the base of the stake, I realized they'd started to shake wildly. "You knew about Leo, didn't you?" I whispered.

Shock still shone on his face as slumped back against the temple door. "Learned everything I could about you…" He clutched the stake in his chest, his eyes fathomless pits of shadow. His body went still, and his head fell forward.

Shaking, I breathed in deeply. I closed my eyes for a moment, trying to refocus my attention. I envisioned what the Pater's face would look like as I stole his last breath. With a clear head, I pulled open the temple door.

I stalked inside, blood-soaked and reeking of death.

The Pater's eyes slid to me immediately, and his jaw dropped. His eyes went wide. Right now, there was no one in here but us and the silent, eyeless torchbearers.

"Help!" The Pater's voice echoed off the stone. "Magister!"

Fury hummed through my bones, and I prowled closer to him. "He can't help you now. Death has come for you."

Fear crackled through the air. The torchbearers stayed in place, committed to their vows. Their torch-light danced over the room.

The Pater, coward that he was, turned to run. "Luminari!"

I broke into a sprint after him, quickly closing the distance. I caught him by the cowl and pulled him back sharply with a hard jerk. He fell down backward on the stone floor, and I pinned him.

Joy slid through me as I gripped both his hands in one of mine. I stroked my fingertips down his face, from his forehead to his cheeks.

His eyes went wide.

"You shouldn't have threatened Leo," I hissed.

Bruise-colored veins shot beneath his skin, and his muscles seized up beneath me. I watched, entranced with my work, as his mouth opened and closed soundlessly. His body convulsed. The sounds of his gasps were a symphony to my ears, his death spasms a macabre dance.

I stared at him, watching the life drain out of him.

With shuddering breaths, I rose off his limp body.

I stumbled back from the sight of the dead Pater, trying to focus on what to do next. All I wanted to do was kill again, but that wasn't part of my greater plan.

The question was, should I free Maelor now?

I turned away from the Pater and took long strides toward the door—

"Serpent's whore." The rasping voice came from behind me.

I whirled, my heart racing.

The Pater stood by the altar, his body glowing. In the torchlight, he cast a long shadow over the floor.

My breath went still in my lungs. I'd just watched him die…I had *killed* him. How was he now standing by the altar?

His gray hair hung in front of his face, but his skin looked clear of the toxins. He peered at me through his lank hair. "Did you really think the Archon would let me die? Me, his chosen one?"

I reached for my sword, and he shook his head. "It's no good. I always come back. The Archon protects me."

Behind me, the door creaked open, and I turned to see Sion stalking in. My heart skipped a beat. I couldn't breathe. Blood poured down his chest, and his clothes gaped open where I'd stabbed him. But he was very much alive, graceful as ever.

His black eyes took me in, brushing up and down my body. "So, your pretty lover told you how to kill a vampire. Except it seems he forgot to mention what sort of wood to use, didn't he? Not very useful. Seems like he doesn't really trust you at all." A note of mockery rang in his deep voice.

"What is this? How are you standing?" shouted the Pater. "My Magister Solaris…"

Sion's dark gaze slid to the Pater. "Do you think I'm yours? Have you never noticed that I'm smarter than you, faster than you, stronger than you? That I'm better in every way?" He sighed. "I suppose you wouldn't have."

All the color drained from the Pater's face. "But you have served me so loyally."

A wicked smile curled Sion's lips, and he glided closer to the Pater, his movements fluid. "I haven't." He moved in a blur of shadows, then reached for the Pater's throat. Sion lifted him into the air. "I'm here to figure out how to kill you. Except our little Mistress of Death over there fucked up my plans." His tone was calm, casual, even as he threatened the Pater.

Sion dropped him onto the floor and knelt on his

chest. He lifted the Pater's head by the hair, then slammed his skull down on the flagstones.

The Magister glanced back at me, and his black eyes flicked up to meet mine. "Here's a skill I feel you're lacking, witch. You just go for the kill, and you don't toy with your prey. You're a hunter. Act like it." He smashed the Pater's head one more time. "But you do have to be careful. Because mortals are so very, very delicate, and they really do die so quickly sometimes." He let out a long sigh. "You know what that's like."

He stood, staring at the heap at his feet. The Pater rolled to his side, his expression stunned. He was trying to crawl now.

Sion's amber eyes met mine again. "This one dies easily, but he always comes back from the dead. None of us know how to stop it. And that *was* my entire purpose here." Gold flecks pierced his black stare.

On his elbows, the Pater pulled himself toward the torchbearers. "The Archon protects me," he rasped.

Sion let out a low, dark laugh that sent an ice-cold shiver up my spine. Then his smile faded. "There is no Archon!"

His blasphemous shout echoed off the temple walls. I stared, stunned. I'd never heard anyone say such a thing.

"And if the Serpent exists," said Sion, "I am he. Am I supposed to feel guilt for being better than mortals? Is it *my* fault you're all sad, slow, and pathetic? I didn't create you to grow more decrepit day by day, and yet the Order seems to believe I'm responsible for your mortality. They tortured me for decades." His voice softened. "I know, I know, that was before your time, but you carry on their traditions so faithfully, don't you, Pater?"

He crouched down by the Pater's side and dragged the man closer to the hole, so that his head hung over the depths.

"Do you see the face of the Archon?" asked Sion. "Do you see?"

"I see the Archon," breathed the Pater. His voice shook. "I see the face of the Archon before me! Glorious Archon!"

"It's supposed to drive a man mad. But the thing is, you already are." Sion gripped him by the robe and dragged him over the edge, shoving him into the pit.

His scream echoed off the dome, then grew faint as he fell.

"Daft cunt." Sion dusted off his hands on his robe. When he turned back to me, he curled his lip to show one of his fangs. "Don't be relieved. He'll be back. And when he is, he will send the entire Luminari force after both of us. Thanks for that. I was able to deceive him for years, but I think stalking into the temple with a giant crevice where my heart should be pushed the bounds of credulity a bit too far, don't you?"

Anger still skittered along my bones. "Why would you tell him about Leo?"

He leveled his piercing stare on me, his body

completely still. "I didn't. That was the boy's uncle. *Hamelin*. You can't trust anyone in Merthyn, don't you know that?"

"Where is Leo?" I demanded.

"Still in Eboria with his wretched plague-sore of an uncle." He narrowed his eyes. "Though again, Leo will probably be one of the first people the Pater will pursue when he returns after what you just did. He's going to have a real vendetta against you, do you realize that?"

"Yeah. He was about to burn me at dawn, so I was aware of his distaste for me." My nerves crackled. I had to get out of here.

"Maelor was supposed to get you out." An edge cut through the smoothness of his voice. "He told you that, but it wasn't good enough for you, was it?"

"No, it wasn't." My fingers slid over my bloody pommel. "Because you two were going to let everyone else burn. There's a boy here hardly older than Leo. You think I could leave him to suffer the flames?"

He folded his arms, looking bored with the conversation already. "What difference does it make?" That lilting Lirion accent tinged his voice. "You're all mortal. They'll be dead in the blink of an eye, no matter what happens."

"'Dead in the blink of an eye'? That's not how it seems to us." I took a deep, shaking breath. "And when it comes to your secret mission of learning how to kill the Pater, it doesn't seem like you were making much headway on that front, were you?"

Shadows spilled off him, ice-cold on my skin. "We were the reason Eboria was prepared."

"We can't keep letting all these Penitents die while you try to figure out how to kill him. We need a new tactic."

He started to circle me, and amusement danced in his metallic eyes. "Who the fuck is *we*? Have you just appointed yourself head of the resistance? How interesting."

I stared at him as he prowled around me. His movements were so eerily smooth.

"How exactly were you able to deceive the Pater?" I asked. "You seemed like an evil creep the first moment I met you. You don't seem remotely mortal."

"Thank you." He went still, then cocked his head. As he took me in, his eyes looked heavy-lidded, almost seductive. "I have ways of bending people's minds to my will. I can convince them of the reality I want them to see. But it has its limits."

"The Archon cursed me after I left an offering out in the woods for the old gods. If there is no Archon, how did I end up cursed?"

He lifted an eyebrow. "Is that really what you think happened?"

"It's logical. I was cursed immediately after leaving food out for the old gods."

He crossed his arms over his chest and leaned back

against a column. His gaze flicked away from me. I'd already lost his interest. "Has it ever occurred to you that maybe it's not a curse?"

"You think the risk of killing everyone I love isn't a curse…though I suppose that wouldn't seem like a curse to you, would it?"

He'd only just thrown the Pater into the hollow, and he already looked bored. "Maybe you just need to spend more time around vampires instead of fragile mortals."

Just above his crossed arms, something caught my eye. It was the tattoo on his healing chest, visible where I'd ripped the fabric.

I stepped closer to him and pulled away his arms. He didn't resist. Instead, he just stared down at me, and I studied the tattoo on his skin. My breath went still. I'd seen this already, in my vision. One of the first times I'd touched Maelor, I'd seen a spiked crown tattoo, blood-spattered. But Maelor didn't have a tattoo. It was Sion's. And just like in the vision, a butterfly pendant hung down, visible in the space where I'd ripped his robe. The memory burst to life in my thoughts, vibrant as sunlight. I brushed my finger-tips over his pendant.

A dark smile curled his sensuous lips as he stared down at me. "Honestly, Elowen. I know vampires are irresistible, but is this really the time to undress me with your eyes?"

Tension coiled through my body as I pointed at his

chest. "I've seen your tattoo before. Just like this. Spattered with blood."

From under dark eyelashes, gold eyes pierced me. Shadows spilled around him like ink through water, and a shiver rippled over my skin.

"I see your memory is coming back," he murmured.

I stared at him. "Memory of *what?*"

"Well, it could be one of two times."

My eyes stung as it slid together in my mind. "I remember blood on the white anemones when Father died. You were there. Is that what you meant when you said you make people believe your reality? Did you force me to forget things?"

He was still as the stone column behind him. The shadows whipped and licked at the space around his broad shoulders. "It's probably a good thing you're all out of stakes right now because I really didn't enjoy being stabbed."

"You killed my father." My voice cracked. "Tell me now, or I swear to the Archon, I will make good on your advice to draw out the pain."

"That's adorable." He gave an easy shrug. "Yes, I killed him. But don't go off on a whole unhinged revenge mission because clearly, you're incapable of killing me. And I might start to lose my patience, my pretty friend."

Molten rage ignited. I blinked the tears from my eyes. "So. You were just hungry? Wanted to fill your belly? Why not? Our lives are over in the blink of an eye anyway, right?"

"You're really not going to like what I have to say next," he whispered.

"I already fucking hate you," I snarled.

I thought I saw him flinch, though I had no idea why, since he clearly had no feelings.

I stepped closer to him, wrath spilling through me. "And I will figure out how to end your life," I added. My voice sounded cold, ragged with pain.

He stared down at me, his expression cold, unreadable. "Maelor and I were members of the resistance after the Order took over the kingdom. It was our job to kill those who informed."

I shook my head. "Absolute bollocks." My voice echoed off the dome. "My father wouldn't work with the Order."

"Not for money, no, but the Order knew a witch lived at the manor. I think you know who that was, don't you? The Ravens were closing in. Your father gave a name to save your life. Leo's father. In the end, they took the boy's mother as well. You know how it is. And that, Elowen, was how you ended up with Leo."

I could hardly see through the blur in my eyes. I jabbed at his steely chest with my finger. "I don't believe you. Why would I believe you? You are the most repulsive person I have ever met. When I look at you, I feel physically sick."

His eyes looked like I'd struck him, and shadows

rippled out from his body. But it was only a moment before a smirk was on his face again. "I don't really give a fuck, Elowen. Why don't you tell all this to your lover? Where is he, anyway?"

"Locked in my room."

His low chuckle filled the temple. "You really fucked him up. I've never seen him so deranged. It's been decades since he's killed like this, and..." His smile faded. "Actually, I kind of like it. He was getting really sanctimonious about not feeding or fucking. And then what's the point of living?" A heavy sigh. "But tedious as he is sometimes, I can't leave him there. He'll never get out. Even a vampire can't scale Ruefield's walls—"

The door slammed open, and Maelor stood in the doorframe. Shadows darkened the air around him, and blood streaked his knuckles. A chill rippled into the temple, a frigid breeze that nearly snuffed out the torches. My gaze flicked to the blood that dripped off Maelor's knuckles. He must have punched the wood between the iron bars until the door fragmented enough so he could let himself out.

"What exactly is happening?" he hissed.

"Your sweet friend here killed the Pater and rammed a stake into my chest. How did she learn about stakes?"

"I never told her the kind of wood." Maelor's darkened gaze slid to me, his expression icy.

I inhaled sharply. "You told me that Sion was deeply

committed to the Order. That I should never tell anyone what we were doing—"

"I said that he's unyieldingly committed to his cause, and he'll kill anyone who gets in his way," Maelor said, finishing my thought.

I stared at him as the pieces slid together in my mind. "His cause being...the resistance." My gaze flicked to Sion. "Bollocks. Is there anyone else I need to know about?"

Sion cocked his head. "Will you stake them, too?"

"I staked you *because* I didn't know you were in the resistance," I shot back.

"Do you have any idea how long it took us to build up the Pater's trust?" asked Sion in a low hiss. "To get into this position?"

Regret coiled through me. "You lot have a very different opinion than I about whether we should be trying to save the rest of the Penitents or letting them burn to death. But your secret is out now. You might as well help us because you need to get out as badly as we do."

Two furious vampires stared back at me, and the air grew cold.

Maelor stalked farther into the temple. "None of that matters right now. There are Luminari on high alert. They found the dead soldiers, the empty prisoner rooms. When the Pater returns, he's going to lead them right here."

Sion glared at me. "What's your plan?" Mockery

sang in his deep voice. "This wonderful plan where everyone gets saved?"

I swallowed hard. "If we're going to survive, we need to work together. With everyone. Allies are an asset, not a liability."

"So we can't eat our new friends, is that what you're saying?" murmured Sion. "I'm always on my best behavior, of course, but as for Maelor here…I'm afraid you've unleashed something of a monster."

Maelor's jaw clenched. "I will be fine. I've already gorged on Luminari."

Sion flashed him a half-smile. "Ah, there's the old Maelor I loved. Because I need you to actually be strong after the chaos your woman unleashed tonight." Sion's amber eyes flicked to me. There was something predatory and catlike about them. "And you, Mistress of Death, might need to be strong, too. If you want to get out of here alive, you need to stop being so terrified of your own power. Give in to the thrill of what you truly love and stop lying to yourself. You're a monster. Maybe it's not a bad thing."

Goosebumps rose on my skin, and I tightened my jaw.

For Leo, I'd do anything. I'd even work with the man who murdered my father. "Let's go."

# CHAPTER 40

The sword hung at my waist, and I touched Maelor's back as we walked through the musty tunnel. Distant torches lit up the passage, but the light in here was dim, and my eyes still hadn't adjusted. From the temple, Maelor and Sion had led me down an old stone stairwell. The wide, torchlit dome of the temple had transitioned into a dark so heavy I might as well be an eyeless torchbearer.

Down here, it smelled of soil and decay.

My mind slid back, turning over what Sion had told me. I didn't want to believe that my father had been an informer…

And why would I believe Sion?

My stomach twisted. It was just that someone *had* informed on Leo's parents, and Sion seemed to know a lot about that. What if it explained Father's absolute determination to take care of a little boy who wasn't related to us? Was it guilt that had made Father so protective over Leo?

I swallowed hard. Whatever had happened, I was more determined than ever to get back to him. I had to make sure the Pater got nowhere near him. And yes, I had to get him away from his *wretched plague-sore of an uncle.*

A sharp coil of metallic fear twined through me. The moment we got out of here—if we got out of here —I wanted to be on a horse, charging for Eboria. Running straight for him.

"You locked me in your room," said Maelor darkly.

"I'm sorry," I whispered. "The Pater told me that he was going to burn Leo at dawn. For all I knew, the Pater actually had him here."

"Do I really have to listen to a lovers' quarrel?" asked Sion. "If I knew this was how my night was going to end, I'd have left the stake in my heart."

I clenched my jaw. "Let's focus on getting everyone out—"

I bumped into Maelor's back—at least, I think it was Maelor? In any case, it felt like running into a brick wall.

"Are you always this clumsy?" whispered Sion sharply from just in front of me.

"I thought I was behind Maelor."

This was what happened when no one would let me light a candle, but they were right about the dark. They were the only ones who could see in this pitch-blackness, which would make it harder for anyone to find us.

"I hear the other Penitents," Sion whispered.

The sounds of his footfalls moved away from me, and I followed, my hand outstretched to feel his back. As we drew closer to the other Penitents, I saw the faint glow of torchlight. Their voices carried through the air, and I exhaled. They were safe.

"Let me go in front," I whispered. "They'll panic if they see you charging toward them. As far as they know, you are still a faithful servant of the Pater."

"Fine." I felt Sion's large body shift as he pressed back against one of the narrow catacomb walls.

I pushed past him, my arm and shoulder brushing by him in the tight space. The faint voices of the other Penitents faded into silence as they heard me approaching.

"Percival," I called out in a loud whisper. "It's Elowen."

"You made it!" Percival grinned at me.

In the narrow space, Hugo huddled with Percival and Godric, while the rest of the Penitents pressed into the narrow space behind them. In here, tombs were inset into stone walls. Low arches swept over us, and old wooden coffins lay on the floor.

Lydia peered out from behind them, and her eyes locked on me.

Sazia pushed her way to the front of the group, and firelight illuminated her face. "I told them you would make it. Did you kill..." She stopped short, her gaze flicking up to the vampire coming up behind me.

I held up my hands. "Don't be afraid. They're both with us. The Raven Lord and the Magister Solaris have been part of the resistance. They're the traitors the Pater was talking about, the people who informed Eboria. Listen, I have a lot to catch you up on, but we don't have much time. The Pater is still alive, and the Luminari are hunting us. We don't have time for questions or arguing, and right now, we don't have time for doubt. I'm just going to need you to listen closely and to trust me."

As if that weren't asking for the biggest miracle of all...

\* \* \*

PERCIVAL and I stood pressed against one side of the crypt door. On the other, Maelor and Sion waited for us.

Percival glanced at me, his scar deepening as he frowned. "I don't know about you, but I'm ready for my life to not be pointless. Even if it doesn't last very long."

"We're going to make it out," I whispered with more confidence than I felt.

The door opened, and the darkness seemed to swallow me. Shadow magic billowed around us, disorienting me completely. It was as if ink had spilled over the dome of the sky, blotting out everything. In the black, shouts rang out—the Luminari screaming, desperate to know why they'd been struck blind. The shadows had a heaviness to them, almost damp, like soil. The wind kissed my skin, cold as winter, stinging my cheeks and bare hands.

Behind me, the Penitents followed, touching each other's backs to stay together. We shuffled through the black like a grim funeral possession.

Someone grabbed my hand, and a moment of panic flickered through me. I was ready for battle, which meant I wasn't wearing gloves. But as I jerked my hand back, I heard Sion's deep voice. "Calm down, it's just me. You were wandering into a wall." On his palm, I could feel the callouses where he held his sword.

I wanted to rip my hand away. And yet, for Leo, I would do anything.

"I hope you can burn things quickly, Percival." Sion's low voice was almost hard to hear with the Luminari screaming in the distance. "Maelor has created these shadows, and I'm going to help him. But we won't be able to keep the entire castle in the dark for long."

"I'll work as fast as I can." Percival's voice sounded clipped. "How close are you taking us to the door? Because it is enormous. To burn that wood down quickly, the heat will need to be…indescribable. A raging inferno. I've never done anything like—"

"Make it happen," said Sion, cutting him off. "We

can stand in an archway that has a view of the door and keep our distance. I'll point you in the right direction. Will that work?"

"I honestly have no idea."

"The answer is yes," said Sion. "Yes, it will work—because if it doesn't, we all die. Understood? Good."

From behind, I felt the other Penitents bump into me. Everyone must have had a well-honed sense of survival at that point because despite the chaos and fear permeating the atmosphere, they were keeping completely silent. In these thick shadows, shouting was the only thing that might identify our location.

On the walls above us, the Luminari were screaming, some that the Archon had blinded them, others that it was the Serpent's work. An icy wind bit at my skin, piercing even the thick wool cloak. I hugged myself for warmth.

People feared the dark because you never knew what monsters lurked in its depths. But when you were the monsters—of fire, death, and blood—the shadows made a good home.

Sion released my hand. "Stand back," he whispered. "Wait for my signal to move forward. When it's time, I'll lead you through the darkness, out the front gate."

Then, nearby, Sion was whispering to Percival, giving him directions. Soon after, from somewhere in front of me, I heard the roar of flames, the crackling of fire. Heat started to thaw the frigid air. In the distance, screams rang out...

I swallowed hard. I'd heard the screams of the burning people, a dreadful sound that still haunted my nightmares.

The scent of burning oak billowed into the air, and even though I couldn't see it, my eyes stung. I coughed in the cinders and smoke, blinking as the heat intensified before us. Then came the faintest glow of light—flames licking at shadows. A dance of dark and light.

My stomach tightened. With the bright blaze, Maelor and Sion were losing their control of the shadow magic. Fiery sparks leapt until the darkness swallowed them again.

"Hotter," said Sion.

The flames roared. I lifted my hands, shielding my face from the heat that scorched the air. Even from here, it heated and dried my skin. I inhaled heavy smoke, woody and tinged with an acrid scent that stung my throat.

Percival's power was astounding. No wonder he hadn't wanted to waste it. Imagine this destructive force on a battlefield, incinerating his enemy…

"That's enough," Sion's voice rang out.

As the heat faded, a burst of shadows and cold washed over me. Sion and Maelor must be freezing the door, trying to put out the fire so we could actually walk through it without igniting ourselves.

The shadows were once again a great beast, consuming everything. Freezing the world around us.

A frost seemed to spread over my skin, and my

teeth chattered. The cold air stung my cheeks, my throat. Panicked shouts pierced the air, screaming all over Ruefield.

"We move out, now." Maelor's voice this time. Where had he come from? "Touch the back of the person in front of you and walk straight. Move quickly. Now! I can't keep it dark much longer."

Frigid wind whipped at us, tossing my cowl from my head. Sion took my hand in his—no! Maelor, smooth and uncalloused. He pulled me toward a wall of heat and smoke until he was practically dragging me at a run. I staggered to keep up with him.

The smoky air stung my eyes and throat, sliding into my lungs, making me cough as I hurried after him. I wanted to ask him if we were leaving everyone behind, but I could hardly breathe. As the shadows receded, orange light glowed before us. Embers blazed in what was left of the wooden doorframe, and my gaze flicked to the smoldering wood that rose up high on either side, towering columns of red cracking black, and the black smoke swooping past it all.

But we were almost free, crossing the blazing threshold—

Maelor cursed.

Something whistled through the night air, and Maelor fell to his knees. An arrow jutted from his throat. Light slid through the shadows as he lost his grip on his magic. The earth felt unsteady beneath my feet as I turned to see the forms emerging from the dark—light glinting off metal armor. A phalanx of Luminari blocking us in, some of them armed with arrows, others with swords.

Maelor ripped the arrow from his throat and staggered forward, but another landed in his chest, just missing his heart. I couldn't breathe.

Sion was a whirlwind of shadows, and he raced for the phalanx. He began ripping apart the Luminari on the right side until an arrow slammed into him. He fell to the ground, pierced in the chest.

Fear slid through my bones as I saw the Pater standing behind the soldiers, mounted on a horse, the smoky wind whipping at his white cloak and hair. He chanted in Tyrenian, words full of fury.

And even if I couldn't translate the meaning, I knew well enough what this meant. He was calling for bloody, holy vengeance against his enemies. It meant Leo would burn. We'd all burn.

But I'd do anything to stop it, even if it meant offering up my soul to the Serpent. Serving it up to him on a platter.

*I am the starving ravages of time, devouring everything before me.*

My gaze flicked over the phalanx, searching for weaknesses. They weren't focused on me, but rather on the staggering, injured soldiers that Sion had attacked. One of those soldiers stumbled forward, screaming. His arm hung by tendons. *Start with him.* The Serpent's voice rang in my thoughts. *Then spread my death like a plague.*

I rushed forward. An arrow pierced my shoulder, but I ignored it. The injured Luminarus staggered, and I brushed my hand over his cheek.

Decay spilled into him, seeping into his veins. His body shuddered, and I shoved him back into the phalanx. He slammed against the cluster of soldiers, and I gripped his face. I thrummed with power in the cindered air.

*I will devour all.*

Death bloomed from my fingertips like roots spreading beneath the soil, from one Luminari to another. Tendrils of rot coiled and wrapped around the soldiers like a lover's caress, gently luring them down, laying them to rest in the welcoming earth.

*The soft embrace of the ground folds the mortals into itself.*

I drank in the sounds of their last breaths. The death rattle was a soothing lullaby to my ears.

*I am death's hunger, and I will never have my fill.*

My mind flashed with bursts of memories. There was Anselm, still just a boy, binding our hands together with a green silk ribbon, promising me it meant we'd marry one day. Lydia, threading together crowns of ivy, meadowsweet, and pale yellow primrose. I wasn't invited to the masque because I wasn't nobility. But she said we'd throw our own masque at night by the sea, and the music would be the nightingale song and the rhythmic crashing of the waves, and no one would be allowed but the three of us.

I saw Leo sleeping soundly, horizontal on his bed with his skinny limbs sticking out of the blankets. Maelor sitting at his desk, frantically writing and trying to feel something again. He turned to look at me, his eyes as dark as the magic spilling from my fingertips.

*Time consumes all in its path.*

The Serpent swallowed my memories, leaving only his own desires.

He wanted me to drape a pall of death over the kingdom, to unfurl a ravenous, withering cloud that spanned from the sea to the walls. Fear blossomed in the air, sweet as honey on my tongue.

A dead army lay before me. A fallen king. I'd march across the earth and take the rest—

Hands grasped me, the scent of sandalwood. Powerful arms pulled me into an embrace. I struggled against the confinement, but his grasp was iron. I heard hooves beat against the earth, and wind whipped at my body. I turned to look back at my greatest work. My masterpiece—the phalanx of corpses, piled so beautifully on each other. Hearts still at last, chests no longer moving.

On foot, the other Penitents ran from the castle until the shadows swallowed the world again.

For a moment, understanding flickered. We'd won. Maelor and I were fleeing on horseback—free. The

Penitents were scattering into the welcoming embrace of the night. I was on my way to Leo, to keep him safe.

But that understanding was gone in the next heartbeat.

Because I'd taken too much. And now, there was nothing left but the Serpent's hunger...

# CHAPTER 41

*T*endrils of shadow bound my wrists. Under my ribs, sharp yearning gnawed. I needed to free myself, to paint the kingdom with ashen hues of purple and gray. I must feed the soil with the dead.

I'd roam the streets, pound the earth amid a symphony of final breaths.

Except there was someone to remember, wasn't there…

Dark hair…

A boy with thin arms and so many questions. *What's your favorite bird? What's your favorite pie?*

And another—a beautiful man in a room of brass instruments, smearing red and orange paint over an ink drawing of a butterfly, trying to bring colors back into his world.

"She's almost back, I think." A familiar feminine voice floated through the air.

Darkness slid over my thoughts again.

*  *  *

MY GAZE FLICKED OPEN, and he was the first thing I saw —eyes violet-blue as the sound of an *O*, bright as the heavens. "You're back, Elowen."

I wanted him to come closer, but he stood across the room. I flexed my sore wrists, frustrated to find they were still bound in his shadows.

"Can you let me go?" Somehow, everything in the room seemed blurry except Maelor.

His eyebrows rose. "I haven't decided yet."

My heart started to race, and my gaze flicked over the room. Small and simple, with white walls and a fireplace. Wood beams crossed the ceiling above. It smelled of a fireplace and also like I hadn't bathed in weeks.

I licked my dry lips. "Where am I? What's happened?"

"We've been in the weald for five days. Lydia has been tending to you this whole time. Feeding you milk, trying to heal you with her magic. She said it was working. You kept talking about the Serpent's hunger, but then you were mumbling about a masque by the sea."

I stared at him, my heart fluttering. "Lydia?"

"I couldn't be around you. Even now, I can't stay

long. Perhaps Lydia's magic can heal your cravings, but it does nothing for a dead thing like me."

"What are you talking about?"

His throat bobbed. "I can't control my bloodlust anymore, Elowen." His expression looked pained. "I'm afraid I'm not the same person I was when you met me. I've completely lost myself."

He looked so different now. So vulnerable. Maybe it was his eyes, or that he was no longer dressed as the Raven Lord. He stood before me in a gorgeous midnight blue shirt and dark gray trousers of a rich-looking material that I wanted to stroke. I wished he'd move closer.

"You're wearing something new."

A half-smile cracked his grim expression for just a moment.

At last, the shadows slid from my skin. I sat up on the bed, flexing my wrists. I wanted to run my hands over the soft fabric of his shirt.

I stared at him. "You said that Sion was loyal to his cause, but you weren't. Except the cause you were talking about was the resistance." I glanced up at him. "So was that what you meant? You weren't as loyal as he was to the resistance because part of you needed the Order?"

He flinched and looked away. "Sion doesn't feel the loss of his soul like I do, but I can never fill the emptiness."

My chest tightened. I wished I could have been that

person for him—the one to fill the void. But we still hadn't fully trusted each other. In Ruefield, seemingly on opposite sides of a war, how could we have?

My muscles ached, and I rose from the bed, taking a step closer to Maelor.

He held up his hand. "Stop. You can't come near me anymore." A sharp command cut under his voice. "You don't know how much I want you, Elowen. I never stop thinking about you. The way you look, the way you smell, the sound of your sighs. And that's exactly why I'm saying goodbye." The expression in his dark eyes was agonized.

Before I could say another word to him, he was gone. The door shut behind him, and only a few wisps of shadows remained.

I stared at the closed door, weighed down by the silent emptiness of the room. I felt as if my chest had cracked open. He could still come back, couldn't he? It wouldn't be the last time I'd see him.

But a new fear was already raking its claws through my thoughts. The memory of Leo came crashing into me like a lightning strike, the little boy waiting for me. My stomach plummeted. Where the hell was Leo?

I flung open the door, and my question was answered immediately.

At a small kitchen table, Lydia sat with Leo. Sunlight spilled in through a window onto them. The pair of them wore flower crowns of ivy, meadowsweet, and primroses. Lydia's gaze flicked up to me.

Leo turned, and a grin spread across his face. "Elowen!" He leapt up and ran for me, arms outstretched.

Panic shot through me, and I held out my hands. "Stop!" I hadn't had a chance to look over myself to see if I was totally covered. With a hammering heart, I glanced down at my leather gloves, the full cloak over my body.

When I looked back at Leo, his eyes had gone wide.

This was what Maelor had just felt moments ago, wasn't it? That bone-deep fear of killing someone you loved. Screaming at them to stay away.

"It's okay," I said softly. I beckoned him closer with gloved hands, and I pulled him into a hug.

With Leo pressed against me, I glanced out the warped, sunlit windows. Two more crumbling stone cottages stood outside, and Percival walked on a path between them, carrying buckets of water.

"How did we end up here?" I asked.

"Percival knew about these cottages," said Lydia. "Abandoned long ago...he doesn't think anyone will find us here. So we're waiting, until it's time to fight back again."

I glanced down at the top of Leo's head, wishing I could kiss it. "And who brought Leo here?"

"Maelor ordered me to get him," said Lydia. "It was actually extremely dangerous since I'm supposed to be in hiding. Honestly, it was fairly heroic."

I frowned at her. "Since when are you taking orders from Maelor?"

She shrugged. "We're in the resistance now, darling. We're all taking orders from those two, whether you like it or not."

"Sion nearly killed your father, you know. And he killed mine."

She glared at me. "War comes with certain sacrifices, I'm afraid. You'll have to get used to it."

"You're joining the resistance?"

"Yes, and so are you."

I released Leo, and he slid away from me to sit at the table again. A pile of crumbs was heaped on a plate before them, and he returned to trying to lick them off his fingers.

I stroked his head with a gloved hand. "My job is to look after Leo, and I'm not letting you fuck that up again."

"I did get him back for you."

"Thank you," I said through gritted teeth. "But I'm not putting his life into danger."

She cocked her head. "So, you two will live in hiding for the rest of your lives? Starving? On the run? Alone and hunted? You think that would be the best life for Leo, instead of using that power of yours to kill the people hunting him?"

Sharp silence filled the room. Lydia was always so bloody persuasive. She always knew *exactly* what to say.

And before I could retort, the cottage door slammed open. My body went cold as Sion stalked into the room, a red cape billowing behind him.

"Maelor tells me you're back in the world of the living." He cocked an eyebrow. "And the dead, I suppose, since I'm here."

"What *are* you doing here?"

"You're going to be joining my army."

I narrowed my eyes. "I truly loathe you, and I have other plans."

He glided closer, and a wicked glint danced in his golden eyes. "I *had* other plans, as it so happens. They were to slowly work my way up in the Order until I could get close enough to the Pater to learn how to kill him. Someone set those plans alight and dumped the ashes in the river." His words were harsh, but his voice was a silken murmur. He leaned down and whispered, "And if you were anyone else in the world, you would be dead right now."

My fingers curled into fists. Maybe I could run from the Order, but I could never run from the vampires. "And what do you need from me so desperately? You want me to let the Serpent take over my soul until I become a complete monster?"

"You're going to need to stop being so terrified of your power." He turned for the door before casting another careless glance back at me. "And Elowen? Don't make the mistake of trying to kill me again."

# ACKNOWLEDGMENTS

The multi-talented Rachel from Nerd Fam contributed in three important ways: she designed the absolutely gorgeous cover, organized all my marketing, and also read the first half of the book to give me feedback on the romance, helping to make it hotter.

Michael, a genius thriller author, read the entire book as I sent him sections of drafts, and he gave me invaluable feedback on improving the writing quality to make it more exciting.

Behind the scenes, three editors helped to refine the text, to make the writing smooth and clear: Noah Sky, Rachel Cass, and Lauren Simpson.

The stunning character art was created for me by Mage on Duty, with interior art by Shayne Rutherford and Saint Jupiter. Additionally, Saint Jupiter designed the naked hardcover and some of the interior art.

Thanks to Emilié Ní Heochagáin for helping us get the pronunciation right on the word Sumaire.

Thank you all for your help in bringing Elowen's story to life.

# COURT OF SHADOWS

If you enjoyed Hallowed Games, you might also enjoy **Court of Shadows**, another series by C.N. Crawford with action, magic and romance:

**Chapter One:**

The vampire bared his fangs, and I knew we'd both be dead by the end of the night if I didn't get him out of here. I leapt over the bar with the speed of a hurricane wind, hurtling toward him. I slammed my fist into his skull—once, twice, three times. He staggered back, then collapsed. He'd fallen so easily I almost didn't feel a sense of victory, but I grinned down at him anyway. The colored lights of the bar stained his porcelain skin red.

I *had* to get him out of here.

I tried to project a calm I didn't feel. "Like I said," I

purred, "a guy like you would be more comfortable in a hipster joint with arcade games and herbal cocktails. You can talk about synthwave or whatever there. Move along. *Now.*" I may have screamed the last word. A sense of urgency was taking over.

It was at that point, I realized that everyone in the bar had stopped talking and were all staring at me over their pints. A pop song crackled through the speakers, and the neon sign in the window flickered on and off. Otherwise, silence shrouded us.

*Easy, Arianna. Easy.* I stood over the fallen vampire, holding up my hands. "Nothing to see here, folks! Just an ordinary Friday night kerfuffle."

I loosed a long sigh. Two thin hawthorn stakes jutted from my messy bun, ready for the vampire's heart, but I restrained myself. My boss would flip his shit if he saw me beating up customers—again. And I definitely wasn't supposed to kill people—even if they were undead—in front of a crowd. Rufus frowned upon things like that in his establishment.

*You can take the girl out of the gladiator arena....*

It was just unfortunate that the vampire had made the serious error of trying to bite me.

As soon as this guy had stumbled into our bar, I'd known he was trouble. In fact, I'd immediately assessed three important things about him.

One, his luxurious Viking beard had told me he was a hipster—not to mention his neon clothing, reminiscent of children's wear in the early 1980s. Whenever guys dressed like him decided to slum it in the Spread Eagle, it usually went down badly with the regulars.

Two, his staggering gait and furrowed brow had told me that he was a mean, sloppy drunk. Given the exceptional alcohol tolerance levels of vampires, he must have drunk his weight in craft beers tonight.

Three, and worst of all, he was a supernatural.

I cocked my head at him as he lay on the floor. He *might* even be old enough that the medieval Norseman beard was actually authentic. Supernaturals like him— like me—were outlawed these days. We had to fly under the radar if we wanted to live. Too bad this one was too stupid to keep a low profile. Four years of executions and assassinations, and this fucker had just brazenly walked into our bar, flashing his fangs around.

As the patrons turned back to their pint glasses, pretending to ignore us, I frowned at the hipster-vampire. Dazed, he still lay on the beer-stained floor, but he'd managed to push himself up onto his elbows. The undead bastards didn't stay down for long. His pale eyes were trained on me, possibly recognizing my own magic.

Ciara, my oldest friend, crept over to us, her brown eyes wide. Her hand was clamped over her grin. I could tell she was stopping just short of clapping her hands. "Oh my goodness, Arianna. You punched him. Do you see his fangs?" She had a sweet but unfortunate tendency to idolize supernaturals, like we were some kind of celebrities. After all, there weren't many of us around these days. "A real, live vampire," she whispered, pointing at him.

"I can hear you," the vamp slurred, now rising to his feet. He staggered closer. "Little girl."

"I need to get him out of here," I muttered. And I had to do it without using any of my magic. You never knew who was watching, ready to turn you in.

Now, my new Viking friend's gaze was locked on Ciara. Red flashed in his eyes. He was after blood tonight, and she was clearly an easier target than me. It didn't help that she was wearing a T-shirt featuring a male model with fangs poking from pouty lips. She gods-damned loved vampires.

"I know your game, little girl." The vampire licked his fangs, swaying on his feet. "You read your little books about teenagers falling in love with thousand-year-old vamps. Our skin is supposed to sparkle like a unicorn's arse, right? And you all get a happy ending. Wrong. Those books are crap. Come with me, and I'll teach you about reading real literature. Hemingway, Kerouac, Bukowski—"

His monologue was cut off by the sight of the thin stake I'd pulled out of my hair. I twirled it between my fingers, and the vampire seemed hypnotized by the movement.

I smiled at him. "Now that you're quiet, let's get one thing straight. I will not have you slandering romance books in my bar." Technically, it wasn't my bar, but that was beside the point. This arsehole thought he was going to feed on Ciara. And moreover, I would not tolerate anyone banging on about Bukowski. "I'd like to just get back to the shots of Johnny Walker I was drinking before you came in, and I don't want to have to keep punching you. I'd prefer not to get your blood on my new miniskirt. So run along. I'm pretty sure an ironic meth-trailer-themed bar just opened up a few blocks away." I leaned closer, arching an eyebrow. "It seems more your scene."

Despite the arse-kicking I'd just given him and the stake in my hand, he seemed unfazed.

He stumbled toward Ciara. "I think I'd be more comfortable if your friend came with me."

I gave him a hard shove, and he staggered back.

The door swung open, and a second vamp came in —this one in a visor, a handlebar mustache, and a pink bow tie. Had someone told them we had a sale on ukuleles or something?

I had to get them out of here. The last thing I wanted was for the Spread Eagle to attract the spell-slayers' attention for harboring supernaturals.

I flashed the two vamps a dark smile. "No supernaturals allowed in here. No supernaturals allowed *anywhere*. Those are the rules. You've got ten seconds to leave this bar," I said sweetly, while calculating all the ways I could kill them. "Or I might start getting angry. And you don't want that to happen."

Viking Vamp snorted, then his irises flared with

red. The air seemed to thin around us. "And what the fuck are you, pretty thing? You're not human."

My blood chilled. I couldn't let anyone overhear him saying that.

He snatched a whisky bottle—my whisky bottle—from the bar, his movements lightning fast. Then, he jabbed a finger in my face. "You're not supposed to be here, either. I think I just might tell the spell-slayers on you. Tick tock. Your time is running out, pretty lady. But give me a look at those gorgeous tits of yours and I might keep your secret."

Rage surged. And then, as I registered the word "spell-slayers," dread slithered up my spine.

Okay. I was done being nice. Now he had to die.

There was only one thing in London scarier than me, and that was the spell-slayers. The fae assassins haunted London's streets in dark cloaks, blending into the night sky like smoke. They terrorized humans and magical creatures alike, ruling the city with the points of their blades, silently slaughtering in the shadows. No one was supposed to look them in the eye, or speak to them, or breathe in their direction. But we all owed them a tithe from our paychecks. Protection money, they called it. They were no better than a magical mafia. In short, they were the worst. I hated them and feared them in equal measure.

I narrowed my eyes at the vamps. "You want me to believe you're brave enough to attract the attention of the spell-slayers? And risk your own necks? Bollocks.

You're supposed to be locked up in a magical realm with all the other supernaturals, not roaming London's streets. I'm now four seconds away from dragging you outside and staking you."

Truth was, I'd stake them whether or not they left willingly. I couldn't risk them turning me in.

I didn't really have time for too many mental calculations, because the next thing I knew, Viking Vamp was lunging for Ciara again, fangs bared.

Fast—maybe faster than I should have—I pivoted around him, pointing my stake at his neck. I wasn't supposed to move too quickly; humans were slow and sluggish. But the sight of him attacking Ciara sent my blood racing, and instinct kicked in.

I pressed the stake against his jugular. Then, I stood on my tiptoes, whispering into his ear. "I know a stake to the neck won't kill you. But I will make it hurt when I jam it into your throat and wiggle it round. Then I'll kill you."

Something sharp jabbed into my back, stopping me in my tracks. A quick glance over my shoulder told me that his friend, Visor Vamp, was holding a knife to my back.

"Drop the stake, darling!" said Visor Vamp.

*Baleros's third law of power: Always let your enemy underestimate you.*

I dropped the stake. I held up my hands as if I were surrendering, adding in a bit of trembling for good measure.

Then, when I felt the point of the knife retreat a little, I pivoted, slamming my elbow into his nose. I brought up my knee into his crotch—three brutal cracks to the groin. Vamps might not be alive, but they were still sensitive in the usual places. As he bent forward, I twisted his arm, forcing him to the ground. I snatched the knife from his hand at the same time. Then, I pointed it at his neck.

My lips curled in a mocking smile. "You still want to play?"

Now, at last, the vamps had the good sense to look scared. Apart from a warbling pop song, the room had gone silent again.

Viking Vamp held up his hands. "We'll leave."

I pulled the blade away from the other's neck. As he straightened, he leaned in close, breathing in my ear. "The spell-slayers will be coming for you."

At that, an icy tendril of dread coiled through my chest.

I watched as the two vamps skulked out of the bar.

I jammed my hand into the pocket of my miniskirt, and I pulled out a lollipop. Cherry, with gum in the center. Nothing like crystalized sugar to calm the nerves. I popped it in my mouth, staring at the door.

Ciara grinned. "Well geez Louise, this has been a heck of an evening." She'd lived in the UK for at least ten years now and still hadn't lost her thick American accent. "I haven't been this excited since my Aunt Starlene drew a clown on my bedroom wall to ease my loneliness."

"It's not over." There'd been something too cocky about those vamps, and their parting shot had told me everything I needed to know. I'd heard of some super-naturals acting as informants to the spell-slayers. Supernatural narcs. Maybe that was how these two idiots had managed to stay alive, biting humans like Ciara with impunity. "Can you cover the bar while I'm out?"

"No problem."

I had a pair of vampires to kill.

Made in United States
Troutdale, OR
12/02/2023

15223641R00248